Things Good Girls Don't Do

By Codi Gary

Things Good Girls Don't Do
"The Trouble With Sexy" in *Kiss Me:*
An Avon Books Valentine's Day Anthology

Things Good Girls Don't Do

CODI GARY

AVONIMPULSE
An Imprint of HarperCollinsPublishers

Excerpt from "The Trouble With Sexy" copyright © 2013 by Codi Gary. Originally appeared in *Kiss Me: An Avon Books Valentine's Day Anthology*, published in 2013 by Avon Impulse, an imprint of HarperCollins Publishers.

Excerpt from *Less Than a Gentleman* copyright © 2013 by Kerrelyn Sparks.

Excerpt from *When I Find You* copyright © 2013 by Dixie Brown.

Excerpt from *Playing the Field* copyright © 2013 by Candice Wakoff.

Excerpt from *How to Marry a Highlander* copyright © 2013 by Katharine Brophy Dubois.

EPub Edition SEPTEMBER 2013 ISBN: 9780062292919

Print Edition ISBN: 9780062292926

JV 10 9 8 7

For my mom.
My rock. My cheerleader. My conscience.
I love you.

Chapter One

IT'S IMPORTANT TO always be a nice girl, Katie. Other-
wise, people won't want to let their kids play with you.

Katie tried to remember her mother's childhood
advice while organizing the Rock Canyon Independence
Day Extravaganza, the annual parade, fair, and fireworks
show celebrating the Fourth of July. The only drawback
was that she had to work with Mrs. Marcie Andrews.
And Mrs. Andrews was trying her patience in a big way.

"I just don't understand why the tattoo booth is set up
next to the kissing booth. Those drill noises are going to
be distracting."

Katie took a breath. Sometimes Mrs. Andrews acted
like she was in her eighties instead of her early fifties. She
was a dairy farmer's wife, had four kids, and attended
church every Sunday, but even Katie's mother had called
her a "gossiping windbag," and her mother had rarely
spoken ill of anyone. Katie, taking a calming breath and

channeling her mother's patience-is-a-virtue mentality, said, "There won't actually be any real tattoos being done, Mrs. Andrews. It's going to be henna tattoos. Mr. Trepasso is just handing out his cards and giving people samples of his work."

Mrs. Andrews harrumphed. "Why Merve rented that space to a tattoo parlor, I'll never know. It always just seems to draw the wrong element."

And the two bars in town don't? Katie didn't say that, though. She just smiled and said, "I'm sure it will be fine."

Mrs. Andrews seemed to realize that Katie wasn't going to agree with her and dropped the subject. "Now Katie, I know that the town council appointed you for this job, but I am co-head of this committee and I have more experience with this event since I'm a bit older than you. I just want to make sure you appreciate my advice, and don't disregard it out of turn. I know how you young people like to think you know everything."

"Of course, Mrs. Andrews, I completely value and appreciate your help. I am so honored that they picked me to help run things, but I am sure there is a lot I can learn from you."

That seemed to pacify the older woman, and she preened. "All right, then, so your shift for the kissing booth is from three to three thirty, and we'll start the fireworks after the Canyon Queen Pageant. I really don't know about doing a big fireworks display. It's a waste of money and so very dangerous."

Katie wrote some notes in her binder, ignoring the fireworks subject for the sixteenth time, and closed it with a forced smile. "Okay, I think that's it! We should be set for Thursday."

Mrs. Andrews frowned a little and worried aloud, "Are you sure there's nothing else? You have your dress for the Canyon Queen float?"

Of course she had her dress. In a small town like Rock Canyon, everyone knew everyone else's business and you didn't mess with town festivities and traditions. At least six people a day asked her stupid questions like "Are you ready to retire your crown?", "Are you excited about riding the float again?", "What's your dress look like?", and "How's Jimmy doing?"

That last question was enough to make her throw everything her mother ever taught her out the window and unleash the fury on someone. Jimmy Lawrence, her boyfriend of seven years, had broken up with her eight months ago. Actually, *broken up* was too mild a term. The dirty, lily-livered jerk had dumped her for a girl six years younger and twice her bra size. She'd tried to just smile and act like it didn't bother her by participating in the Valentine's Day singles auction—where she'd ended up spending the Sweethearts Dance with Carl Anderson, a nice enough guy when he didn't think his rotten-egg farts were hilarious. After that, she'd gone out with a few men from church, but the men of Rock Canyon were just so . . .

She couldn't come up with the perfect adjective to sum up the disgusting, irritating, and even boring antics of the six dates she'd had.

So Katie threw herself into one project after another,

and this parade was only the latest. She tried to keep busy at the salon, and it helped that Jimmy and his new girl-friend had moved to Twin Falls, so she didn't have to see them walking around looking happy and in love. If she had to suffer through that torture on a daily basis, she might drive her car into the canyon—after running the cheating bastard and his little tart over with her 4Runner first.

Was she bitter? Well, no one could blame her. She had put her heart and soul into a relationship that had gone nowhere. All the years she'd spent grooming Jimmy, supporting him, and now someone else got to enjoy the benefits.

Which brought her here, listening to Mrs. Andrews go on and on about the marching band, when a deep voice interrupted, "Excuse me, ladies, I just wanted to hand over my check for my rental booth."

Katie's gaze snapped up to meet a pair of steel-gray eyes. She could hear the disapproval in Mrs. Andrews's voice as she drawled, "Mr. Trepasso, we were just talking about you."

Those amazing eyes didn't stray from hers as he replied, "Please call me Chase, Mrs. Andrews. I hope you ladies were saying good things about me?"

Katie's gaze shifted away from him to Mrs. Andrews, who looked like she'd smelled something vile. Katie, afraid the older woman would open her mouth and tell him exactly what she'd said, smiled, took his check, and quickly said, "Thanks, Chase, and of course it was good. I was just telling Mrs. Andrews what a wonderful job you did on my friend Stephanie's rose tattoo. It's lovely."

Chase's handsome face, with his slim nose, sensual mouth, and dimpled chin, lit up with a wicked grin. His brown hair was short, spiky, and a pair of studs adorned both of his ears. "Then why haven't you been down to see me, Katie?" He lowered his voice and leaned closer. "I can do something really small and feminine, where no one would ever see it."

Katie fought the urge to fan herself as she heard Mrs. Andrews's gasp. She remembered the first time she'd seen Chase after he moved to Rock Canyon five months ago. He'd been moving through the crowd at Buck's Shot Bar, handing out business cards for his parlor. He'd stopped in front of Steph and her, holding out a card to each of them, and when Chase's hand had touched Katie's it had been electric. Too bad he hadn't seemed as affected by it as her; he'd moved on to the next group without so much as a backward glance. She'd been a little disappointed at his dismissal, and when she'd seen him in the crowd at the Valentine's Day singles auction, she had secretly hoped he might bid on her. It was an idiotic hope, though. She went off with Carl, and Chase got into a bidding war with Gregg Phillips over Ryan Ashton. He'd lost out, and since then she'd seen him out with several women, but never the same one twice. It seemed Chase preferred a certain type of woman and none of them had a reputation for being a "good" girl, unlike Katie, who couldn't even seem to return a library book late.

It was just as well that he had never looked at her like

that. Chase was a heartbreaker, the kind of guy everyone in town disapproved of, but that didn't mean he didn't get her blood pumping anytime he came near her. Only last week he'd joined her best friend Stephanie, her husband Jared, and Katie for a friendly game of pool. When she kept missing shot after shot, he'd taken her aside, bent her over the table, and whispered, "Now, what you want to do is . . ."

She honestly couldn't remember what else he'd said as he'd folded that tall, muscular frame over hers and she'd felt every breath of his words against her hair, cheek, and neck. Her butt had been cradled perfectly against his jean-clad crotch and instinct had screamed at her to wiggle against him, but good girls didn't do that. It would have been vulgar, and nice girls were never vulgar.

He'd finally backed away from her and she'd told everyone she needed to leave, that she'd forgotten to feed her cat. She'd figured her crazy attraction to him was just a side effect of her stagnant sex life and she just needed to put some distance between them, but the memory of his body flush against hers was something that gave her ideas. Naughty, naked, sweaty ideas.

Katie realized both Chase and Mrs. Andrews were staring at her.

"I'm sorry, I have so much to get done, I guess I spaced out for a minute. I'll get this to the bank tomorrow, Chase, and thank you for renting a booth."

He gave that sexy I-know-how-hot-I-am-smile and said, "Sure, Katie, anything to help the town."

Katie tried to keep her head down so he wouldn't see

her bright red cheeks or the dirty thoughts lurking in her eyes. What was wrong with her?

Turning away with a mumbled good-bye, she walked toward the patch of dirt used as a parking lot and shook her head at her own stupidity. It didn't matter that Chase Trepasso was probably one hell of a good time or that those gray eyes held enough heat to light a barbecue. Thinking about him in that way was a mistake.

Katie got into her 4Runner and headed to her little two-bedroom house on Oak Avenue. It was affordable and had plenty of room for her and her big, fat black cat, Slinks. She'd bought it seven months ago, after Jimmy had told her he was leaving their little apartment at the edge of town.

Her hands clenched every time she thought of that morning, when he'd calmly told her over a stack of waffles and black coffee that as much as he cared about her, he had met someone else. Seven years together. Seven years of washing his clothes and making him birthday cakes. Seven damn years of talk about marriage, kids, and their life together, and he had dumped her as casually as if he'd asked for the syrup. And Katie had sat there, trying not to cry because her mother had always said, "Good girls never make a scene."

But she'd wanted too. She still did. Every time someone mentioned his name, she pictured slapping his face or busting out the windows on his stupid truck, or what he always referred to as his "baby," right in front of him. She must have listened to that Carrie Underwood song "Before He Cheats" a hundred times a day for a month after Jimmy had come by to get his stuff with a few of his buddies. She'd left the apartment while he was there, gone to Steph's house and bawled like a baby. Steph had tried to cheer her up, threatening all kinds of castration and venting her own hatred, but nothing had helped. When she'd learned Jimmy had rented an apartment in Twin Falls with Selena—ugh, even her *name* was better than Katie's—she hadn't even been relieved that she wouldn't be bumping into them. All she could feel was rage that he had said he wasn't "emotionally mature enough" for marriage with her, while little Miss DD just needed to wiggle her butt and *boom*! Two months later they were picking out curtains.

That was when she'd decided to buy the house and salon, and even though both had needed quite a bit of work, she'd valued the distraction. She'd spent months updating the house— which had needed all new fixtures and paint—and organizing all of her things the way she liked them. She could put her decorating skills on Pinterest, they were so cookie-cutter-esque.

One good thing about Jimmy leaving: no big, muddy work boots mucking up her clean floors. And she definitely had more room for her clothes and her craft corner. Her mother always said, "Idle hands are the devil's tools."

Katie parked her car in the carport and went to the end of her drive to get her mail. She pulled open the little white box decorated with trees and flowers, an impulsive buy from T.J. Maxx, but she loved it. Thumbing through the stack of bills, she found a large white envelope. Flipping it over, she opened the seal and pulled out the off-white invitation curiously. When Katie read the names in the perfect, swirly script, she felt like she'd been hit by a bus.

Mr. and Mrs. Harold Lenier
request the honor of your presence
to celebrate the marriage of their daughter,
Selena Marie Lenier
to
James Thomas Lawrence

How could he? She couldn't read anymore, her vision was so blurred by angry tears. Seven years and all she had was a couple of necklaces and a pair of emerald earrings. What had Selena done that had gotten her an engagement ring in just a few months? And *why* would he send her a wedding invitation? To hurt her? There was no reason why he would want to, at least none that she could think of. He had cheated on her, not the other way around, and the worst thing she had done was keep his favorite Toby Keith T-shirt before shredding it with a pair of scissors. What man in his right mind would think it was okay to humiliate her all over again by flaunting his happiness?

Katie stuffed the invitation back into the envelope and pulled out her cell phone.

Steph picked up on the second ring. "That low-down, no-good son of a bitch!"

Katie smiled at her best friend's outrage and said dryly, "I take it you got one too?"

"I don't know why in the hell he thought either Jared or I would want to go to his wedding. We only tolerated his no-good cheating butt because you thought you loved him! I tried to tell you he was shifty! Didn't I tell you he was shifty?"

Katie rolled her eyes as she unlocked the door. "Yes, I heard shifty several times."

"Want me to come over? I can bring a bottle of wine and some brownies from The Local Bean. We can get stuffed and wasted. Maybe even look up how to make a voodoo doll."

Katie dropped the mail down on her table and sighed, "Thanks, but I think I'm just going to have some dinner, take a bath, and pop in a DVD."

Katie could hear exasperation in Steph's voice. "Katie, you cannot sit at home all the time and mope. You need to go out, have fun. Get your mind off Jimmy the Jerk-off! Maybe even meet someone new."

Katie choked. "I don't think I'm ready for anyone new yet. Still getting over the old one, and pretty sure I'm not going to meet anyone new in Rock Canyon."

"So maybe you'll meet the right one. Maybe you've been so blinded by Jimmy and his deceitful charm that you haven't noticed him," Steph suggested.

Maybe the right one doesn't exist. "Maybe, but I doubt it. It's a good thing you met Jared in kindergarten, otherwise you'd be fishing in the same slim-pickins pool as the rest of us."

Steph and Jared had known each other their whole lives, started dating freshman year of high school, and married right after graduation. They'd gone to college to-gether and were the epitome of what Katie wanted: her better half. Her soul mate.

Instead she'd gotten Jimmy, and now she didn't even have him anymore.

"Hey, if I was single, I would be making waves in that pool, let me tell you! Your problem is that you're such a good girl, you just try to please everyone. Name one thing you've done wrong. One person you've pissed off besides me or your mother."

"As much as I'd love to play let's-make-Katie-feel-worse-on-the-third-crappiest-day-of-her-life, I'm going to go. Maybe drown myself in a bathtub," Katie said, emotionally drained.

"Shut up, you will not. Seriously, if you're feeling that bad, I'll be there in five."

Katie took a deep breath and counted to ten. She adored Steph, but she hovered sometimes. What Steph needed was a couple of kids to worry about; then maybe she wouldn't worry so much about her love life. Or lack thereof.

"I'm just kidding! I love you, but I just want to be alone," Katie said as she opened up her bare cupboard to reveal a lonely can of green beans and a box of cake mix.

"Okay, okay, but you know I love you, right? I just like to give you a hard time. After all, someone's got to shake up that goody-goody thing you've got going on."

"Good night," Katie said.

"'Night! And don't . . ."

Katie hung up the phone without waiting for Steph to

finish, but she already knew what she was going to say: don't mope.

"I don't mope," she muttered to herself as she searched through her fridge for anything edible. There was something green and fuzzy growing on the fajitas from three days ago. Ick.

She grabbed her notepad off the counter, a pen from her pink poodle mug, and started a grocery list. She hated having to go out again this late, especially after being on her feet all day at the salon and then dealing with Mrs. Andrews, but she was starving and the occasion called for alcohol. Quite a bit of alcohol.

Suddenly, a better idea struck her. Dropping the pad on the counter, she grabbed her purse and headed back out to drown her sorrows in mojitos and fries at Buck's Shot Bar. Drinking alone at a bar on a Monday was better than grocery shopping. The grocery store held sympathetic looks and well-meaning advice. At least at Buck's she'd be left alone to dwell on her future of twelve cats and spinsterhood.

CHASE TREPASSO HAD thought a city of 19,000 people was small, but the culture shock of Rock Canyon's barely 4,000 citizens was crazy. It was like Mayberry married the NRA and they had a baby: that would be Rock Canyon. He'd laughed the first time he'd walked into the liquor store and saw that you could buy a gun with your beer.

Moving here had been on a whim. He'd been looking to sell his tattoo parlor in Elko, Nevada, and relocate, so he'd grabbed his map and started searching. When his finger had fallen on Rock Canyon, he'd checked out the real estate and the town, figuring a little small-town charm was just what he needed. That first month of getting everything set up had been hectic, but it was worth it for the peace. Now he was able to work on the next issue of *Destructo Boy*, the comic book series he'd started when he was eighteen, which was due to his editor later that month.

It was a benefit and a curse, that peace.

He'd spent a lot of time at the parlor, or at one of the local haunts, Buck's Shot Bar, networking and making a few friends, but he was finding it hard to break into a new town. Especially one as close-knit as Rock Canyon.

Despite the size of it, the people who lived there were the same as every other town he'd lived in. The same narrow-minded older generation, same tough college kids wanting something "cool" on their biceps, and the same women looking for a man to take care of them.

He'd tried to avoid those types by going out with a few bad girls, or as bad as they got in a town like this, but all of them had been the same. Girls who drank too much, dressed a little wild, and were up for anything. But in the end they'd all wanted the one thing he had no desire to give: commitment. He just didn't seem to have it in him. He couldn't even believe he'd actually bought a house in Rock Canyon. He'd always rented, but something about the old farmhouse had spoken to him. Still, just because he was thinking about settling for a while didn't mean he wanted to settle down for good. Especially not with any of the girls he'd dated so far.

Chase tried to stop thinking about his love life and take his pool shot, but then Katie Connors walked into Buck's Shot Bar, her honey-blond hair curling over the shoulders of her red short-sleeved top.

She smiled at Grant Henderson, the bartender, and said something to him before moving on to one of the booths. Katie was put together real nice: just enough up top to balance out her bottom half, and with hair so thick and long Chase couldn't help imagining what it would feel like to have his hands buried in it.

The first time he'd met her, he'd been very attracted to her, but he knew her type. An angelic good girl on the outside but nasty and self-righteous on the inside. He avoided girls like her for a reason, and so, after handing her his card, he'd moved on.

Not for very long, though. In a small town like Rock Canyon, it was hard to avoid someone, and Chase found himself bumping into Katie everywhere: at the grocery store, the gas station, the coffee shop, and especially at Buck's. It also hadn't taken him long to learn that whatever his preconceived notions had been, there wasn't a mean bone in Katie's body. He'd watched her help an older lady out with her groceries, just to be nice, and when someone's dog had been running down the middle of Main Street, Katie had rescued it. He only knew that because he'd watched her crouch in the middle of the road, pat her legs and call the mutt to her. After that, he had doubled his efforts to stay clear of her. A good girl with a kind heart? Both were too easy to break.

A couple weeks ago, he'd joined Katie for a game of

pool with her friends Steph and Jared, telling himself that no one else was playing, but when she'd missed her shot, he'd been an idiot and offered to show her how to make it. The smell of her hair and the way her butt had fit back against him had given him an hour-long stiffy and an even longer conversation in his head about why getting involved with Katie Connors was a really bad idea.

Despite his resolve to ignore her, he'd caught himself studying her today when he'd dropped his check off. The way she bit her lip when she'd obviously had something to say to the cranky old hag, Mrs. Andrews, but held it back, even when she was irritated. He'd seen her do it before with others and wondered why she kept it in. She was never obvious with her annoyance, but it was there, just a slight tightening in her smile. Did she keep quiet because she wanted everyone to like her? Because they did. People in Rock Canyon might walk all over her, but they held Katie Connors up as all that was goodness and kindness.

He'd bet his chopper, though, that Katie might be all cool sweetness on the outside, but she was a firecracker on the inside.

And boy, had he fantasized about Katie Connors letting that sharp tongue loose and maybe using it on him. In some real fun ways.

She sat down out of his view and he took his pool shot, wondering why he was so fascinated by a small-town hairdresser who bottled up her emotions like a shaken soda pop.

'Cause she's out of your league, and that makes it all the more interesting. You always want what you can't have.

When the game ended, Chase headed back up to the bar and noticed her doodling on a napkin while she munched on some chili cheese fries. The way her eyebrows knit together in concentration made him want to read what was on that scrap of paper. Something told him it wouldn't be her grocery list. He leaned over the bar and asked Grant, "Hey, what's Katie drinking?"

"Sorry, dude, but there's no way in hell you're making it with Katie Connors," Grant said.

"Maybe I just want to talk," Chase offered.

Grant snorted and made a clear drink with a lime wedge and some leaves, then handed it to him. "Uh-huh. Well, whatever floats your boat, dude, but if I was buying Katie a drink, it wouldn't be because I was looking for conversation."

"Thanks, man," Chase said, taking the glass. "Can I get a beer too?"

Grant handed him the beer. "Good luck. You're gonna need it."

THE MOJITO HAD not improved Katie's mood. She shoved another chili fry in her mouth and thought of how bleak her life looked. It wasn't like Rock Canyon was swimming with eligible men who had steady incomes and nice manners. Her mother had always put a lot of stock in a man with manners. Jimmy had always been polite to her mother, and she had never said an unkind word against him, except that he was *charming*. Her mother's tone had been less than complimentary when she'd said it and, looking back, she had probably been trying to tell her something. Even Ted Bundy had been charming.

She doodled on her napkin, her thoughts dwelling on her mother. Her strong, capable mother, who had raised her by herself after her dad had left when she was two. As far as she knew, they had never divorced, and her mother had never considered remarrying. She'd seemed fine alone, holding on to her manners and her morals like a security blanket.

Katie wondered what her mother would say about everything that had been happening the last few years. When she'd lost her to breast cancer three years ago, Katie had felt broken and lost. Her mother had been her rock. Her cheerleader. Her conscience.

Had her mother ever gotten tired of being good, tired of doing the right thing? If Katie could do anything she wanted, without repercussions . . .

Struck by an inspiring idea, she put the pen to her napkin and started making a list of the things she had always wanted to try or had always been told she shouldn't do.

One. Get purple streaks in my hair.

When she was sixteen, she'd wanted to dye her hair purple. Her mother had told her no, that it was vulgar and a fad.

She bit the end of the pen and remembered the night after graduation, when she'd gone with all of her friends to Twin Falls and everyone had gotten a tattoo but her because she was terrified her mom would see it.

Two. Get a tattoo.

In ninth grade, when her friend Brittney Richards had stolen a pair of cheap sunglasses from Hall's Market and been caught, her mother had told her she couldn't hang out with Brittney anymore. Katie had tried to explain that Brittney had only taken the glasses because she and Steph had dared her to, but her mother hadn't relented.

Three. Steal something.

On and on the list went, her mother's voice ringing in her head with "Ladies don't do this" or "Good girls don't do that." She had to unfold the napkin just to make more room.

"You looked like you could use another."

Katie's head snapped up from her list and she covered the napkin quickly. "Hi, Chase. What are you doing here?"

Stupid question. Why else did someone go to a bar? To drink.

He slid into the seat across from her and passed her the mojito. "Shop's closed Mondays. Didn't feel like hanging out at home."

"Oh. Well, thanks for the drink, but I probably shouldn't. I need to head out soon so I can get up early. You know what they say about worms and birds." She could tell she sounded like she was rambling, but she couldn't help it. It happened when she got nervous.

"So you have to be up early, which begs the question . . . What brings *you* here?" he asked.

"I didn't have any food in my house and didn't feel like grocery shopping." She tried to act casual, but the way his eyes kept shifting toward her hand was making her heart pound with anxiety.

"So you chose to come to a bar on a Monday night?" he said, his dark brow arched.

"They have great chili fries and I was in the mood for something greasy and really bad for me," she said defensively.

He nodded toward her hand with a grin that was nothing short of evil. "What were you writing? You looked like you were thinking really hard."

"Just my . . . to-do list. I have a lot of things to do for the Extravaganza. I was trying to remember everything, but this mojito's really getting to me. Besides, my handwriting is so messy, I can't even read what I wrote anyway." She swallowed and let out a nervous giggle.

"Huh. Well, if you're feeling a little tipsy, I could finish writing it for you."

She watched his hand creep across the table and yelped in terror. "No thanks! I think I'll just save it for tomorrow, you know, go after it with a clear head."

She started to slide the napkin closer to her, but quick as a snake, Chase pulled the napkin out from under her hand. Panic rose up, tightening her throat, and she cried hoarsely, "No!"

But Chase had already brought it under his nose, and those teasing eyes shifted as he scanned the first line. "'Number one. Get purple streaks in my hair.'"

She wanted to die. She wanted to curl up in a ball and die a slow, horrible death. Grabbing her purse, she threw some bills down for Grant before bolting for the door. She couldn't just sit there and listen to him read off each idiotic idea that had come into her head after one mojito.

Note to self: Next time you decide to make a crazy list of things you want to try someday, do it at home.

CHASE WAS TOO startled by Katie's abrupt departure to stop her. He hadn't meant to upset her; he'd only been playing around. He looked over the list again, and could see why she was so spooked. A surprised smile spread across his face as he read:

One. Get purple streaks in my hair.
Two. Get a tattoo.
Three. Steal something.
Four. Say the first thing that comes to mind.
Five. Go skinny-dipping.
Six. Go to a sex shop.
Seven. Try handcuffs.
Eight. Tell Jimmy exactly what I think of him.
Nine. Drink and flirt too much.
Ten. Have a one-night stand.

Chase folded up the list and put it in his pocket. Who would have thought little Miss Play by the Rules would make such a naughty list?

Smiling as he left the bar, he decided that first thing tomorrow he would call K.C.'s Salon and get an appointment with her. This was the perfect chance to satisfy his curiosity, and get over his crazy attraction to the uptight blonde.

If the only way he could get her undivided attention, and pitch his master plan to help her complete any and all of the items on her list, was to get a thirty-dollar haircut, then so be it. Besides, he couldn't wait to see prim-and-proper Katie Connors get a little hot under her collar.

Chapter Two

KATIE ENJOYED HER little salon, loved the laughs that came from being in a room with a bunch of women. She'd rented a chair in a larger salon for years, which hadn't been cheap but was a lot less than owning her own place. The problem with renting a chair was that you had no say about who would be renting next to you, and Katie had gotten tired of the backstabbing and client stealing. She wanted to be able to choose who she worked with. She'd always planned on buying a salon someday, but she'd also planned on being married before that ever happened.

So she'd saved every tip, every extra penny to pay for a dream wedding that never happened. Instead of using her money on the perfect dress, she'd put a down payment on her house and rented the salon space from Maeve Kettle, who'd done the rinses and styles of the ladies of Rock Canyon for forty years. Katie had done some painting and updated all the equipment, but it had been hard finding beauticians and manicurists who wanted to work in such a small shop, let alone a small community. After six months, though, she had two other stylists and two manicurists who were all easygoing and worked well together, and she'd just hired Kitty the month before to help organize their schedules. Overall, K.C.'s Salon was doing great.

Katie had a pretty light day on Tuesday and was just finishing up a cut and highlight when Chase walked in. Ducking down and slinking off to the storage room seemed like the best plan, but she couldn't leave Daphne O'Neal's hair wet, and with her luck, someone would ask her what she was doing, thus drawing more attention to herself. She didn't know how she would face him, though, knowing he had probably read every word on her list and laughed at her expense. She was mortified and yet ticked off that he had the nerve to poke his nose into her business.

When Chase caught her gaze, he smiled with so much sexy arrogance her cheeks burned.

"Be right with you!" she called shakily.

Turning her back on him to finish blow-drying Daphne's hair, her eyes kept straying to his reflection in the mirror. He had on a pair of loose jeans and a blue T-shirt tight enough to show off some very drool-worthy pecs. Jimmy had been short and stocky, whereas Chase was tall, with lean muscle. He leaned over to say something to Kitty, and Katie noticed that every female eye seemed to be watching him, and if the way he flashed that pearly white smile around was any indication, the cocky jerk knew it.

Bigheaded jerk. Showing up here with his charm and his hotness, all to tease her. Well, she wasn't going to give him the satisfaction of letting him fluster her. Turning off the dryer, she smiled at Daphne and said, "You're set. See you back in a couple of months. Make sure the shampoo and conditioner you're using is for color-treated hair, okay?"

Daphne turned her head from left to right and gushed, "Of course, Katie. You do such a good job on my hair. I love it!"

Katie smiled, although her eyes were on the hunk of juicy male resting against the reception desk, watching her every move. Turning away from the mirror and his blatant perusal, Katie grabbed her broom and started her post-appointment cleanup. Daphne left her tip on the station desk, and despite her resolve to not let him get under her skin, Katie looked over in time to see Daphne flashing him an inviting smile. Chase just nodded at her, ignoring her disappointment, and turned his unnerving gaze back on Katie. He gave her a knowing grin, and imagining what he must be thinking about, she swept harder.

When she couldn't stall anymore, she put the small broom back and tried for casual, but it sounded a little squeaky to her ears. "Hey, Chase, what brings you by?"

Kitty, always so helpful, answered, "Oh, Chase is here for a haircut. He called this morning."

Katie's nerves went from frazzled to haywired. She eyed the already short strands and could tell that it hadn't been too long since his last haircut. "Looks like you just had one."

"Yeah? I did a few weeks ago." He stood up and moved closer to her until she had to look up at him. She tried not to think about how good he smelled as he said, "Is it a problem that I like having my hair cut? For me, nothing feels better than having someone's fingers run through my hair." Lowering his voice, he added, "Well, almost nothing."

At his suggestive words, her heart pounded like a hundred hoof beats and she tried to ignore the way his mouth tilted up in a small smile, a smile that said *I know exactly what I'm doing and you want me bad, don't you?* The guy thought he was so irresistible.

Well, he kind of is. I mean, between the eyes, chin, and that body, who wouldn't go a little gaga over him?

How could she be attracted to the man who had taken something so personal from her last night and was here now, teasing her, taunting her with his presence? When had she gone completely cuckoo for Cocoa Puffs and started lusting after any hottie with a body no matter how despicable he may be?

Trying to regain some composure, she said, "Oh well, sure. Come on back. Do you know what you want to have done?"

"Just short on the sides and a little longer up top so I can spike it," he said, easing into the chair of the washing sink, his lips still twisted in that annoying smirk.

Sliding the cape over him, she tried to focus on her irritation and not on his very nice lips. She turned on the water to hot, slowly decreasing the temperature until it felt good on her skin.

"All right, just let me know if it's too hot or cold." She ran her hands through his already short hair and over the skin of his neck, helping him lean back. She relaxed as those gorgeous eyes closed, no longer looking at her like he could see inside her head, and said, "Feel good?"

"Awesome," he said.

Filling her hand with shampoo, Katie began to work it into his hair, using her fingers to massage the scalp and give gentle tugs on the strands. She leaned closer to him, watching his handsome face soften, and when she heard a small groan escape him as she found the two pressure points on the back of his neck she tried to remember he had read some very personal things about her and as a result, had come to her place of business to mess with her. Only a mean-spirited snake would harass someone he hardly knew.

Despite her suspicions as to why he was there, she couldn't help noticing that he was one of the best-looking guys in town. With his mouth slightly open and his full lips looking soft, she wondered if he was a good kisser. Jimmy had been more of a bird with his kisses and it had made her crazy, until she'd finally grab him by his head to keep him still. Somehow she had a feeling Chase knew how to kiss without any direction.

I bet this is what he would look like during sex.

"Holy shit, that is amazing. Where did you learn to do that?" His voice broke into her disturbing thoughts, rough and raspy. It was the sexiest sound she'd ever heard.

What is wrong with me? Stop thinking about him. He's

just another turd with nice eyes . . . and lips . . . okay, so his
chest and arms are pretty great . . .

Pulling at his short strands again, she tried to control her hormones and prayed he wouldn't open his eyes. The last thing she needed was for the man who had already seen a list of her biggest regrets catching her with flushed cheeks and wondering why washing his hair was getting to her. The guy was not a nice man, and he didn't deserve her lusty thoughts. "In school, and I also got my massage therapist license. Just let me know if the pressure is too much."

"It's perfect," he said, opening his eyes. She silently prayed her cheeks were no longer rosy, but if they were, he didn't mention it. Instead, he surprised her by adding, "I actually came in to apologize. I didn't mean to embarrass you last night. I was trying to be playful, and I crossed the line."

Jerking her gaze up to meet his, there was no mockery on his face and he sounded sincere. Maybe she had been wrong about him and he wasn't such a bad guy. She felt a little guilty for all the angry thoughts she'd been having about him.

She rinsed the shampoo and rubbed the conditioner in, starting the scalp massage over again. While she worked, she decided to follow her mother's advice about graciousness and said, "Thank you for your apology. I appreciate it."

They were both quiet for a few minutes, and she assumed it was because that was all he had needed to get off his chest. But while she was rinsing the conditioner out, he said, "I've been thinking about your list."

The hand holding the sprayer slipped and she gasped in horror as the full force of water hit him smack in the face. She turned off the water quickly as he flew up sputtering, wiping water from his eyes. Grabbing a towel from the cupboard, she started patting his face dry, blurting, "Oh my God, are you okay? I didn't mean to do that, you just . . ."

He opened one of his eyes and grimaced. "I was going to say that if you want to come by tonight, I'll help you out with number two, but if you're going to drown me, I take it back."

She tried to remember what number two was. Then it clicked. *Two. Get a tattoo.*

She brought down another towel from the cupboard and started drying his face and hair, avoiding his gaze. "I was just playing around when I wrote that list. Things I would never do, you know."

He blinked both of his eyes open and grinned. "Right."

How dare he not believe her? Biting her tongue and counting to ten, she finished cleaning him up and said calmly, "Okay, why don't you follow me, and we'll get your cut started."

She walked in front of him to her chair, aware of everyone watching them curiously, and motioned for him to sit down.

"So that list you wrote was just for fun? Stuff you would never, ever do?" he said as he slid into her chair.

"Yeah, that's right. Just me being a lightweight," she said, pulling out her clippers and comb.

"Huh. That's too bad." She couldn't stop her head from

jerking up and locking eyes with him in the mirror. "A couple of those items I'd be happy to help you out with."

CHASE CHUCKLED AS she flipped on the clippers, her cheeks bright pink. She worked on him in silence and he decided to bide his time until she finished. Teasing Katie was starting to become one of his favorite activities. She'd been angry with him; even when she'd tried to hide it, he could tell, but there was something else there too. A little spark of interest maybe? Something that made him certain good girl Katie wanted to try her hand at being very, very bad.

His eyes followed the swell of her breasts as her chest came close to his face. They were a great size and shape, just big enough to fill his hands, and those lips were soft, pouty, and had a promise of bliss. He wondered if she'd slap him if he just happened to kiss her right now, in front of everyone in the salon.

Chase didn't have a shy bone in his body and he especially didn't mind going after what he wanted. The only other woman in town to tempt him for more than a quick release was Ryan Ashton, but he'd lost that battle. Ryan had been a good girl too, a bit on the shy side, but he had been interested in her because they'd had similar interests. By the time he had met her, though, she was already spoken for.

Despite his efforts to stay away, good girls had always been a huge draw for him, ever since he hit puberty. But those types of girls hadn't wanted anything to do with trailer-trash Chase. If they had looked at him at all, it was because they had a score to settle with Daddy and he fit the bill of "big mistake." Those girls may have been good, but they didn't have a nice bone in their bodies, whereas Katie had this way about her. She genuinely seemed to care about the people in her life, even the ones he thought really didn't deserve anyone's consideration. It was like she was constantly trying to dig deep inside everyone else and find the good in them, something he would never dream of doing. He barely knew her, but he found her to be an enigma, a puzzle he wanted to solve.

She turned off the clippers and cleaned him up, styling his hair into short spikes. He watched her in the mirror, her champagne-blond hair in a sassy knot on top of her head.

When she finished, she smiled too brightly and said, "All done. You can just pay Kitty up front."

Chase pulled out his wallet and slipped her a ten, with his card underneath. "The offer still stands. Come by tonight and I'll help you out," he said, his voice lowered, "with anything you might want."

Those full lips tightened and he saw her hand was shaking as she took his money and card. Tossing them into the top drawer of her station and snapping it closed, she said softly, "Thank you. I'll see you back in a few weeks."

"Or sooner," he said confidently.

Her blue-eyed gaze was no longer friendly as he turned away, grinning his way up to perky Kitty. He was going to get to the real Katie Connors sooner or later. He had a feeling she was going to be a lot of fun.

Once she pulled that giant stick out of her ass.

KATIE FINISHED HER last appointment and headed to the grocery store to do some shopping. She drove past The Local Bean and Chloe's Book Nook, and looked to the left at Chase's place, Jagged Rock Tattoo Parlor. She was still fuming about him coming into her salon and playing with her, even if he *had* apologized. Telling her he could help her out with anything on her list. Of all the conceited, high-handed, jerky things to say. He obviously hadn't been too sorry, since he made that outrageous proposition. And after she had just started to think he wasn't that bad of a guy.

Who did he think he was, Iron Man? That he could just ooze charm and she would fawn all over him because he was handsome, successful, and single?

Like she would ever really do anything on that list, and for him to suggest it made her feel cheap. Like he had no respect for her, or maybe it was just women in general. Was he one of those guys who thought all women were easy prey, just waiting for some big, handsome guy to move in with a few suggestive ideas and they would just drop their panties and say, "*Come on, big boy . . .*"?

Without really thinking about what she was doing, she pulled around the corner and parked. She slammed her door and marched into the parlor just as he was coming out of the back with a sterile tray. His pleased, lazy smile only added fuel to the fire.

"Hey," she said, "I don't appreciate you coming into my salon and baiting me with things you really know nothing about."

Setting his tray down slowly, he said, "Actually, I know quite a bit about tattoos, and let's see . . ." He pulled something from his pocket and unfolded it slowly. Recognizing the bar napkin, Katie lunged forward and tried to grab at it, but he held it out of reach, reading, "Sex shops, stealing—although I don't recommend that—drinking, skinny-dipping, flirting, and oh yeah . . . one-night stands." He brought his arm down and she snatched the list from him. Before she could move away, he reached out and grabbed her wrist, running his thumb over her skin slowly.

Attempting to pull away from him, she cursed the tingles his warm hand caused. Glaring, she tried to sound firm. "Let go of me. I'm tired of your games. I don't know why you think it's funny to play with someone's emotions, but I've never done anything to you and I find it humiliating that you would make fun of me over something I did when I was having a bad day. It makes you a bully, and I want you to leave me alone."

Chase didn't release her, just reached out with his other hand and started to pull her toward him. Her heart pounded as all that mouthwatering muscle drew closer to her and he slipped his arm around her waist. *She* might think Chase was lower than pond scum, but her hormones sure didn't agree.

Katie stopped struggling and tilted her face up just as he said, "I can't do that."

Letting her wrist go, she froze as he trailed his hand up her arm slowly, making every single cell in her body scream to get closer, but a lifetime of good breeding and manners kept reciting, *Good girls don't . . . good girls don't . . .*

Still, the part of her that hadn't been held by a man in a long time wanted him to kiss her until her brain shut up.

He didn't kiss her like she wanted him to, though.

Chase ran one hand through her hair and cupped her cheek with the other. "Sweet Katie, the last thing on this earth I'd want to do is upset you, but I have to say, it is really hot to see you all riled up." He slipped his thumb over her bottom lip and continued, "Your mouth purses when someone irritates you and you're trying not to say anything. I've noticed you do that a lot. But your eyes heat up when you're ticked off, and that's hard to miss. Like now."

Katie was holding her breath as she swayed toward him, and he whispered, "Do you know what you want?"

Did she? "Yes." She drifted a little closer, like she couldn't resist him. It was his eyes. No, the way he smiled. Maybe . . .

"Do you know where you want it?"

His words were penetrating the fog of desire and she blinked at him. "What?"

Sliding his hand from her lip to over her shoulder, he asked, "Do you want it here?"

It finally registered what he was asking and she said, "I don't want a tattoo."

"Are you sure?" he said teasingly. "'Cause I have a binder full of things you might like. Of course, there are some things we could check off the list that don't involve binders, needles, or tattoos. Let me think . . ."

She needed to move away from him so *she* could think. She took a breath, but that was a mistake. He smelled amazing, and she was so tired of being good all the time. She was thirty years old and the man she was supposed to spend the rest of her life with had picked someone else. Maybe if she had been more daring and less rigid, Jimmy wouldn't have dumped her. She would never know now. She couldn't change the past, but she could let go now, just this once.

Slipping her arms up around his neck and ignoring his wide-eyed expression, she said, "Chase, if you want to kiss me, will you just do it already?"

OF ALL THE things she could have said to him, that wasn't what he'd been expecting.

Despite his initial surprise, Chase, never one to disappoint a lady, dropped his mouth to hers and took her lips in a soft, searching kiss.

Damn.

She tasted like peppermint and heat. Using his arm to bring her against him, his other hand slipped to the back of her neck. He liked that she didn't just let him kiss her, but she kissed back with enthusiasm. Katie's hands ran over his neck, reminding him of her scalp massage, and he imagined those hands on other parts of his body. The intimate image and the feel of her pressed so closely to him made his cock harden with need.

Her hands traveled over his back, down his sides, and up under his T-shirt. Her nails skimmed his bare skin, sliding around to his stomach and between their bodies. Anyone walking by could look in and see them.

"Maybe I should lock the door," he said between kisses, "pull the blinds."

He knew it was a mistake to break the spell the minute he spoke the words. Her eyes popped open and she stared up at him in horror. She tried to move away from him, but he didn't want her to leave, not yet. "I just didn't want someone to walk by and see you. This town is like a festering pool of gossip, and I'm not exactly Mr. Popularity."

"I'm sorry. I don't know what came over me . . ." she said, fiddling with her cute, lopsided bun, which was starting to come down.

"Hey, no complaints here. You don't have to apologize for anything," he said, wondering what exactly she was apologizing for. Asking him to kiss her? Kissing him back?

He would have asked, but he figured it might just tick her off, and right now she looked like she was thinking hard about something. Like whether or not she wanted him to do as he'd suggested and get back to making her soft and willing . . .

Her voice was so quiet, he almost didn't hear her ask, "Does it hurt?"

Kissing? No, wait, not kissing. Oh.

"Getting a tattoo?" She nodded and he laughed. She just kept surprising him. "A little, sometimes a lot, depending where you get it, but then the pain goes away after a bit and it's just uncomfortable."

"Hmmm." She pulled away from him, much to his disappointment, and turned. Katie walked over to the wall of photographs, pictures of women and men showing off his work. He was proud of his art, not just the tattoos, but his graphic novels too. She stopped in front of his framed copy of *Destructo Boy*, his first graphic novel, and he said, "I did that one years ago, when I was barely eighteen."

She turned to him with surprised eyes and asked, "You did? Did you do anymore?"

"Yeah, I do artwork for several series, but this one is all me. I do the illustrations and dialogue."

"That is so amazing. I've never met anyone famous before," she said, adding, "except for Travis Bowers. He's a country music singer I went to high school with."

"I don't know if I'd call myself famous. I just write comics, not like I do cartoons for Pixar or something." Her inspection was actually making him nervous. He picked up a binder of tattoo samples and held it out to her. "Here. Why don't you look and see if there's something you might like while I close the blinds and lock the door?" She gave him a startled look and he teased, "We wouldn't want everyone in town to know that Katie Connors was doing something so out of character like get a tattoo, would we?"

She blushed and took the binder from him as he walked over to close up the front of the store and turned over the OPEN sign. When he came back toward her, he was dazzled by the smile on her face.

"That's cute." She flipped to the next page and made a face, "Ew, who would put that on their body?" She turned the page again, stopped, and ran her finger over a picture with a smile. "This one."

Coming around to stand behind her, he pressed against her back to see the picture. It was a daisy with a ladybug hovering over it. Very girly, and not his taste, but it wasn't his body. Leaning over until his mouth barely hovered over her neck, he said, "And where do you want it?"

KATIE HAD NO idea where to put a tattoo. It had been a fantasy, a rebellious fancy when she was eighteen, but now the warm body of the man behind her and his softly asked question was making it all too real.

Trying not to lean back into him, she said, "Somewhere that no one will see unless I want them to." There, that sounded safe.

"All right, then. Go ahead and unbutton your pants and slide them down to your hips," he said, moving away from her.

"Excuse me?" she said, turning around to see him transferring the sterile tray he'd held earlier from the counter to a metal table just behind an armless chair.

"I said, unbutton your pants, slide them to about halfway down your hips, and straddle the chair," he said, slowly and deliberately.

"Why?" she asked, thinking there was no way she was going to pull her pants down in front of him and show him her butt. Especially under bright, fluorescent lights.

"I was just thinking you'd probably like it on your lower back. That way your jeans will cover it most of the time." His face was blank, but she could hear the humor in his voice and she felt like an idiot.

Reaching for the button on her jeans, she unsnapped them and eased them down a little, pulling her T-shirt down to cover her skin. He pointed to the chair in front of his stool and said, "Go ahead and straddle the chair while I set up."

She did as he asked and heard him fiddling behind her. Just the fact that she didn't know what was coming made her ask, "Are you sure this isn't going to hurt a lot?"

His hands moved beneath her T-shirt and when they touched her skin, she jumped. "What are you doing?"

Katie was sure she heard a sigh before he said, "It will hurt for a bit until the area becomes numb, then it shouldn't hurt anymore. And to answer your second question, I am tucking your T-shirt up so I can see where to put the stencil."

Taking him at his word, she didn't protest when he stuffed her shirt up under the clasp of her bra, even though she felt awkward sitting in front of him with her butt crack hanging out. She wasn't even wearing sexy underwear, just a pair of pink cotton briefs. Those big hands trailed across her skin and she felt her whole body tighten at the sensation. Having her back stroked and kissed was one of her favorite forms of foreplay, but Chase wasn't being sensual, he was just doing his job.

Nothing he was doing was meant to make her heart pound, her stomach knot, or her eyes close; it was all in her head. Her body didn't know that, though. All it knew was that there was a pair of very rough, strong hands causing some very private areas to throb and dampen. And he wasn't even aware of the quivery feelings he was eliciting from her. If he had even the slightest clue that his touch was making her hornier than a rabbit, he would have probably teased her about that too.

The instruments of her hormone-induced trip to crazy town stopped their innocent exploration, and he said, "Now I'm going to get started. Try not to tense up." She heard the sound of snapping latex behind her and a whining buzz.

He ran his hand over the small of her back again and she closed her eyes, enjoying the sensation but knowing that just behind it there was a rapid-firing needle. She felt him lean closer to her and his breath rustled the small hairs that curled along her nape as he whispered, "Are you ready?"

"Yes. I'm ready," she said. The first prick felt like she'd been burned, and she bit her lip, trying to hold back her cry as her back caught fire with pain. "Owowowowow! Okay, when does the not-painful part kick in?"

"It's different for everybody. Just try to relax." *Bzzzz* went the little gun again and Katie tried to suck it up, but her eyes teared.

Stupid nearly midlife crisis!

All she felt was pain. Pain . . . pain . . . *pain*! It seemed like she'd been sitting there for hours when in reality he'd barely begun.

"I can't believe you don't use some kind of numbing agent," she griped loud enough to be heard over the tattoo gun.

The gun clicked off, and she heard Chase sigh followed by the clink of the tray, the snap of his glove, and his steps behind her. She turned to glance over her shoulder to see where he had gone, winced as her lower back stung and faced forward again. Suddenly, a bottle of whiskey was being held four inches from her nose. "Take a couple of swigs."

She eyed the rim dubiously and asked, "Really? From the bottle?"

He grinned at her. "That's good Scotch. I don't share that with just anyone. Plus it's not just one of the oldest forms of anesthesia. It's also an awesome sterilizer. And just to reassure you, I'm clean. I swear."

She blushed and took a swig, the liquor burning her throat. "Smooth."

Laughing, he went back to his work, gloves snapping and then that irritating buzzing again. She took another drink of the vile brew, hoping the foul taste and burning throat were worth it.

A moment later she heard the gun click off. "Why don't you tell me what prompted the list? It'll distract you from the pain."

Or just make things worse, sharing my humiliation with a virtual stranger.

But what could be more humiliating than him reading every stupid thing she'd never done and always been too scared to do?

Trying to take her mind off her tender back and said, "I got dumped about eight months ago. We'd been together almost seven years."

"So why the list now?"

"I just got his wedding invitation in the mail yesterday."

The *bzzzz*-ing stopped and Chase slid round on his wheelie stool to look at her face. "Is it the same girl he cheated with?"

"How did you know he . . ."

He waved his hand. "Because he's an obvious douche bag. Only a giant douche sends his ex-girlfriend a wedding invitation, unless they were friends for a long time before or after. Is that the case?"

Katie smiled for the first time since yesterday. "No, we haven't talked since he left. And yeah, he was pretty much a douche during our whole relationship. I was just the only one who didn't notice."

"Then I'm really glad I shared my whiskey with you. Sounds like you needed something stronger than a sissy girly drink." He slid back behind her and said, "That's how it usually is. You don't see how fucked up a relationship is until you're out."

"It wasn't all bad. We really were happy, most of the time." She didn't know why she was defending Jimmy, but the whole situation made her feel stupid. How had she not realized how *broken* their relationship was? How had she not seen that he had one foot out the door and his boots under someone else's bed?

Chase interrupted her descent into self-loathing when he said, "Any guy who doesn't marry you after three years isn't going to. My mom taught me that."

She took another gulp of whiskey and it no longer burned, just increased the warm sensation in her tummy. "Gee, I've never heard of the three-year rule; please teach it to me."

"After my dad left, my mom had a lot of boyfriends," he said loudly over the gun. "Some even lasted longer than three years, but once she brought up the word *marriage*, they were gone. Then she'd lie in her bed for a week or two, crying, and start all over again. By three years you should know everything there is to know about a person, or close to it. And if you know everything and you still can't take the leap, then you need to get out."

"What about love at first sight? Or people who fall in love and get married after six months? Do you really think they're going to last?" she asked, starting to feel a little tipsy.

"As long as they go into it with their eyes open, knowing the other person's flaws and loving them anyway, who am I to judge?"

Katie, feeling loose, asked, "What are your flaws?"

"Why? You want to know if I'm your perfect match?" he asked, and Katie could hear the humor in his voice.

She scoffed. "No, I was just curious." Taking another gulp, she marveled as pain-free warmth spread through her limbs, and prodded, "So what are they?"

More whirring behind her until he finally stopped and said, "I'm stubborn as hell."

Katie rolled her eyes, even though he couldn't see her. "Most people are stubborn."

"You're not. You give in to everybody."

His words stung. If he hadn't been jabbing a needle in and out of her back, she would have gotten up and let him have it. Instead she snapped, "I do not! I just pick my battles."

"I've been here less than six months and I haven't seen you really hold your ground on anything."

She turned her head enough to look over her shoulder and said, "I'll have you know, I told Mrs. Andrews we were keeping your booth where it was, next to the kissing booth, and that was that."

He raised his eyebrow at her. "Where did she want me moved?"

The angle was hurting her neck, so she turned her head forward again. "She didn't want you to have one at all. Thinks tattoo parlors bring around a bad element."

Chase was quiet after that, only the sound of the tattoo gun echoing in the parlor. When the gun finally went silent, she felt him dabbing at her back. "All done." Handing her a small mirror, he helped her stand up. "Here, can you see it?"

Katie looked at her spanking new tattoo, and part of her was excited and exhilarated that she had done it. But the small, sober part of her brain screamed, *What did you do, you idiot?*

"Just keep a piece of plastic wrap over it for the next three days until it heals," he said.

Katie heard his coolness and knew something was wrong by the look on his face, but couldn't really recall what she had said to upset him. She set the whiskey bottle on the counter and the room was a bit hazy around the edges.

Lightweight.

Had it been the thing with Mrs. Andrews? Why would a guy like Chase care what some small-minded woman thought? Still, if that was it, she didn't want him feeling bad, especially since she shouldn't have said it in the first place.

"Look, I'm really sorry for what I said. I shouldn't have repeated that conversation," she said.

He picked up the tray and his eyes were glacial. With a tone just as cool, he said, "It's nothing I haven't heard before."

She crossed her arms over her chest and said quietly, "Those were her words, not mine. I don't agree with her."

He gave her a little half smile. "I appreciate that. Not all people share your high opinion of me."

The whole conversation was awkward and uncomfortable, and she wanted out of it. "How much do I owe you?"

"Don't worry about it," he said, turning his back to her as he went into the back.

She stood there for a minute, not knowing what to do or say to make things better, before pulling out several bills from her purse and leaving them on the counter. She felt awful about hurting his feelings, but she had drunk too much whiskey too fast and wasn't in control of any of her finer brain functions. Even if she could figure out the right thing to say, she couldn't stop the irrational urge to giggle, and somehow she didn't think that would make her apology sound very sincere. Better to wait until to-morrow, when she had all her wits about her.

Katie pulled her pants back up, but when she tried to button them, they dug into her back, making her suck in a sharp breath of pain. So with halfway-zipped pants and a little wobble in her step, she walked out the door and pulled out her cell phone. The warm summer air hit her face but did nothing to sober her. She dialed Steph and cursed when it went straight to voice mail.

There was no way she was driving, even if it was just around the corner. Katie passed by her 4Runner and kept walking down the side streets toward home, her thoughts lingering on Chase. He was weird; there, she said it. One minute he was sticking his nose into her business, then showing up to apologize and two minutes after that he was offering to help her complete her list. It was frustrating to admit when they went at it verbally, he was quick-witted and kind of funny. He acted tough, nonchalant, and carefree, but one negative comment from someone he didn't even know had shut him down. He was like a big, hot slice of cake with all kinds of yummy layers to savor.

Picturing that cake, she realized she'd forgotten to go grocery shopping. *Crap.* That would teach her to let Chase Trepasso distract her. It wouldn't happen again, no matter how good a kisser he was.

Chapter Three

CHASE HADN'T MEANT to take his frustration out on Katie, but it was the same thing everywhere he went. People too high up on their fucking horses thought that tattoo artists were lower than dirt, and it pissed him off.

He came out from the back of the shop and started, "Look, I . . ." but Katie was gone and there was a wad of crumpled cash on the counter. Cursing, he shoved the bills into his wallet and went to turn off the lights. She was in no condition to drive, and if one of the hard-ass Barney Fifes in blue decided to pull her over, she'd be screwed.

Admiring his motorcycle's beauty in the evening sun, he swung his leg over to sit astride the powerful vehicle. He had a Chevy Blazer he drove when the roads were bad or he needed to haul something, but the chopper was his pride and joy. He saw Katie's SUV still parked on the side of the street and started the chopper up. He flipped the motorcycle around and was surprised to see her up the street, walking unsteadily.

"Let me give you a ride," he yelled as he pulled up alongside her.

Stopping and turning to face him, she asked, "I thought you were mad at me?"

He was surprised she'd even picked up on his irritation. "No, I'm not mad."

"Really? 'Cause you seemed like you were teed off . . ."

"I'm not mad," he snapped, and, at her hurt look, took a deep breath. "I'm sorry. Just come on. I don't like you walking home by yourself."

"It's still light out, and really, it's not far," she said, and she was right. It was past nine, but the sun hadn't fully set yet. He had a feeling though, that wasn't what was stopping her.

"God, will you stop being so stubborn and get on the damn chopper?" He pulled in front of her and cut the engine. "Look, just let me take you home. It will make me feel better." She seemed to be weighing the dangers as he reached out to grab her hand. "Trust me."

Why that worked Chase didn't know, but she took a deep breath and climbed on behind him. He liked the way her arms wrapped around his waist and the feel of her breasts pressed against his back. Patting her hands comfortingly, he said, "Hang on."

Starting the chopper back up, Chase headed down the street, following Katie's directions as she shouted them. When he pulled in front of her house and parked in the drive, she released her death grip on his waist and scrambled off. He rubbed his ribs where her fingers had dug in and couldn't help grinning at her as she tried to shake off her obvious terror.

"First time on a motorcycle?" he asked.

The little smile she gave him was just a small lift of her lips, but he thought it was sexy as hell. "Yeah, sorry, I just can't seem to help it. It just doesn't feel right to have nothing between me and everything else. How do you keep from getting bugs in your teeth?"

"Actually, one time, I went to pick a girl up for a date and the whole night she acted weird. I couldn't figure out why." He started chuckling as he continued, "When I went to kiss her at the end, she literally started gagging and finally told me that I had a smashed bug on my face."

Katie's sweet laughter joined his. "I'm guessing you didn't go out with her again?"

He shook his head. "I was eighteen and angry. I just roared off, and when I saw her around, I ignored her. Another flaw I guess. I don't like to be made a fool of and I don't let people treat me like a joke."

Katie cocked her head and said, "I don't really think that's a flaw."

He shrugged. "Let's just say it doesn't make me popular with most people. I'm not really a filter kind of guy. You piss me off, I'm not going to pretend it's all fine and dandy. Guess that's one way we differ."

He saw that flare again, the one he noticed every time she had something to say but held it in. It started to cool and he grabbed her around her waist, pulling her to him.

"Don't. Don't hold it in with me. I've got a pretty thick skin: I'm sure I can take whatever you wanna dish out."

When she didn't respond right away, he figured she was going to bottle it up anyway. Instead she blurted, "I am not spineless. I was just taught to always put my best behavior out there and not just say whatever comes out, no matter how much I may want to sometimes. I can have an opinion without being rude."

"Fine, so if I was to ask myself inside for a nightcap, what would you say?" he asked.

She seemed to be struggling with her answer. Her mouth started to open but snapped shut again before she could get anything out.

"You want to tell me to go to hell?" He said, smirking. It really was fun to fluster her.

She shook her head. "No. I want to tell you that I don't have any alcohol and I didn't get to eat dinner. I meant to go to the grocery store because I have no food in the house, but you distracted me! Coming by my work to embarrass me, and then again with that kiss . . ."

"Hey now, you came by *my* work and distracted *me*. As for the kiss, you wanted me to. And that was a good kiss, an amazing kiss. And it's definitely something that we should do again very soon."

"No! No more kissing. I shouldn't have asked you to kiss me," she said.

"Actually, it was more like a demand . . ." he said.

"The point is, it was wrong and . . ."

Abruptly, her protests stopped as he slipped his hands up and under her jaw to lift her blue eyes to his. "We are two single, consenting adults, and if you want to keep kissing me, let me be clear"—he brought his mouth closer to hers—"the feeling is completely mutual."

Chase went in slowly, giving her every opportunity to stop him, but she didn't. When his lips finally covered hers, she opened her mouth, their tongues meeting and melding together. He started to wrap his arms around her waist, but, remembering her tattoo, slipped his hands down to her ass instead, squeezing it and using it to press her against his aching cock.

Gasping, she yanked away from him. "What are we doing? We hardly know each other."

"I thought we were getting to know each other really well," he said.

The look in her eye told him the momentary lapse in judgment was over. He shoved his hands into the pocket of his jeans and said, "I'm not going to apologize, if that's what you're hoping for. You want me, just like I want you."

"I don't even know you!" Her voice hit a shrill note and the neighbor's dog started barking.

Chase shook his head and said, "Unless you want to be the hot new topic for the masses tomorrow, you should probably keep your voice down."

Her eyes darted around frantically and she hissed, "Please leave."

"I thought you were hungry. I could come in and we could order a pizza?" He gave her his best innocent smile and held his hands up. "I promise I won't try anything else."

"I don't think it's a good idea," she said, hesitating slightly.

He was going to take that as a yes. "I think it's a spec-fucking-tacular idea. You go inside, I'll go get food."

Not giving her a chance to protest, he took off on his chopper and headed toward Hall's Market. Hopefully he got back before cautious Katie had a chance to take the reins again.

THIS IS CRAZY. Absolutely certifiable. He isn't even your type.

Okay, so she didn't really have a type. She had only really ever been serious with her high-school boyfriend and Jimmy. All the other dates had been setups, or men she'd known forever and didn't want to hurt their feelings when they asked her out. Chase wasn't like any of them, though. He did what he wanted, despite how much other people's low opinions might bother him. She envied that.

Her first boyfriend had been a high-school baseball player who went to the same church and her mother had adored him. He'd been cute as a bug, but nothing compared to Chase's raw sexuality. Her mother had definitely never worried about them being alone together, even though he had been her first.

Of course, he had left for college and broken up with her for a sorority girl named Tiffany who he'd met during pledge week, so maybe she did have a type.

Dirty, rotten, cheating jerk faces.

Katie could hear her mother now: *Katie, if you invite a man into your home he'll have certain expectations.*

It's not like she had really invited Chase, he had just kind of invited himself and she hadn't said no. So, technically, she hadn't done anything wrong . . . yet.

All of these thoughts rushed through Katie's head as she paced her very neutral living room, picking up her bra off the back of the couch and cleaning up a pile of cat puke Slinks had left by the entryway. She winced as the skin of her back pulled tight and her tattoo throbbed, cursing the cat silently. Sometimes she thought he did it on purpose, just to make her life more difficult.

As she was washing her hands, a knock made her jump and run for the door nervously while Slinks, who had been quietly munching on kibble, puffed up and ran for her bedroom with a hiss.

"Sorry, Slinks!" She opened the door and had a grocery bag shoved into her arms. "What's this?"

"You said I distracted you from your evening of grocery shopping, so I picked up a few things." Chase walked past her with two bags of his own and set them on the counter.

She was still standing in the entryway, unsure how to proceed. "How did you get all this on the back of your bike?"

"Whoa!" He turned to her with a dark scowl. "That is a gorgeous piece of machinery, not some tricycle. Show some respect."

She shut the front door and set the bag she held next to his. "You didn't have to buy me groceries."

"I didn't. You left money on the counter when I told you not to, so I used it to buy some food." He opened up her fridge and she heard him tsking. "Geez, when you said you had no food, you weren't kidding. Is that a Chia Pet?"

Katie pushed past him to grab the forgotten fajitas and threw them in the trash. "I left you that money to pay for my tattoo." The man was making her dizzy and frustrated, unloading groceries in her kitchen. Groceries he'd bought for her. It was high-handed. It was overstepping. It was . . .

Okay, it was kind of sweet.

Another knock sounded and she jumped. "Who in the name of Brad Paisley is that?"

He started laughing and wheezed. "You are too much . . ."

She walked to the front door and pulled it open. Clinton Hammond stood on her front porch with a Rico's Pizza box and a plastic bag of plates in his hands, his egg-sized Adam's apple bobbing in his stork-like, teenage throat. "Hi, Katie. Got your pizza and bread sticks."

Now she was doubly confused. "Thanks, Clint, but I didn't . . ."

"Ah, perfect timing, kid." Chase came up beside her and reached out for the boxes. He handed Clint some money and said, "Have a good night." Clint's eyes were wide and his Adam's apple bobbed quickly as Chase slammed the door in his face. "Come on, I'm starving."

Katie felt like her head was going to explode. "*You* called in a pizza order and had them deliver it to *my* house?"

Chase handed her a slice on a paper plate and looked at her like *she* was the crazy one. "Yeah. You said you were hungry, and I was starving."

"Well, so much for avoiding gossip! Clint's going to head back to Rico's and tell Rico, who will tell his wife, Regina, who has a bigger trap than Marcie Andrews." She wanted to fill the sink and drown herself just thinking about what people would say tomorrow. What was she doing? Her mother must be looking down at her and shaking her head in disappointment. Not only had she gotten a tattoo, but now she was standing in her kitchen, at night, eating pizza with a man who would make a nun sweat.

He pulled another piece out of the box and said, "Then I think there's only one solution."

Chase took a bite and she wished he would chew with his mouth open or maybe even belch. Anything to make him less appealing.

"And what's that?" she asked, setting her plate down.

He closed the gap between them and pressed against her, his arms slipping through hers to grab the tile countertop behind her. Grinning down at her wolfishly, he said, "We give them something to talk about."

His nearness was wreaking havoc with her plan to resist him. Especially with those great lips so close to hers. "What do you mean?"

As he moved against her suggestively, her body started humming with desire, especially in the places that hadn't been touched since months before Jimmy left. And Chase knew what he was doing to her; she could tell by the heat in his eyes.

"I think your little list was about more than just brain-storming a bunch of out-of-character fantasies. It was a cry for help. I think you need to have a little fun and cut loose. And I'm just the guy you need."

"Oh yeah? And how does it benefit me for the whole town to know we're dating or hooking up or whatever you have in mind?" Her eyes almost crossed with lust as he moved his hips into hers again, causing a throbbing ache between her legs.

"Maybe because people will stop seeing you as this perfect little miss with no substance and start taking you seriously." He swirled his hips against her again and she had the urge to jump him, wrap her legs around his waist and grind back.

But she wasn't going to. No, she was going to take the high road, resist temptation . . . as soon as she could get him to stop that grinding motion.

"People do not think that about me," she said, grabbing his hips.

He snorted. "They think you're a kitten. A ball of fluff that they can push around. But I see you when you think no one notices. You've got a spark inside you, and if you let me, I can make you burn."

Her breath caught as his voice lowered. She tried to remain in control, but the images and feelings he brought to mind were not helping her resolve. "God, you think a lot of yourself. So I'm getting all this great exposure that's going to make my life better. What do you get?"

He leaned down, putting his mouth a hairsbreadth from her ear. "I get to do something I've been thinking about since the first time you walked past me with your little nose in the air and that sweet-ass swaying."

She pushed at his shoulders. "You're a pig."

Laughing, he went back to his side of the kitchen. "Oh come on, you are wound too tight. You need to relax and just have a fun. You do know what that is, don't you?"

Grabbing her pizza, she shoved some in her mouth, biting down aggressively. "Of course. I have fun all the time. I am the epitome of fun."

He grabbed a Coke from the counter and laughed. "Whatever you say, Firecracker."

"Firecracker? Why Firecracker?" she asked, ignoring the giddy thrill the nickname gave her.

"'Cause you're all wrapped up, just waiting for someone to light your fuse and make you heat up, start to lose control and finally, explode," he said, grinning as he popped his Coke lid and took a swig.

"And you think that someone's going to be you?" she asked.

"I like my odds," he said.

"Are you always so sure of yourself?" she asked.

"No, but I don't think I'd still be here if you weren't a little interested," he said, taking a bite of his pizza.

Watching him while she gnawed absently on her own slice, she considered his proposal. It would be nice to have somebody to call up to hang out with, and not have to sit at home twiddling her thumbs. She *was* fun, except she hadn't really met anyone to be fun with. Almost every weekend she went with Steph to Buck's or Hank's Bar, or to the movies, but she was sick and tired of playing third wheel with Steph and Jared. Even when Justin Silverton, Jared's best friend, came along, she could never think of Justin in that way. Not that he wasn't nice to look at, being a former marine and already quite hunky, but he had never been more than just one of the gang. He certainly didn't make her heart pound or her palms sweat like Chase. Maybe he was exactly what she needed. Someone who wouldn't lie to her about what he wanted, and who she wouldn't dream about getting serious with.

Lord knew her mother would have disapproved. It was a sobering thought, her mother. She would have definitely told her to steer clear of Chase.

She also doesn't have to spend her nights alone with a fat black cat and whatever bad reality crap is on TV. She would want you to be happy and live your life, not mope around because your plan A didn't work.

Mind made up, she threw the paper plate into the trash and asked, "So say I'm interested. What are the ground rules?"

He crossed his arms over his chest. "Rules? We have to have rules?"

"Of course there need to be rules. For instance, this is going to be fun. Casual. So no holding hands. No kissing in public. No romantic gestures like flowers or chocolates," she said, counting off each item on her finger.

Chuckling, he said, "Ah, Firecracker, I have never made a romantic gesture in my life. And I'm not exactly the type to skip about town holding hands and playing footsy under the table."

That's not true. Going to the grocery store for a woman

because she forgot is pretty romantic and chivalrous. She didn't mention it, though. Instead she ignored his sarcasm and continued, "And if and when we . . . you know, it will be on my terms, and I don't want you spreading it around to your buddies at Buck's."

He lost his smile. "First of all, if you're old enough to 'do it,' then you should be able to say it. Sex. Screw. Laid. Fu—"

She slapped her hand over his mouth and growled, "Stop. Don't be vulgar."

Reaching up, he removed her hand and nibbled on her palm. "Stop acting like such a stick. I'm not the type of guy to kiss and tell."

Jerking her hand back, Katie snapped, "I'm sorry I impugned your honor, but I'm not used to this. I wasn't raised for this, and I certainly wasn't prepared for you. It reminds me of my first internship in college, at the police station." She could tell by the surprised lift of his brow that he didn't believe her. "What? I wanted to be a cop. I even took a class on firearms and takedown tactics."

"So, why didn't you?"

She blushed. "The detective I worked under wanted me to read a statement to him, but every other word was a curse and my mom had always told me that ladies didn't talk like that. So I was blanking and bleeping out all the bad words and when I finished, he took the paper from me. I thought he was going to yell at me, but he just read it to me, every effing word of it, then handed it back and said, 'Now read it right or maybe you should rethink your career path.' I finished up the semester and transferred to cosmetology. It was just a better fit for me."

"Surprised you didn't pick kindergarten teacher or nurse. Cosmetology is kind of a big jump, isn't it?" he said.

"Not really. I wanted to be a cop to protect people, and help them. I'm just helping them in a different way by making them feel good about themselves. And the pay is way better," she said with a smile.

"Fair enough," he said. "So, your list is all about breaking a bunch of rules, right? Whose?"

Katie flushed. "My mom's rules. She had certain ideas on what a lady did or said, but following the rules hasn't exactly gotten me what I wanted."

"What is it you want?" he asked.

Katie's laugh was bitter, even to her ears. "What does any girl want? A big house with a wraparound porch and a few rocking chairs facing the best view. A couple of kids running around, making mischief, and a husband who loves me and wouldn't hurt me for the world." Sighing, she walked over to the box of pizza and asked, "Do you want any more?"

Chase just shook his head and she went to slip it into the fridge.

"If that's your goal, then why the list? How are purple streaks and a one-night stand going to help you get those?" he asked.

"I have pretty much given up on finding the guy of my dreams. The list was just about living my life, and not playing it safe anymore," she said.

"What are you, thirty? You've got plenty of time to get married and have kids," he said.

"Not in a town like this. If you don't find someone to marry in high school, or maybe even college, you have to move away 'cause Mr. Right's not here," she said.

"So why don't you move?" he asked.

"Because this is my home. I love it here. My friends are here and honestly, I've accepted my lot in life," she said.

"No you haven't, and you shouldn't. A girl like you is supposed to get married and you'll have buckets of kids someday. Trust me," he said.

"A girl like me?" she said, smiling.

"Yeah, you know. Pretty. Sweet. Likes kids. Helps old people across the street. Every man wants to marry a Girl Scout," he said.

"You make me sound boring," she said, losing her smile.

His face split into a grin. "Not trying to. I just mean most guys want to marry a girl who acts like a lady, but when the doors close . . ."

"I get your point," she said quickly. "How do you know I'll be like that? Behind closed doors, I mean."

His voice went dark and smoky. "Just a feeling I get."

She shivered at his suggestive tone and was nervous about disappointing him. It would have been better if he had just walked away, but deep down, she was glad he hadn't.

She wanted him bad. She wanted to live and have fun and just be . . . wanted. And she could just tell that Chase wanted her. Simplistically, maybe, but he wanted *her*.

"Well, I hope I live up to you expectations," she said softly. Clearing her throat, she added, "I think that's it

for boundaries on our arrangement. No PDA and no romance. I mean, it's not like either one of us is looking
for something serious, right?" Seeing him shake his head
in agreement, she asked, "So should we do something to
seal the deal?"

Moving closer, he reached up and trailed his fingers
over her temple as he pushed some of her long bangs
back behind her ears, making her knees turn to jelly.
Just when she thought he was going to give her another
heart-stopping kiss, he said, "Sure. What did you have in
mind?"

"A handshake?" she said, holding her hand out between them.

His amusement reached up to those gorgeous eyes
and she wanted to take it back. Why was she being such
a dork?

"A bit formal considering what we're talking about,
but okay," he said, taking her hand in his, squeezing it
gently. "We have a deal."

Disappointed that he still hadn't tried for a kiss, she
said, "Deal."

"So do we start now or . . ." Chase started.

"No!" she said loudly. Clearing her throat, she added,
"I just mean I'm not ready yet. I would like to get to know
you a little better before we . . ."

"You do know that casual works better when we don't
know each other, right?" he said.

"I know, but I just can't hop into bed with some
strange guy, okay? I have to at least know a little bit about
you," she said.

"I hate peas, don't enjoy long walks on the beach, eat my burgers with mayo, and I wear boxers, not briefs," he said, grinning.

Great, now I'm picturing him in nothing but a pair of boxers. "That's not what I meant ..." Taking a deep breath for strength, she said, "Look, can you just take me back to my car? I think I'm sober enough to drive and I have a lot to do tomorrow. Plus, I need a night to process."

"Whatever you say, Firecracker," Chase said, walking toward the door with a slow amble that would have done John Wayne proud.

Still in shock over what she had agreed to, Katie followed him out the door and down the steps to the dreaded beast of metal and mechanisms. He climbed on first and she swung up behind him, wrapping her arms around his waist again as if her life depended on it. Squeezing her fingers, he started up the motorcycle and headed back toward town. She liked the feel of his muscles bunching under his T-shirt and caught herself rubbing her cheek against his back, shivering. Whether it was from the wind as they sped down the street or Chase's proximity, she wasn't sure.

It took only a few minutes to make the trip back to her car, and she was surprised by the depth of her disappointment when they arrived. He parked the motorcycle across from her 4Runner and she climbed off a bit more gracefully than the last time. This ride hadn't been as terrifying, although she still didn't like the feeling of vulnerability she experienced with nothing between her and rough, deadly asphalt.

Walking across the street, she unlocked the 4Runner and was just about to escape inside when she heard his heavy boots behind her.

"Wow, that eager to get away from me, huh?"

She turned to him and smiled nervously. "No, it's just, it's getting late, and I have a lot to do tomorrow, so I just figured we'd start our little . . . experiment . . . tomorrow."

He put his hand against the side of her car and leaned over to kiss her, teasing her lips with his. "I think whatever you have going can wait a few more minutes. And who says we can't start our little experiment tonight?"

Trying not to lean into him, to stand firm when her body wanted desperately to melt into his kisses, she said, "Because if I'd wanted to do anything more than sleep, I could have asked you to stay at my place. Remember the rules: sex on my terms."

Chuckling, he said, "But you didn't say we couldn't do other things. And at my place, no one would see your car, whereas everyone has probably already seen and heard my baby."

"Seriously? You're one of those guys who gives his toys pet names like *baby*?" she said, groaning with disgust. Were all guys the same?

Without warning, he kissed her again until her eyes crossed and she leaned back against the car for support. "Again, you are trivializing my motorcycle, but it's okay. By the time I'm done with you, you will be one hot motorcycle loving woman and if you're really sweet to me, maybe I'll even let you drive it." He slid his leg between hers and rocked against her as he nibbled his way across her throat. She sucked in her breath and tried to control the urge to press down on his hard thigh to ease her throbbing arousal.

She realized her jeans were still unbuttoned when he moved his other hand down her body and slipped one finger down along the opening, leaving blazes of heat where his skin touched hers. Struggling to keep her eyes open, she lost the battle when he laid his palm against her lower stomach and started to slip down, a breathy moan escaping her at the sensation.

"Believe me, once you get that kind of power between your legs, you'll crave it."

Holy cow, what am I doing? She was leaning against the side of her car, letting a man stick his hands down her pants and basically just saying *take me now.*

This wasn't what she'd signed on for. Casual fling, yes. Destroying her reputation? No. Before she lost her resolve, she reached down and grabbed his wrist.

Chase pulled back, his breathing coming a little faster and his eyes looking dark in the fading light. She tried to soften the rebuke. "Like I said, you have a high opinion of yourself and your skills."

He shrugged. "Never had any complaints before."

"Well, there's a first time for everything," she shot back, feeling a little more in control of her body, although the heat of his leg between hers was still distracting.

Chase's eyes widened and he shook his head with a grin. "There might be hope for you yet, Firecracker." He kissed her hard once more, then stepped back with a little salute. "I'll see you tomorrow."

As he sauntered back to his chopper, she stayed propped up by her 4Runner until he climbed on and tossed her that same smug grin before taking off.

Arrogant, obnoxious, egotistical, high-handed . . .

She ran her fingers over her swollen lips and smiled. He might be a hundred different negative adjectives, but if his kisses were any indication, his skill probably wasn't exaggerated.

At least she hoped not. Because she was starting to really look forward to finding out if Chase Trepasso could walk the walk.

Chapter Four

KATIE WAS TIRED, her tattoo hurt, and she had a raging headache, which hadn't gotten any better after having Mrs. Andrews's high-pitched, nasal whine ringing in her ears.

"Hey, pretty, want a coffee?" Steph called as she walked across the grass.

They had decided to have the Rock Canyon Independence Day Extravaganza at Liberty Park. The large, grassy field held the town pool and a playground already, so all they needed to do was add a bunch of booths and a few bouncey houses to make it the perfect place.

Steph's long, dark hair swayed around her hips and her green eyes were sparkling as she handed Katie the cup. "You look like you could use this."

Katie could have kissed her when she took a drink of the sweet, blended caramel mocha. "Have I told you today that I love and adore you?"

"No, but I'll forgive you for the lapse," she said.

Katie checked to see where Mrs. Andrews was and whispered, "I swear, I was three seconds away from strangling the old bat before you showed up."

Steph scoffed. "Yeah right, you? You wouldn't hurt a fly."

Chase's description of her came back in a flash. Playing with her clipboard, she asked, "Do you think I'm Jell-O? That I don't have opinions?"

Steph looked at her in surprise, but there was a bit of guilt there too. "No. I just meant that you spare people's feelings. You're kind."

"I'm a pushover." Katie took a sip of her coffee to help fill the empty place her stomach's sinking had caused. Even her best friend thought she was a marshmallow.

"No you aren't! You give people your opinions. You just do it in a nice way."

Katie shook her head and decided that this was it, this was the day she was going to unclog her filter. The next person to even look at her cross-eyed was going to be in for the sharp edge of her tongue. She could still hear her mother telling her to be nice, to respect her elders, but another voice had joined in. A very male, very sexy voice. She didn't know why Chase's opinion of her kittenish ways bothered her, but they did. She didn't like that Chase, someone she hardly knew, had observed people treating her like she would just take whatever crap was dished out. If he had noticed it, then he was right about the rest of the town. They knew how to get around her.

She saw Mrs. Andrews heading back toward her with a bee in her bonnet, and Katie stiffened her spine.

Bring it on, you opinionated, gossiping old hag. I'm ready for you today.

"Katie, you have to do something! That ... that woman wants to buy a booth! We can't have her with all of those ... things out for all and sundry to see!"

Katie looked past Mrs. Andrews to Becca Easter, standing about fifty feet away, watching them blandly. Becca had moved to Rock Canyon a month ago and bought the building next to Hank's Bar. She'd opened a women's clothing store called Sweet Tart's Boutique, featuring intimate apparel and a black-curtained area in the far back. Some of the older people were having a wall-eyed fit about it, but Kate admired Becca for her screw-you attitude.

"Mrs. Andrews, Becca would never have anything in her booth that couldn't be viewed by all." Katie smiled at Becca, who watched them with dark eyes and a riot of black and red curls. Katie's mother would have called her look strange, but Katie envied her brazenness. "Becca's money is as good as anyone's. Please apologize and put her next to the Jagged Rock booth."

Mrs. Andrews drew herself up and snapped, "I will not be a part of this! It's shameful what kind of derelicts we're allowing to pollute our town."

And with that, Katie unleashed the fury. "That's enough! If you don't want to help out, then leave. You're being rude and insufferable and I'm done with it!"

Katie almost slapped her hand over her mouth as she

took in Mrs. Andrews's outrage, Steph's drop-jawed expression, and Becca's wide smile. It was the smile that gave her courage to walk past the other women to where Becca stood several feet away. "I'm sorry about the misunderstanding. We'll put your booth between Chloe's Book Nook and Jagged Rock Tattoo Parlor."

Becca handed her the check. "Thanks. You know, you're a lot cooler than I thought you would be."

"Well thanks. I think," Katie said, smiling.

Holding out a small white card, Becca said, "Come by my shop. It's not all dildos and thongs. I've got this belt and a pair of jeans that would look awesome on you. You've got a great ass. It deserves to be shown off."

Katie blinked at her and Becca winked, leaving Katie standing there, bewildered, with a two-hundred-dollar check in her hand.

KATIE HEADED BACK to the salon, feeling freer than she ever had. Even after apologizing to Mrs. Andrews for her outburst, she had been proud of herself for finally telling the cranky woman how she felt, and that she needed to stop being rude to people just because she didn't approve of their lifestyle. If they paid, they got a booth. Mrs. Andrews continued to grumble, but that was the worst of it.

Steph had given her a big hug and told her how awesome it was to watch someone tell "Battle-ax Andrews where to stuff it"—out of Mrs. Andrews's earshot, of course. Katie had to admit it had felt pretty incredible to speak her mind for once.

She walked in the door of the salon and Kitty looked up from the *Rock Canyon Press*, frowning. "Didn't you get my message?"

Katie reached into her purse and searched around for her cell. "No, why?"

"Your three o'clock canceled," she said.

"I didn't get it. What are you reading the paper for? I thought you only liked reading celebrity gossip magazines," Katie said, dropping her purse on the counter to continue the search. Chase was right; she really did have too much stuff inside.

Kitty flipped the paper over. "It's a new gossip column called *Small-Town Scandals*. The author calls herself Miss Know It All and she is pretty dead on. It's way better than celebrity gossip because these people, I actually know." Pointing to a picture, she said, "Did you know that Kirsten Winters went home from Buck's last night with Doug Dooly? I mean, I know she's a little dim, but she could do way better than that dork."

Katie looked at the paper and shook her head. "Just what this town needs, more gossip. Only this time it is in print, so it's got to be gospel."

She finally found her phone in the small pocket, next to a white napkin. Pulling out the crinkled paper, she read through her list for the first time since Chase had stolen it at the bar. Curiously, she saw that there was another task added to the end, and it wasn't in her handwriting.

Eleven. Call Chase.

Katie tried to fight a smile, but it couldn't be stopped; the guy was a charmer. So, he had added his own little item and just waited for her to demand it back? The whole thing was actually kind of . . . sweet.

An idea popped into her head. "Kitty, when's my next appointment?"

Kitty looked up from the paper distractedly. "Actually, Michelle was supposed to be a cut and highlight, so you had blocked out three hours for her."

"Hey, Holly!" Katie called as she came around the desk.

The short, round stylist with a cute A-line cut called, "Yeah?"

"After you finish Charlie's cut, wanna do something crazy?" Katie asked with a grin.

Holly gave her an are-you-serious look and said, "Girl, you know I'm always down for crazy! What did you have in mind?"

KATIE CALLED STEPH from her cell phone as she walked down the street. The call went to her voice mail and after the beep, she giggled. "Dude, call me! You are never going to believe what I did."

She hung up and caught a glimpse of herself in a shop window, her champagne-blond hair streaked with bright purple strands. Holly had twisted some of the hair away from her face and curled it down her back in tight ringlets. Katie hadn't felt this good in a while and, with a flip of her new hair, she walked down the street with attitude.

Digging into her purse for her keys, she got a hold of that list again. Maybe she would go by Chase's shop, see what he thought. Turning around and heading in the other direction, she felt bold. Punching in Chase's number, she texted, *What are you doing?*

She walked past Becca's store and heard her phone chirp, but before she could read his reply, a voice said from right behind her, "Hey! You were just going to walk by and not come in?"

Dropping her phone with a cry of surprise, Katie bent over to pick it up quickly, checking it for cracks. She turned to glare at a grinning Becca, standing in the doorway of her shop. "Hasn't anyone told you it's not nice to jump out at people?"

"Hey, if it gets you into my store, then my job is done," Becca said.

Katie hesitated. "I really need to get going."

Becca rolled her eyes. "Relax. You may be hot, but you are way too type-A for me. I'm digging those streaks, though." She stepped back and held the door farther open. "Come on."

"I didn't think you were hitting on me," Katie grumbled, walking by the other woman. Once inside, she looked around at the rows of clothes. "Oh man!" She picked up a black, flowy halter top with red cherries on it. "This is so cute."

"Hell yeah, it is, and it would look awesome on you with . . ." Becca walked around to another rack and held up a pair of jeans. "Size seven?"

"Yeah, how did you know?"

Becca pshawed. "I went to design school. You've got too much ass for a five."

Katie's hands drifted down to her butt and asked, "So, why aren't you off in New York, living large?"

"I went after graduation," Becca said as she grabbed some other things off the rack. "And I did well for a while. I didn't want to be famous or even rich, though. I just wanted people to love my clothes and bask in my awe-someness. But all the suits wanted me to make changes to my designs and charge so much that only certain people could have afforded them and it just got too political. So I packed up my designs, put my finger on a map, and here I am."

Katie looked at the label of the halter and was amazed. "You designed this top?"

Becca beamed. "I designed everything except the lin-gerie and shoes, but I only order from small designers. No big labels."

"You have some super-cute stuff." Katie eyeballed a pair of jeweled wedges as she passed the shoe wall. "Why did you want me in here?"

"Because if I can get a girl like you in my shop buying clothes, then other people are going to check me out," Becca said, opening up one of the dressing rooms.

Katie scoffed. "People don't care what I think."

"You're the queen bee without having to be a mean girl. People talk about you like you walk on water. I've only been here a month and I know that."

"Really? 'Cause I've been told I let people walk all over me." Thinking of Chase, Katie pulled out her phone and let out a rather large gasp.

His text read: *I'm watching this hot girl with purple*

hair walk into a sex shop. I told you I would take care of you. ;-)

Becca hung up the clothes in the changing room and said, "Well, either someone sent you Smurf porn or it just got really hot in here."

Katie's cheeks flushed darker. "Neither, just ... men are stupid."

Becca closed the door on her and said, "Preaching to the choir, baby. Preaching to the freaking choir."

"BECCA, I LOVE it, but I can't afford all of this!"

Katie had been in Sweet Tart's Boutique for over two hours and the counter was covered with shoes, pants, skirts, shirts, dresses, tops, and Becca had even tossed some bras and panties into the mix. Everything was to-die-for adorable, but now, Katie was staring at the $553.49 total in horror.

Becca waved her off. "I'll make you a deal. I'll give you forty percent off, if you wear everything around town for the next month and tell everyone where you got it. I'll even throw in this." She handed Katie a little black paper bag with hot pink tissue and winked. "Just wait until you get home to open it."

Katie stared at the black bag with a mixture of curiosity and fear. "I don't know."

"You just spent two hours telling me how you were sick of people treating you like a doormat. Think of this as your coming-out party. A party to celebrate the new, take-no-crap Katie." Becca did a little dance behind the register.

Katie shook her head and held up a lavender off-the-shoulder top that ended above her belly button. "Or they're going to think I've lost my mind. Maybe this is too much."

Taking her hand, Becca said, "Katie, the people who mock you or make you feel bad never respected you in the first place. At least this way you'll know who they are and get on with telling them to go eff themselves."

Katie's eyes widened and she burst out laughing, imagining telling Mrs. Andrews to eff herself. She eyed her bounty, especially the leather belt with the rhinestone buckle that read ROCK, and pulled out her purse.

"Do you take Discover?"

Becca ran her credit card and said, "You know, I haven't really made many friends here. Maybe we could grab a drink after I close up?"

Katie stared at her mountain of clothing and grinned. "Why the hell not? I should probably change though, right? If I'm going to be a walking advertisement, no better time than the present."

CHASE HAD DONE a couple of tattoos and lost track of whether Katie had come out of Sweet Tart's Boutique. She hadn't texted him back yet and he figured she was sore at him for teasing her. Katie didn't seem to take innuendos or a little dirty flirting well, and she probably hadn't appreciated his text. Maybe he'd stop by her place on his way home and try to get her to let him in. Make it up to her.

Apparently he was one of those guys who loved a challenge.

Chase tried to push Katie from his mind and work, but then he glanced up and saw her coming out of the shop, loaded down with bags, including a little black one. Becca followed behind, locked up the shop, and two women walked up the street laughing. Katie was dressed in a strapless black dress that hugged her curves and gave a great view of those mouthwatering legs.

Well, well. Look at Firecracker all grown up.

KATIE, WHO KNEW she was pretty in a sweet, wholesome way, was prepared for shock, dismay, and even disappointment when she walked into Buck's Shot Bar with Becca. There had been a few shocked looks, mainly from the table of older men who had known her mother. Mr. Hall had actually asked her if she'd lost a bet, in his backward attempt to be funny.

Before she could react to his insensitive comment, she was surrounded by several women she'd known forever, all talking at once.

"I love your hair, Katie! Who did it?" Gabby Hazelton said.

"Those shoes are soooo cute!" Kimmi Hazelton said.

"Holly did the streaks, and the shoes I bought at the Sweet Tart's Boutique. Becca has the cutest clothes! I got the dress there too. You guys should check it out," Katie said, giving Becca a wink. After the introductions were made, the Hazelton sisters bombarded Becca excitedly with questions about her shop and Katie slipped away to see about grabbing a drink.

Kirsten Winters's got Katie's attention when she said, "You look fantastic! I bet you wish Jimmy was here to show him he made a mistake."

Her smile dimmed a bit, until she caught movement at the door. Chase walked in, and little tingles of excitement spread through her body. "Actually, I'm so over Jimmy."

Sliding off the stool and adjusting the pencil skirt of the dress, she walked toward Chase. She had never worn anything so tight or so revealing, and the strapless bra underneath gave her an abundance of cleavage. She had to keep reminding herself not to put her hands over her chest to cover herself.

Katie smiled nervously as his eyes moved slowly over her, and when they finally met hers, they were so hot she nearly stumbled. He met her at the edge of the bar and said, "I thought you were pissed at me."

"Why did you think that?"

He pulled out his phone and held it up. "You never texted back."

She shrugged. "I got busy."

His eyebrow hiked up along with his smile. "You too busy for a drink?"

"You buying?"

"Yeah."

She laughed. "Good, 'cause I just spent all of my extra income on clothes."

Leaning over and putting his mouth so close she could

feel his warm breath on her neck, he whispered, "So what was in the little black bag?"

He watched me leave. "Are you stalking me?"

"Not stalking, just interested," he said, still close enough for her to see the black flecks in his gray eyes while he played with one of her curls.

The way he was admiring her made her feel powerful and brazen, and it was going to her head in a big way.

"Hmmm. In taking care of me, you mean? Maybe taking me home and using this very impressive body to get me all hot and bothered?" she said, surprising herself as she trailed her finger over his chest suggestively.

He froze, staring at her like she was wearing an donkey head, and she tried not to blush or look away.

"You can't be drunk already," he said.

Laughing, she said, "Nope, just trying out the no-filter thing."

"How are you liking it?" he said with a rich chuckle.

"Definitely saves time from thinking about what not to say."

He leaned against the bar. "You don't have to get rid of your filter. It's what makes people like you. I just think you should stop letting the assholes treat you like dirt."

The comment hit too close to home and Katie, wanting to change the subject, tossed her hair and said, "So what do you think of my dress?"

"I like it. But do you?"

His question gave her pause and as he ordered them a

round of drinks, she thought about the sudden changes she'd made. She'd sat down and written that list at a low, self-loathing moment. The streaks were fun, the tattoo stung, and the clothes were cute, but would she regret them later? She had no idea. She didn't want to think about the future; she just wanted to live in the moment. She wanted to feel good for the first time in months, not just try to get through the day.

"Yeah. I think I do."

CHASE LIKED UNFILTERED Katie. She was funny; she got loud and lost that bit of prim and proper attitude. And right now she was looking at him like a kid waiting to unwrap her shiny new bike.

He just hoped she really wanted to take him for a ride, because every minute he spent with her, the more he liked her. She was the type of girl a guy could just hang with, relax, and not have to put on a big show. She wasn't like any other girl he'd ever been around.

The Band Perry's "Better Dig Two" came on the jukebox and Katie gushed, "Oh my God, I love this song." She grabbed his hand and pulled on it. "Come on, dance with me."

Chase looked out on the empty floor and shook his head. "I think you've had too much to drink."

"I've had one beer." She tugged his hand harder.

"There's nobody dancing!" he said, wondering if he should bring up the no-holding-hands-in-public rule.

When she batted her eyelashes and pouted her full

lips, though, he dropped his guard long enough to laugh and she jerked him off his stool with an evil grin. He gave up reasoning with her and let her lead him out onto the dance floor.

He had always associated her with being bashful, but he was quickly figuring out that just because she was a reserved girl didn't mean she was shy. She finished maneuvering him smack into the middle of the room, slid her arms up over his shoulders, and moved against him. His hands settled on the small of her back, minding her tattoo, and he had to admit she did feel really good pressed against his front.

She was singing the lyrics softly and he joked, "Kind of a morbid song, isn't it?"

Something passed through those blue eyes when she looked up, and a strange feeling ran through him. Protectiveness. He knew she'd been hurt, and he wanted to take away that pain.

What the hell is the matter with you? She's just a girl you might have some fun with. Nothing else.

"Maybe, but at least the girl got to have her wedding," Katie said.

He didn't like the sadness in her voice either. Trying to get himself out of his head and distract her, he reached up and tapped her nose. "Why are you getting sad on me? Do you need me to kiss you again? 'Cause we both know you like that."

"Now, that would be breaking the rules. No kissing in public." Her smile chased away the sad look.

Chase leaned real close so only she could hear him

over the music. "I think we can make an exception this once."

"Do you really want to?" she asked, her tone seductive as a siren's call. "'Cause even if we bend the rules this once, people might get the wrong impression."

Suddenly he didn't care what the people of Rock Canyon would think or say. "Let 'em talk."

Dipping his head down to kiss her, he loved the feel of her fingers tickling the back of his neck as she kissed him back. He wanted to get the hell out of there, take off that sweet little dress, and get his hands on . . .

"Hey, Katie, I'm sorry to interrupt, but I need to get home."

He pulled back to give Becca the eye, but she just returned his look with a knowing smile. Becca had come into the parlor a few days after she'd first moved to town, and he'd given her a tattoo of two red cherries still on the stem low on her right boob. When she'd caught him eyeing her with interest, she'd told him he wasn't her type. He'd asked her what her type was, she'd said, "Probably the same as yours."

He'd laughed and liked her immediately, but right now she was cock-blocking him hard, and that smirk said she knew it.

"Oh sure. Sorry, we rode together." Katie turned to Chase and looked so disappointed that he wanted to find Becca another ride, just so she would stay.

He slid his hands off her waist and said, "It's okay. We can pick this up another time."

She gave him a brilliant smile as she followed Becca

out the door, and Chase jumped when a heavy hand fell on his shoulder.

"So, Katie Connors, huh?"

Chase grinned at the bigger man standing next to him. "Where have you been all night?"

Eric Henderson was Grant's brother and ran the day-to-day operations of the bar for his dad, Buck. Chase and Eric had become pretty good friends, despite the way Gracie McAllister, the object of Eric's interest, tended to flirt with Chase outrageously. Especially when Eric was in the vicinity.

"Had stuff to do." Eric turned his dark, I-want-to-intimidate-you stare on Chase and said, "Katie is the kind of girl you marry and have kids with."

Chase didn't argue. He knew what kind of girl Katie was. It didn't stop him from wanting her, and it definitely didn't change the fact that she wanted him too.

"Yeah, but even girls like Katie need to sow some oats before they settle down with their Prince Charming, right?" he said.

Eric's frown would have sent a weaker man scurrying for safety, but Chase knew Eric. He liked people to be scared of him. It was his way of controlling his world, but under all that snap and snarl, Eric was a marshmallow. At least with certain people.

But Chase must not have been on the marshmallow list tonight, because Eric just nudged him and growled, "Just make sure you don't hurt that girl or the people of this town might make you disappear."

Chase looked around, caught several unfriendly looks,

and tried to resist the urge to gulp. Visions of torture and crazy men with guns were not on his list of fantasies. Nor was being the cause of any pain in Katie's soft, blue eyes.

"Trust me, hurting Katie is the last thing I'd want to do," he said.

Chapter Five

KATIE WAS FLOATING on air as she hauled all of her bags into the house and set them on her bed. She adored Becca already, and most of the people at Buck's had loved her new look. She'd even caught several of the guys watching her with interest, which might have thrilled her more a few days ago, but now that she had this thing going with Chase . . .

Well, she didn't know exactly what it was yet, but there was something there. It was like lightning every time they were in the same room; sparks flew all over the place. And the way he kissed her, she felt her toes curl and steam come out of her ears like a cartoon character. Well, maybe not the most romantic description, but no one ever made her feel that way before.

She pulled everything out of the bags, humming as she checked tags for washing instructions, and then the little black bag with the hot pink tissue caught her eye.

Reaching out for the thin paper sack, she lifted the tissue and peeked inside. She stuck her hand in and pulled out a jar, then read the label.

Plumeria Bath Salts. Okay, not too scandalous. She twisted off the top and took a whiff; the smell was subtle and lovely. She put those aside with a smile, planning on trying them out very soon.

There were a couple vials of liquid and she pulled them out, reading the sides. Strawberry and chocolate edible massage oils. Heat traveled up her neck to her cheeks as she read the instructions, but they weren't as bad as she was expecting. She put them next to the bath salts and looked at the next little plastic container.

"Little Helper Gel," she read out loud, eyeballing the tiny bottle suspiciously. "'Add one to two pumps of Little Helper to the clitoris for added pleasure during manual stimulation or sex.'"

That one she practically threw across the bed, trying not to fan her cheeks. She was terrified of what else was left inside. Reaching in, she pulled out a package containing a little remote with a long cord attached to . . . her eyes flew up to the description. "'The Terminator Two Waterproof Vibrator. Back and better than the original.'"

Dropping the package on the bed, she gave up trying not to feel horrified and shook her head. She was going to give Becca a piece of her mind. Grabbing her phone, Katie texted, *Why did you give me that bag?!*

Several minutes went by before her phone beeped. *Cause you looked like you could use some stress relief ;-)*

She snorted. *I do not need a vibrator.*

Beep. *Okay, you don't have to use it. It's part of my new promotion. Spend $100, get a goody bag. :-) You should try the bath salts, though. They rock.*

Katie laughed; she couldn't help it. She liked Becca. She was outrageous, honest, and not afraid to say what she thought.

Thank you. I'll try them. Good night.

The phone beeped again, but she didn't bother checking it. Pulling off her clothes and slipping into her robe, she decided to take Becca's suggestion and run a bath with the special salts. She was too wired to sleep and she'd been dying to read the new romance she'd picked up at Hall's Market.

She was in the kitchen pouring a glass of water when a knock sounded at the front door.

What in the world? She walked over and peeked out the peephole.

Jerking the door open, she said, "Seriously, have you ever heard of a telephone?"

CHASE'S EYES MOVED over Katie in her thin bathrobe and guessed she was naked underneath. The deep V of the robe gaped to show off the sweet valley between her breasts, and the bottom hit just high enough to draw attention to the shapely legs beneath. Swallowing hard, his Johnson went from semi to rocket in seconds, and the thought of getting his hands on that silky skin just about undid him.

He tried to think of anything besides the fact that her

nipples were hard under the light fabric and held out a bag with a bottle in it. "I just remembered I never got you any alcohol when I picked up your groceries. Thought maybe we could have a drink together."

"I was about to take a bath," she said, eyeing the bag longingly.

So much for not thinking about her naked. He grinned. "I could join you."

When she laughed, he watched certain areas jiggle freely and he knew all his good intentions were going to fly out the window. No way was he going to be able to walk inside her home, with all those curves just waiting to be touched, tickled, and tasted, and not try something.

After a moment's hesitation, Katie moved back and waved him in. "Just wait in the kitchen while I turn off the water and put some clothes on."

"Hey, don't bother on my account. I like what you're wearing," he said, wiggling his eyebrows as she closed the door.

"I'll just bet you do." She said, watching him through lowered eyelashes—it was a come-hither look if he'd ever seen one. Those purple streaks were sure giving her sass.

Setting the bag with the wine on the counter, he stuck his hand out, and pulled her against him. "I do."

Putting her hands on his chest, she squeaked, "Chase . . ."

He ran his fingertip over her bottom lip. "I can't help it. Every time you come near me I have to touch you." Feeling her melt against him, he continued, "Do you know you have the most expressive face? I can read every little thought behind those beautiful eyes."

Her lips pursed. "Oh yeah? Then what am I thinking right now?"

Kissing her mouth before slipping his lips over her cheek and along her neck, he whispered, "You're thinking how much you wish I'd just take you back to your room and have my way with you."

He felt her soft sigh as she protested, "That's not what I was thinking. I was think—"

Chase lowered his mouth to the V of her robe, nuzzling the fabric away to expose one beautiful, pale handful, and covered her sweet, pink nipple with his lips. Katie ran her hands through his hair, tugging the strands softly as he slid his own hand around and under her robe to grab her bare ass. Releasing her breast, he kissed her, slipping her tongue inside to tangle with hers as his other hand grabbed her other cheek under her robe. Lifting her onto the kitchen counter with ease, he wasn't prepared when she ripped her mouth away, squealing, "Ahhh cold!"

"Sorry," he mumbled and brought her down to her feet, dipping his head to kiss her again. When she put her hands against his chest, he stopped and asked, "What's wrong?"

"The water. Bathwater," she cried, jerking out of his embrace.

He let her go, watching as she ran out of the kitchen and out of sight.

"Oh no!"

Following her cry down the hallway to her bedroom,

he saw what she was hollering about. Water was all over the floor of the bathroom, about to leak onto the bedroom's hardwood floors.

"Shit. Where are your towels?"

"In here." She reached up into the cupboard, pulling out the towels frantically and tossing him a stack. Chase knelt down and started mopping up the water, soaking through his first towel in seconds. He stood up to kick off his shoes and socks, and looked up in time to see Katie slip across the floor and fall hard on her ass.

"Ow!" she cried, rubbing her injured butt with a pout.

"Want me to kiss it and make it better?"

"You're such a funny guy." She stood up slowly, wincing a bit as she moved to the tub and bent over to turn the water off. He got a good look at the rounded pink part of her plump rear end now that her thin robe was sopping wet. When she grabbed a towel from the stack and got down on her hands and knees facing him, Chase could see down to her navel, and if it hadn't been for the water seeping up his jeans, he might have been tempted to kiss her until they were rolling around on the bathroom floor.

Making short work of his stack of towels, Chase stood up and stepped toward the draining tub to ring them out. Suddenly, his feet slid out from under him, and as he fell on the hard tile, he knocked Katie over. He groaned as his elbow hit the floor hard. "Son of a bitch."

"Are you all right?" There was laughter in her voice despite her words of concern.

He rolled over to face her, ignoring the throbbing

pain in his elbow and hip. "I don't know. Want to examine me?"

"Ugh. That's what I get for being nice." She grabbed at her robe and pushed her damp hair out of her face as she struggled back up to kneel on her towel.

"You call making faces at me nice? Now taking care of a man who was wounded while assisting a lady? That's nice." He held up his elbow. "I have an owie. Kisses?"

"What are you, five? I didn't make you kiss my boo-boo," she said.

"But I offered, so brownie points for me." He could feel the water that was left on the floor seeping into his shirt and sat up.

"Please, Brownies are always girls. Now if you had said badges that would have made sense, although I doubt you were ever a Boy Scout," Katie said, starting to gather the wet towels. "Do you want me to throw your clothes in the dryer? That way they aren't wet when you ride home."

"You mean you don't want me naked and using this . . . how did you put it? Oh yeah, this 'impressive' body to make good on our deal?" His teasing had the desired effect and her cheeks turned rosy. Liking the way she reacted to him, one minute a sassy flirt and the next sweetly innocent, he had pity on her. Reaching out to tuck a stray wet curl behind her ear, he said, "That's okay. The wind will dry them. I'll be fine."

The pink in her cheeks didn't lessen. Moving away from him, she laid the last two dry towels down before standing up with an armful of wet ones.

"Do you mind just finishing up the last bit while I wring these out and throw them in the dryer?"

He shook his head and watched her leave, that thin, wet fabric still clinging to her as she walked out. His erection was throbbing painfully and the only thing he could think about was stripping off that scrap of satin and licking every droplet of water off her curves.

Trying to distract his wandering mind, Chase soaked up the last of the water, picked up the sopping towels, and squeezed them over the tub. He made his way out of the bathroom, trying not to drip on the floor, and came around the corner to find Katie bent over with her head in the dryer.

The sight had him gripping the wet towels hard, little droplets escaping between his fingers to drop on the floor. She stood up with an armful of dry clothes and put them in the laundry basket on top of the machine. He watched her transfer the laundry out of the washer; such a mundane chore, but in her wet robe, with its peek-a-boo neckline . . . it made him look at washing clothes in a whole new way.

In fact, it made him think about taking her by the waist, turning her around to face him, and lifting her up onto the dryer. Kneeling in front of her, he'd slip those shapely thighs over his shoulders and . . .

"Thanks for the help," she said, breaking into his wicked daydream to take the wet towels from him. "I'm really glad you were here or that might have taken me a lot longer. If that floor got ruined, I would have had to kick my own butt."

One thing was for sure, he wasn't made of stone. And when Katie bent over again to toss the last of the towels in, he started to reach for her, but she was already standing on her tip toes, trying to get something from the cupboard above the dryer. Chase couldn't stop himself from moving behind her, pressing against her back as he whispered, "It was my fault. I distracted you."

Leaning over and kissing her shoulder, he ignored her stiffening body and slid his arm around her waist, gently trailing kisses up her throat and nuzzling her ear. "If you want me to go, I will. Or I can stay, and make you feel good. Even if you aren't ready to take the next step in our . . . arrangement."

What made him offer he had no idea, except that at that moment, he would do anything just to touch her.

His other hand crept up to play with her breast through the satin of her robe, and Katie didn't stop him. She actually melted back against him as he slid her robe off one shoulder and licked at her warm skin. He slipped his hand inside, skimming his finger teasingly over her skin. Using his thumb and forefinger, he played with her hard nipple until soft moans met his ears. Chase opened his palm and squeezed her gently, loving the soft texture of her breast.

Rubbing against her, he ran his other hand down her body until his finger found the folds of her femininity already wet. He slipped his finger inside, over her clit, and she moaned. He kept kissing wherever he could reach as he massaged and stroked her, and he watched her hands grip the side of the dryer until her knuckles were white.

He tugged and tickled her as she rocked back against his teasing fingers.

It was the hottest thing he'd ever done with anyone.

It wasn't just that she had perfect-sized breasts or that her little noises were soft and eager. Or that she smelled amazing and the taste of her skin was heady. It was when she let go of the dryer and reached up to wrap her arms around his neck, arching against him as she came, that he wanted to come with her. Be with her.

He wanted her to want to be with him too.

HOLY MOLY, IT's never been like that.

Her first time had been down by the river, and it had been awkward and awful.

With Jimmy, she'd thought sex was good. Compared to her first, he was a rock star.

But Chase had made her come with only his fingers. That had never happened to her. Ever.

She felt like her legs were going to give out any second and her heart was pounding. Why had she let him do that? She could have said no. She could have stopped him.

You didn't want to. You wanted him to touch you.

But she barely knew him. She'd known Jimmy all her life and they'd waited six months before having sex.

That was a long time ago and you're older now. There's nothing wrong with sex between two consenting adults.

Not according to her mother. Katie had waited until after her mother died to press the issue of living with Jimmy. Mainly because she'd been busy taking care of her mom and hadn't wanted to leave her, but she also knew her mother didn't approve of couples living together before marriage. Old school or not, it had been a strong point of contention between them. As for casual sex, that was a big no-no. Her mom had preached long and hard that sex was intimate and should only be shared with someone you loved and trusted.

Like a husband.

But her mother had lost that battle when Katie was two weeks shy of eighteen, just before her high-school boyfriend left for college. They'd talked about marriage and kids, as teenagers did with their first loves, and she'd had this romantic image of them telling their kids how they were high-school sweethearts someday. So she'd had sex for the first time on the bank of the Snake River, and it hadn't been magical or sexy. It had been painful, awkward, and quick.

With Jimmy, she had wanted to wait a year, but he had given her a load of bull about how he was used to having it with his ex-girlfriend, and if they really loved each other, what did it matter how long they waited? Six months later she started staying at his place overnight. Her mother never said anything about her "sleepovers," just "I can only guide you; I can't force you."

Funny how a little motherly guilt went a long way. Jimmy had complained often and loudly about their non-active sex life and all because she didn't like disappointing her mother. And it wasn't like sex was something she couldn't have lived without, considering it was nothing like how the romance novels described it.

Well, at least it never had been with Jimmy. Chase, however, was a whole different experience, and she had no idea why. She had always been told love made sex better, but she had loved Jimmy, hadn't she? And she certainly didn't love Chase, but he had just given her the best orgasm ever. Had her mother been wrong about sex? Was it really about feelings, or more about how talented the man was? Maybe a bit of both?

Wanting out of her own head and where her thoughts were headed, she came back to the present. Sliding her hands down Chase's neck, she turned to face him. Staring up into his strained expression, she blushed. "I . . ."

He reached out to pull her robe together. "I'll help you finish cleaning up."

Kissing her once more softly, Chase turned and left the small room. She was puzzled that he hadn't pushed the issue of sex, but a large part of her was relieved. She had expected to be pleased with Chase, maybe even orgasm during sex if she was lucky.

She hadn't expected to completely come apart during a little foreplay.

Turning on the dryer and washer, she picked up the laundry basket and followed him back to the bedroom. He was standing by the bed and holding the rectangular package that had so appalled her. "You got a vibrator?"

Katie cried out and grabbed the package from him, shoving it into the black bag, but he picked up the edible gel before she could stop him.

Chase opened the top, put a little on his fingertip, and licked it. The flash of his tongue made her feel hot and melty, even when he made a noncommittal face and said, "It's okay. So this was what was in the black bag? I had no idea you were this kind of girl."

Embarrassment replaced the gooey feelings, and she reached out to pluck the gel from his clutches. "I'm not. It was a gift with purchase."

He held up his hands in surrender. "Whoa, I'm sorry. I really didn't mean anything by it. I just never thought I'd find something like that in your room. Nancy Drew novels, sure. Maybe even a few *Cosmo* mags, but sex aids?"

Katie felt like a horse's behind jumping down his throat, but after what they'd done only a few minutes before, she was on edge. She'd never done anything like that with anyone. It had been overwhelmingly passionate: her whole body had been on fire, and then it had felt like she was floating. A guy she barely knew, who she'd allowed to touch her however he wished.

She should be ashamed of herself. She knew her mother would've probably been shaking her head saying, "*Now Katie, I've told you a million times, no man's going to buy the cow when she's giving her milk away to every Tom, Dick, and Harry.*"

Pulling herself out of her silent admonishment, she said, "I'm really tired. I think I'll take a rain check on that drink."

She wanted to take it back the minute the words were out, but Katie really did need time to think. Yes, she had agreed to a casual affair, but did she really want to go down that road with him? And then . . . what? Just part as friends? Acquaintances? Or would they avoid each other as best they could?

She didn't know if the flash of disappointment was real or her imagination, but Chase's face settled into a cool mask quickly. "Look, I didn't mean to piss you off . . ."

"You didn't. I am just really, really tired and I want to go to bed," she said, wishing she wasn't making it sound so much like she was kicking him out.

Studying her solemnly, his blatant scrutiny made her squirm. At last, Chase covered the two steps between them and gave her a quick, hard kiss. She barely had a chance to close her eyes and enjoy it before he turned to walk out the bedroom door. She heard the front door open and close, and then the roar of his motorcycle moments later as he took off down the road.

Way to go, spastic. Just what every man wants, a prude with mommy issues.

With a groan of disgust, Katie threw herself across the uncluttered side of the bed, buried her face in the mattress, and screamed her frustration.

CHASE WAS KICKING himself for rushing out of Katie's last night, but he was feeling raw from their little encounter too. He'd wanted her so badly, he'd gone home, taken care of himself, and still dreamed about her. It was crazy to get so caught up in a woman like her. She'd get over her little crisis of character and go back to looking through him, the way girls like her usually did.

The next day he'd worked on his new graphic novel

and then gone into the shop at five. He stayed open all day on weekends, but Tuesday through Thursday, he went in at five until nine or ten, depending on walk-in clients. Some people in town might not approve of his business, but he'd built enough of a clientele to make Jagged Rock Tattoo a success. Word of his art had spread all the way to Twin Falls, and comic lovers would drop in to shoot the shit. So some of the older, stodgier crowd would have loved to run him out of town, but that was their problem.

He was cleaning up in the back when the front door chimed. He came out and saw Katie standing there, her streaked hair held back in a ponytail. She had on a black tank top with a loose red skirt and a black belt with the word ROCK on the buckle in rhinestones. A bag of Styrofoam containers sat on the counter.

"I thought you might be hungry," she said shyly.

Moving toward her, he smiled. "Might be. What did you get?"

She opened a container and said, "I got a bacon burger from Jensen's for you."

"Then yeah, I'm hungry." He didn't know why he did it, but Chase kissed her cheek, lingering over the soft skin. He pulled back slowly, taking the smell of her with him as he said, "Thanks."

She seemed surprised by his gesture and he wished he could take it back. The last thing he wanted was for her to think he was hoping for something serious. She had laid down those rules in the beginning and he wasn't going to be the one to scare her off by acting boyfriendly. Nice as she might be, he didn't want her to have any kind of power over him.

Too late for that.

"I'm sorry about last night. I was embarrassed about the . . . you know, things on the bed."

He shrugged. "It's fine, I wasn't mad."

She cocked her head. "Really? 'Cause you rushed out and it just seemed like . . . but if you say you're fine . . ."

"I am. And I didn't rush out; I was respecting your wishes." *Shut up, asshole, and stop making things worse.* He took a bite of his burger and groaned. "I love Jensen's."

He caught her frown changing to a smile and almost released a sigh of relief. Just what he needed: to act all butt-hurt. That would be a surefire way to end things before they'd even started.

Katie took a bite of her burger and moaned. "Mmm." Swallowing and dabbing her mouth with a napkin, she said, "No one makes burgers the way Jensen's does. I love that he puts fry sauce on them."

"I don't know, there's this diner my mom has worked at for twenty years and it has this special sauce that might make you change your mind," he said.

"I'll have to taste this sauce for myself. Can't take your word for it," she said.

"Why not?"

"'Cause, I'm still getting to know you. I don't even know if you're a Coke or Pepsi guy," she said.

"Coke," he said quickly, before stuffing a French fry in his mouth.

"Hmmm ... I'm a Pepsi girl. Although, the truth is, my favorite soda is Dr. Pepper," she said.

As strange as it was for her to put so much stock in his choice of pop, it wasn't the weirdest conversation he'd ever had. Although he was a bit surprised when, in mid-bite, she followed it with, "So, have you been tested for ... stuff?"

He raised his eyebrow, knowing exactly what she was talking about but loving the way she nervously stuttered. "Yeah. I'm clean." She looked relieved and he laughed. "What about you?"

She nodded. "After I found out Jimmy had ... cheated, I got tested."

"And there's been nobody since your ex?"

She shook her head, and he was secretly pleased she didn't just hop into bed with anyone, although it wouldn't have mattered if there had been someone else. He wanted her too much and he wasn't exactly a saint.

They finished their food, and he got down from his stool, taking two steps closer to stand between her legs. She leaned back on the counter and he put his hands on her thighs as he asked, "So does this little interview mean you want me to come over tonight?"

"I don't know." She nibbled on her lip and he leaned over to kiss it, taking the plump flesh into his mouth and sucking gently. He slid his tongue over it, happy to be able to taste her like this. He had been worried when he left last night that he'd blown it, and the thought had been like a sucker punch. Katie had wormed her way under his skin, and he just couldn't seem to shake wanting her.

"Do you have your list?" he asked, pulling back from her.

Her eyes still closed, she tried to bring him back to her. "It's in my purse."

Chuckling, he reached out to grab her purse off the counter and gave her a quick kiss. "Hmmm ... why do women keep so much shit in these things?" he asked as he started rummaging through the bottomless pit of change, lip gloss, and other odd items only a girl would think she'd need.

"Because we like to be prepared, whereas men would rather MacGyver their way through life," she said.

Looking up with a grin, he said, "Struck a nerve?"

"No, I'm used to hearing that kind of thing from men, and with you being such a guy's guy, I figure you probably call women 'chicks' and slap barmaids' butts," she said.

"Guess we'll have to go out and find a barmaid. See if your theory is right." He found the napkin and held it up. "Aha!"

"Look at that! You managed to find something through all my ... stuff," she said.

Grabbing a pen off the counter and handing it to her, Chase said, "Here you go, sassy Sue. You need to check off your tattoo, your streaks, the sex shop, and saying the first thing that came to your mind."

She took the pen. "But I didn't go to a sex shop," she argued.

He grinned. "You have everything you need from one. Except the handcuffs."

She hit his arm and he grabbed her hand. "And Becca

told me about how you went off on Mrs. Andrews. You said the first thing that came to mind. I bet you apologized afterward, but it still counts."

She didn't pull away as he stroked her hand but said, "Which reminds me, I have to call her tonight about the weather. There's supposed to be a big thunderstorm coming in, so we will have to move the pageant from an outdoor stage to the community center. And reschedule the fireworks. Knowing Mrs. Andrews, she'll probably call it a blessing."

"Does that woman like anything? What kind of person hates fireworks? You get to play with fire and watch things explode," he said.

"Why are all men such pyros?" she asked, laughing. "She doesn't hate them; she just thinks they're a waste of money."

"I see. Well, back to your list. All you have left is to steal something—which, again, I do not recommend— skinny-dip, get drunk and flirt with a bunch of guys— not a big fan of that one either—have a one-night stand, and buy some handcuffs. Oh, and tell your ex that he's a jerk off. I don't know why you need to explain that; it should be obvious to him."

"It's therapeutic for me, and no, I don't think Jimmy considers himself to be anything less than awesome." Running her hand over his chest, she said, "I could just text Becca about the handcuffs."

"Great, okay, so now a one-night stand. I do remember offering my services for that." He dropped her hand to move closer.

Reaching up, she wrapped her arms around his shoulders and said, "But it wouldn't work with you."

That gave him pause. "Why the hell not?"

Katie ran her hand over his cheek. "Because a one-night stand is supposed to be a stranger that you have sex with and never see again."

"I see the problem. So maybe we could modify your list. Instead of one-night stand, we'll have a torrid affair," he said.

She laughed. "I can't believe you know the word *torrid*."

"What do you think, I'm just a dumb tattoo artist who dabbles in comics?" he said, his pride pricked by her comment. "I went to college and I graduated with a three point eight GPA."

Why people always assumed he was stupid just because he liked doing tattoos he didn't know, but Katie looked like he had told her he was an alien. It was pretty insulting even though he was used to it, but coming from Katie it stung more. She didn't seem like the type to be so judgmental.

She blinked at him. "Where did you go?"

"Berkeley, on scholarship," he said, trying to keep the testiness out of his tone.

"That's amazing! What did you major in?" she asked.

"Amazing? Like you're amazed that I was smart enough to get a scholarship?" he said.

"No! I just meant it's really hard to get a scholarship. You are really special, Chase."

His irritation dimmed a bit and he said, "I majored

in art and minored in English. I had already written and sold my first comic before I graduated, and I've been doing tattoos since I was eighteen, so I just stuck with what I knew. Saved my money, bought run-down parlors, turned them around, and sold them for a profit."

She ran her hand down his arm and asked, "What else?"

"What do you mean?"

She stared at him so intensely it made him squirm, then asked, "What other little secrets don't you want everyone to know?"

"I'm not hiding anything."

"You let all of these people believe you're just a tattoo artist, but you're so much more than that," she said.

He couldn't look away from her. "What am I?"

"You're smart, and creative, and—"

He cut her off. "All of those things should be obvious. I run my own successful business and I can draw. I own one of the nicest houses in the area and I keep my nose clean. The only people who don't know me are the people who don't want to."

Realizing how much he'd revealed in that one sentence, he started to draw away from her, but Katie tightened her arms and wrapped her legs around his waist. The look in her eyes was kind and understanding, a look that told him without words that she wasn't in the latter category.

"I didn't see through you, Chase. I saw *you*. I saw you at Buck's the night you were handing out your business cards, and again at the Valentine's Day auction, when you bid on Ryan Ashton, and I remember thinking how lucky she was. There have been a hundred different instances since you moved here when I have seen you and wondered about you."

"Right," he said, even though her words made him want to smile.

"It's true. I've been a total mess for half a year, Chase, but I wasn't dead. I noticed you. But a guy like you? Guys like you aren't interested in girls like me," she said.

He looked at her in disbelief, then scowled. "What does that mean, guys like me?"

She gave him a teasing grin. "You know, cool guys. Tough guys. Rebels. You all think I'm a goody-goody."

His tension eased as he laughed. "You are a goody-goody."

Giving him a dark look, she said, "And guys like you don't like that. You like girls who can drink whiskey straight and who wear fishnets and . . ."

"Well, I'm not going to find many girls like that here, except maybe Becca, and I'm not really her type." Wrapping his arms back around her, he said, "Guess you'll have to do me now that you're so bad."

He caught her giggle in his mouth and leaned her back on the counter. Her legs and arms were still around him and he rubbed against her as he delved into her mouth.

The jingle of the front door pulled him back as two guys walked in with wide grins. "Hey, Chase, we were hoping to get a couple of tattoos, but if it's a bad time . . ."

Chase didn't like the Coulter brothers, and he especially didn't like the leers they were giving Katie. Helping her pull her long skirt back down, he stepped out from between her legs and stood a bit in front of her. "If you boys will just wait over there, I'll be with you in a bit."

Katie let him go and slid off the counter. Seeing the red stain of her cheeks, he said, "Why don't you head on home and I'll text you when I leave?"

She nodded and didn't even look at the other men as she left.

Wayne, the uglier and meaner of the two, sneered. "Well, I never thought I'd see sweet little Katie in such a position. What's your secret, Trepasso?"

Chase still possessed some self-control because he didn't punch the vile son of a bitch right there. "Did you guys come in for tattoos or not?"

KATIE PULLED UP to her house and laughed. Standing on her front porch were Becca and Steph, talking animatedly.

"Well gee, if I knew you girls were coming over, I'd have grabbed margarita mix," Katie said as she climbed out of the 4Runner.

Steph held up a bag. "Got it. And since when are you fooling around with Chase Trepasso?"

Becca threw up her hands when Katie glared at her. "Don't look at me; you're the one who was making out with him on the dance floor last night."

"Nobody told me, I read about it in the new gossip column! They even have a picture of you!" Steph said, holding up the paper.

Katie took it from her and read the headline: GOOD GIRL GONE BAD? Underneath was a picture of Chase and her with their faces close together. The first sentence read, "Could Katie Connors be shedding her golden-girl image to hook resident bad boy, Chase Trepasso?"

"What a load of crap," she said, scowling.

Handing the paper back to Steph, she pulled out her house keys and walked past them to unlock the door. Becca and Steph followed her inside and closed the door behind them.

Tossing her keys on the kitchen counter, Katie walked over to the cupboard to pull out the blender, stretching onto her tiptoes to reach it.

"Are you going to answer me or not?" Steph insisted.

Katie shot Becca a grin over her shoulder. "Not without some tequila in me."

Steph sighed loudly but handed her the mix and tequila. Katie put the blender on the counter and plugged it in. She poured in four shots, the mix, and ice before replacing the lid and pushing the power button. When there was a smooth mix of ice and alcohol, she got down her good margarita glasses and led them to the table.

Steph pointed at her hair. "Holy shit, your hair has purple in it."

"Yep," Katie said.

"What is up with you?" Steph looked at Becca accusingly.

Becca laughed and said, "Sorry, it wasn't me. She walked into my shop with her hair already like that."

"Don't you like it?" Katie asked, a little upset Steph

was acting like her mother and not her best friend. Steph
had always been protective of her, but she had never been
unsupportive.

Steph's mouth dropped open. "Of course I love it! It is
freaking awesome sauce! I just want to know what's happened in the last two days to make you go all punk-rock
princess on me."

"I'm guessing that it had something to do with Chase,"
Becca said mischievously.

Katie took a big gulp of her margarita and yelled,
"Ahhh! Brain freeze."

"Don't change the subject! Tell me!" Steph got all
shrieky when she was excited.

Katie knew there was no help for it except to tell the
truth. Clearing her throat awkwardly, she said, "I was
feeling a little low on Monday and I wrote a list. A list of
things I've never done."

"Okay, with you so far."

Katie took a smaller drink and continued, "Well, Chase
got a hold of it, and we've just been kind of . . . hanging out."

"What was on the list?" Becca asked.

Must drink more. Katie took another swallow of the
slushy margarita. "You know, stuff. Like shoplifting.
One-night stands."

"What are you, thirteen? That is when you shoplift,
not when you're a grown-ass woman! They arrest you and
throw the book at you when you do juvenile shit!" Steph
said.

"I just made a list of things I had always wanted to do.
I didn't say I was going to do them all," Katie said.

THINGS GOOD GIRLS DON'T DO 109

"What about one-night stand? Have you done that? Did you sleep with him?" Steph asked. Her voice was now several octaves above soprano, and Katie resisted the urge to rub her ears.

"No."

"But she wants to bad," Becca jumped in.

"You are not helping," Katie growled.

Becca shrugged. "I'm not a very helpful person."

Katie stood up to get the pitcher and nearly jumped out of her skin when Steph shrieked, "Oh my God, I love your belt! Where did you get that?"

Katie smiled. You had to love Steph. She had always been easily distracted by cute clothes.

"Becca's place. Sweet Tart's Boutique." Katie refilled her glass and asked, "Wanna see what else I got?"

"Uh, yeah!" Steph turned to Becca with a smile that said *you are welcome here and I accept you.* "I'm going to have to check out your shop!"

Walking ahead of them toward the bedroom, Katie heard Becca ask, "You're a size five?"

Stephanie gasped. "How did you know?"

"It's what I do."

CHASE FINALLY GOT done with the Coulter brothers at a little after ten and called Katie. She picked up on the second ring, laughing.

"Shut up!" Katie said.

He heard his name being screamed in the background, along with kissing noises, and asked, "This a bad time?"

"Yeah, Steph and Becca stopped by with margaritas."

Damn. He had been thinking if he dropped by her house, she might invite him in, and maybe they'd get back to where they were before the Coulter brothers had interrupted.

"So I guess I'll see you in the morning at the Fourth of July thing?" he said.

She giggled. "Oh yeah! I'll be the one on the float with the poufy dress and the tiara."

He grinned at her slurred words and the image she created. "All right, I'll look for you."

"'Bye, Chase! Muahahaha!" High-pitched squeals and laughter followed, then the line went dead.

Chase shook his head, not sure he ever wanted to experience Katie and her friends up close and personal on a margarita night. His ears were still ringing from the sounds they'd made.

Now, Katie one-on-one after a few margaritas might be fun.

He cleaned up the rest of his tools and was getting ready to lock the door when his phone rang. Recognizing the number, he picked up with a deep breath. "Hey, Mom, what's up?"

"Hey, Chase honey, I was just calling to see how you were."

Her voice sounded far away and he asked, "Mom, are you okay? You sound weird."

"Yeah, I'm good. I just wanted to see if there was anything new and to hear your voice."

The sound of a loud speaker and a voice announcing, "Code blue," came from the background.

"Are you at the hospital? Did something happen?"

"Oh, Buzz and I just got into a little fender bender. We're fine, though. Tell me about you. You seeing anyone?" she asked.

He shook his head. His mother and he had a weird relationship, but she was always worried about him meeting someone. Since marrying Buzz eleven years ago, her son's lack of serious relationships seemed to be on her mind a lot.

But the one thing he wasn't going to do was talk about Katie with his mother. "There's one girl, but it's too early to tell. Do you need anything?"

Her voice sounded almost disappointed as she responded, "No, baby."

A conundrum, that's what his mother was. She had ignored him for most of his childhood, giving him food, shelter, and everything he could need except her time and attention. Instead she'd worked double shifts and dated her men, while he'd sat with one babysitter after another. Buzz was the first man in his mother's life that he'd actually gotten along with, and if she had only met Buzz when he was a kid, maybe his childhood would have been better. But he had been an adult and already out of the house when Buzz had come along, and Chase knew he was just indulging in wishful thinking. His mother hadn't wanted to get close to him and he had no idea why.

Yet when she called, it was almost like she wished things weren't so strained between them. Like she wanted there to be more.

She's had thirty-three years to talk to you. You don't owe her a thing.

"Hey, Mom, I've got to go. Closing up the shop and I can't talk and ride, so . . ."

"Sure, I get it. I love you, Chase."

"Yeah, me too." He hung up and stared at the phone. She had sounded weird. It wasn't abnormal for her to say she loved him, but it was the way she had said it. He thought about calling Buzz to see what was up, but shook off the idea.

His relationship with his mother was complicated and he doubted it was going to change anytime soon.

Chapter Six

———————————————————————————

THE FOURTH OF July kicked off with Katie having a slight hangover and being fifteen minutes late to help set up the craft fair tents. She was now on her third cup of coffee, and the dress she'd picked out for the Canyon Queen float still wasn't looking better. She'd picked it up off the rack at an after-prom sale, and now that she had it on, she looked like one of those women who tried too hard to look young and wished she'd gone with something less juvenile. It was too late now. But the poufy strapless gown in an iridescent teal did make her eyes seem bluer, and made her purple streaks more noticeable, as they fell down around her shoulders in thick ringlets.

She'd brought a bag with a change of clothes and her makeup for later, and slipped on the cute, simple black heels she'd bought at Payless.

As she slid the tiara on top of her head, it took her back to her first Little Miss Magic Valley Pageant, when she'd been barely five. Her mother had loved to do her hair in stylish up-dos and bought the puffiest princess dresses for her, telling her the pageants would give her grace, poise, and confidence. She hadn't minded really, although she had wanted to stop once she'd turned twenty-one, feeling too old to prance around singing Patsy Cline or answer ridiculous questions about where she saw herself in five years.

But she'd continued to do them for her mother's sake until she was too sick to go with her, and when she'd died, Katie had assumed her pageant days were over. But Jimmy had bugged her and bugged her until finally last year she'd done the Canyon Queen Pageant one last time. When she'd won, he'd paraded her around afterward like a prized pig at auction and she'd felt like an idiot. Now here she was, about to get up on a float covered in cotton and streamers, in a huge, puffy taffeta skirt the color of fake seaweed. Every year the Canyon Queen gave her title to the next winner, and even though the pageant was for ages fifteen to thirty, most of the contestants weren't over twenty-five. She'd be glad to never have to live through this sort of thing ever again, but the thought of standing up there and being compared to all the younger women competing . . . well, it just sucked getting old.

She walked out of the bathroom reluctantly and heard a wolf whistle from behind her.

"Whoo-ee, you clean up pretty."

Turning, she found Chase leaning against the stone wall of the outbuilding, his smile neither teasing nor mean. She felt less awkward and picked up her skirt like a princess, curtsying. "So, you like?"

He pushed off the wall and walked toward her, inspecting her dress. "Oh yeah, I like. Reminds me of this fantasy I used to have about hooking up with the prom queen."

She grabbed him and laughed. "Stop it. You're going around me like a vulture over carrion."

Wrapping his arms around her waist, he pretended to look hurt. "Now that isn't very nice."

Katie was suddenly aware of the people around them, talking quietly, and said, "We shouldn't do this here."

He dropped his arms and gave her a blank look. "Do what? Tease? Flirt?"

She felt like a jerk and said, "What about the rules? I'm sorry, I just thought we had decided casual. To me, casual means no public displays . . ."

"Hey, don't sweat it. I'll see you after the parade," he said.

"Wait . . ." But he was already walking away, without even looking back. Had she really hurt his feelings? It certainly hadn't felt good on her end to have him just go marching off in the middle of their conversation.

Mrs. Andrews broke her trance by yelling, "Come on, Canyon Queen, get a move on! You are the highlight of this parade!"

Following her, Katie hurried to get on the fluffy float, and was greeted by a group of giggling teenagers and young women, all hoping to be the next Canyon Queen. They stood along the sides, sacks of candy in their hands, as Katie climbed up to the big throne and sat down. She kept thinking about Chase's reaction to her PDA protest. They had said they would keep things casual, but somehow they'd been caught kissing in public twice. If she openly kissed him in the middle of a town event, it would be . . .

Well, people would think they were serious about each other.

The parade started, and she waved while the girls on the float tossed candy to the crowd. Her eyes scanned the faces for Chase, but she didn't see him. By the time the monstrosity was over, all she wanted to do was find him and apologize. But first she needed to make sure the booth for her salon was set up and ready to go.

She went back to the bathroom to change and Mrs. Andrews came in right behind her. "Oh Katie, that was wonderful. The parade went off without a hitch. Now don't forget to be at the booth at three for your kissing shift!"

As the woman left, Katie found herself muttering, "Yeah, I know when my shift is. I organized the damn thing."

Too bad Mrs. Andrews hadn't heard her, rushing from the bathroom like her skirt was on fire. The woman was like a hurricane: fast and emotionally destructive.

Katie changed into her new white halter, jean skirt, and cowboy boots, and hoped Chase would love the top, which tied behind her neck, and once across her back with thin shoe lace straps, leaving most of her back bare. Another sexy and adorable buy from Sweet

Tarts. She left the bathroom to make sure everything was set for the fair. After that was done, she would find Chase.

Like every other business in Rock Canyon, K.C.'s Salon had a booth, and all the employees were taking shifts. They had set up a ring toss where people could win little sample bags of products or free haircut coupons, and a table was covered with products and accessories for sale. Katie's shift was from twelve to two, and then the kissing booth at three.

It was eleven thirty when she headed toward Chase's booth. Katie saw him sitting down, putting a henna tattoo on Kirsten Winters, and felt a stirring of jealousy. Kirsten was very pretty and one of those girls who would do anything to get a man's attention.

She almost kept walking, but he looked up and saw her, his gray eyes dark. He was just so damn beautiful, she couldn't look away from him.

He patted Kirsten and said something to her with a smile. She stood up with a smile, handed him a few bills and said hello to Katie as she passed. Katie liked Kirsten, had been doing her hair for years, but she didn't like the invitation in her eyes when she'd looked at Chase. After one last wave, she walked her cute size-two butt away with an exaggerated sway of her hips.

Katie raised her eyebrow at Chase and said, "Guess I'm not the only one who noticed you, huh?"

He shrugged. "She's not my type."

"Since when is cute, blond, and perky not every guy's type?" she said.

He gave her a small smile. "I have cute, perky, and blond. Well, mostly blond."

A warm feeling spread through her chest. Stepping into his booth to stand in front of him, she said, "About before . . . I'm sorry. I wanted to kiss you, it's just we said casual, and I've never done this before, so . . ."

He pulled her into his body and cupped her face, kissing her hard. When he finally let her up for air, it was to whisper, "I've been waiting to do that since last night."

Katie realized that little things Chase did or said were starting to make her forget. Forget about her rules and that they weren't supposed to be serious. If she didn't stop melting every time he said something sweet, she was going to forget that he wasn't the type of guy you lost your heart to.

Needing to get off the dangerous track her thoughts were taking, she said, "Well, I'm glad you did, because I'm going to be thinking of that while I'm being kissed by every toad in town. Blech."

He lost his smile. "You signed up for the kissing booth?"

She blinked at the deep growl in his voice and said, "I'm the current Canyon Queen, I have to take a turn. It's only a half hour."

His scowl didn't lift, and she kissed him on his frowny mouth. "You're not jealous, are you?"

Running his hands over her bare back, he said, "No, I'm just going to have to sterilize your mouth before I kiss you again."

"Well, if I'm that distasteful . . ." she said, playfully trying to pull away.

He leaned down to kiss her, but she turned her head away and all he caught was her cheek. Next he grazed the little spot below her ear, leaving invisible heat marks long after his mouth was gone. "I was only kidding, Firecracker. I'd kiss you if you ate dog shit and barfed fish guts."

Her mouth twitched as she tried not to laugh, coughing instead. "You would not, and that is disgusting."

Laughing, he said, "But it's true. I love kissing you. In fact, I think it may just be my new favorite hobby." He moved his head as if he was coming at her from the right and when she turned away, he caught her mouth from the left. She laughed against his lips; she couldn't help it.

"Ahem!" They broke apart to look at a very disapproving Mrs. Andrews, who snapped, "Katie, I need your assistance, please."

Katie started to pull away and follow Mrs. Andrews obediently, but at the last minute she went back for one more quick kiss. Forget her rules. Forget other people's opinions. She liked kissing, flirting, and just being with Chase. She didn't have to explain their relationship or their lack of serious intentions. She could loosen the reins and let go.

Quickly, before the older woman had a coronary, she broke off the kiss and caught up with her. She looked back at Chase over her shoulder for a moment, and he blew her a kiss. Warmth spread through her that had nothing to do with the sun or the embarrassment of being caught kissing a man she wasn't really dating, and had everything to do with happiness. She was happy for the first time in—if she was being honest—years.

And anyone who had a problem with that ... well, New Katie would just tell them to go to hell.

THE K.C.'s SALON booth was hopping and Katie was so relieved when two o'clock came around, she nearly ran to get away from it. She grabbed an elephant ear pastry and snacked on it as she explored the different booths, slowly making her way over to see Becca's. The fact that it was next door to Chase's was a happy coincidence that in no way influenced her. She saw Steph snooping around Becca's goods, walked up behind her grinning, and yelled, "Boo!"

Steph jumped and said, "You're a dumb ass."

"So what are you buying?" Katie asked, eyeing the pile of clothes in her arms.

"Everything in my size." Steph grabbed a cute tank top with little pink butterflies on it as if it might disappear at any moment.

Becca laughed from inside the booth and asked, "Do you just want me to make you a bag back here so you don't have to hold on to all that?"

Steph nodded vigorously, handing her load off to Becca. "Thank you."

"No, thank *you*," Becca said, smiling.

"Jared is going to murder you," Katie said.

"I make money too, and I haven't spent very much

this month," Steph said, reaching to rip off a part of Katie's elephant ear.

"Thief!" Katie laughed, holding her food away from Steph.

"Come on, you'll never finish that thing by yourself," Steph said.

Katie ripped the ear in half and handed her some more. "Mooch."

"Thanks, sugar mama," Steph said, giving her a sugary kiss.

Laughing, Katie walked around the large table display of modest lingerie and trinkets, her gaze landed on several pairs of fuzzy handcuffs.

Katie shoved the last bite of the buttery pastry in her mouth, wiped her hands on a napkin, and pointed to the pink pair. "Becca, I want these. Can you set them aside for me?"

Steph made a howling noise, and Becca grabbed the handcuffs, teasing, "Ooooh, Chase is going to be surprised."

Katie blushed and would have given a very smart comeback if she hadn't noticed a cute straw cowboy hat with little purple and white charm beads on it. She reached out and picked it up by the brim at the same time that a high, whiny voice said, "Excuse me, but I saw it first."

Katie turned to face a short blond woman with a sour-lemon expression on her face. She looked familiar, but Katie couldn't place her immediately. Until she saw Jimmy standing next to her.

Selena. Jimmy's fiancée.

Katie froze as Jimmy's wide eyes traveled up and down her body. "Katie?"

"Is there a problem here?" Becca asked.

Selena looked between Katie and Jimmy, completely ignoring Becca. "Katie, your ex?"

It wasn't like they'd never seen each other before, so why Selena was acting like she didn't know her was beyond Katie. In fact, she was pretty sure she had gone with Steph a couple of times in high school when she'd babysat for Selena and her brother Kyle. Selena had gone off to Boise State after her graduation five years ago and hadn't come back until last year, right before Jimmy left. They had hardly seen each other since Selena was a snotty teenager walking around with her nose in the air like her daddy had never shoveled cow manure. And she obviously hadn't matured with age.

Katie realized she was still gripping the side of the cowboy hat and said, "Can you please let go of my hat?"

Selena yipped like a little dog. "You mean *my* hat."

"No, you little bitch, she means her hat," Steph said, coming up beside her.

"Who are you calling a bitch?" Selena said loudly.

"You, Selena, and considering what a little brat you used to be, I can't believe you haven't heard the term lately," Steph said, bristling like an angry dog.

Katie wasn't really listening to Steph and Selena bait each other. She couldn't look away from Jimmy, whose chocolate-brown eyes had once been able to melt her with a glance, and she just felt humiliated all over again. Fighting over a stupid hat with an obnoxious, high-pitched, tramp. She almost let go of it, but Becca stepped in.

"Sweetheart, I'm sorry, but I've had that hat on hold for Katie for a week," she said in a friendly but firm tone. Katie wanted to kiss her.

Selena glared at Steph and Katie, whining, "But there's no hold sign on it."

Becca reached out and removed the younger woman's groping fingers. "Come look over here; there are some really cute ones on this side too."

Selena hesitated, looking at Katie with a sour, pinched look. "Honey bear, are you coming?"

Katie wanted to gag at the sickly-sweet tone. Jimmy kept staring at her like she had horns and a tail, even while addressing his fiancée. "I'll be right there, sweetie pie, I just want to talk to Katie for a minute."

The little witch actually pouted and leaned up to kiss Jimmy, right in front of her. Someone grabbed Katie's hand, probably Steph, trying to comfort her, but it wasn't that she was jealous of Jimmy; Selena could have him. It was that they both seemed to be oblivious to everyone else's feelings but their own. They were perfect for each other, that was for sure.

Selena walked to the other side of the stand, completely ignoring them, and Katie got the message loud and clear. Whatever Jimmy had said about her to Selena, she obviously didn't see Katie as a threat.

"You look great. Different," he said.

"And you look like the same old stupid asshole you've always been, genius," Steph said.

Jimmy didn't even flinch. "Nice to see you too, Steph. Can I talk to Katie, please?"

"Not after the way you treated her, you . . ."

"Steph, it's okay. I'm fine," Katie said.

Steph kept glaring at Jimmy. "Are you sure? 'Cause you don't have to talk to him. In fact, I can probably have his ass thrown out, if you so desire."

"Steph . . ."

"Fine. I need to go check on my husband anyway, but in case I wasn't clear with my RSVP card, there is no way in *hell* I would go to your wedding," Steph said, before giving Katie a hug and whispering, "I'm coming back in a few minutes with reinforcements."

Shaking her head, Katie watched Steph go for a minute before facing Jimmy again. Her gaze met his, and she noticed how mild his eyes were. Steph's obvious hatred hadn't fazed him. But what really got under her skin was that he acted like he had no idea that seeing him here, with the woman he had left her for, would tear her up inside.

"What are you doing here?" she asked a little accusingly.

He looked defensive, something he always did when he knew he was wrong, and said, "This is my hometown. I have a right to be here."

Her first reaction was to suck down her fury and be nice, keep the peace.

But that was the old Katie. The new Katie didn't let anyone treat her like she didn't matter.

And Jimmy was in for seven years of her unfiltered temper.

"Fine. Stay and have a good time. Just stay away from me." She said it in a cold tone and was pleased when he looked taken aback again.

Which lasted all of three seconds before his face turned red and he snapped, "Oh, real mature, Katie. I thought after six years together you could . . ."

Katie exploded. "We were together for almost seven, jerk, when you started having private peekaboo parties with little Miss DD over there. I don't owe you anything. And how dare you send me a wedding invitation like we're just old friends? We're not friends; we're not anything anymore, Jimmy."

Katie realized she had drawn a crowd with her outburst, and she would have turned to run if she hadn't seen Chase come out of his booth, his expression concerned. He reached her side swiftly, slipping his arm around her waist and said, "Hey, Firecracker, was that you I heard yelling?"

Jimmy's face darkened. "Who is this clown?"

Katie was happy to see Chase and kept her gaze on him while she made introductions. "Jimmy, this is Chase. Chase, this is my ex."

Chase didn't even look at Jimmy, just kissed her forehead and said, "Come on, let's get out of here."

"Hey, man, we were having a conversation," Jimmy said.

Selena came up alongside Jimmy and slipped her arm through his. "Everything okay, honey bear?"

Jimmy mumbled something Katie couldn't hear as Chase led her past them.

"Where are we going? What about your booth?" she asked.

"Eric's watching it for me. Thought you might need to go somewhere quiet to cool off." Chase squeezed her waist and she felt better just having him near.

"Can you believe he just acted like it was no big deal? Like we had just been classmates or something?"

He took her around the side of the bathrooms and leaned back against the stone building. "I told you he was a douche."

"Serious douche," she agreed.

"King of the douche nerds."

She gave a little laugh and looked at her cell phone. "Ugh, I have to be at the kissing booth in thirty minutes."

He grinned and set her new hat on top of her head, to her surprise. She had forgotten she was still gripping it. Bending his head down under the brim, he waggled his eyebrows and asked, "Don't suppose you want to practice a little?"

She laughed as she leaned against him, her anger ebbing away as they kissed. Chase made her laugh. Made her feel good about herself. And both of those things were going to become very addicting.

CHASE DIDN'T WANT to let Katie go. They leaned against the concrete building, oblivious to the titters and whispers. Eventually, Chase had been the one to pull back, knowing if he made her late, there'd be hell to pay. Katie seemed to be one of those rare souls who kept her word.

It was an admirable quality in most instances, but being punctual so she could kiss a bunch of other dudes was not one of them.

"We better get going if you don't want to be late."

She looked disappointed, but said, "Yeah, you're right. Everyone's going to want to kiss the soon-to-be former Canyon Queen."

He knew she was making a joke out of it, but he didn't smile. He didn't want anyone else getting a taste of Katie's sweet lips.

Walking her to the booth, Chase said hi to Gracie McAllister, who owned The Local Bean Coffee Shop and currently occupied the kissing booth. The petite blonde gave one of the Rock Canyon High School football players a little kiss and waved him off. "That's it, Jake, move on."

The next kid moved up and said, "Ready to rock my world?"

"No, Tommy, you're too young for me to rock." Peck. "Okay, shoo."

Just watching it, putting Katie in Gracie's place, made Chase growl. "I'm right next door."

Katie smiled up at him so sweetly it hurt his chest and he wasn't sure why. He walked back into his booth and said to Eric, "Thanks for watching my booth."

Eric grinned. "Anytime, buddy. Now if you'll excuse me, I'm going to see if I can get in a last-minute kiss with Miss Gracie Lou."

Chase laughed. It was a well-known fact that Eric had been carrying a big, flaming torch for Gracie since he had carried her out of the Valentine's Day singles' auction over his shoulder. No one knew what had happened that night and neither of them had talked about it, but Eric hadn't stopped looking for ways to antagonize Gracie ever since. The two acted like arch-nemeses in public, but sometimes Chase wondered if they didn't have something going on they didn't want anyone to know about.

Like you and Katie?

Chase kept checking his watch until it reached three and Gracie's voice pealed out over the megaphone. "Changing of the lips! Changing of the lips! Come give your Canyon Queen, Miss Katie Connors, a smooch! Only a dollar!"

Chase glared when he saw the kid who had delivered their pizza walk by and turn right.

It was just a fund-raiser. No big deal. What did he care who she kissed?

A line started forming past the front of his booth and Chase was grinding his teeth and clenching his fists after five minutes. When the two guys he'd beat playing pool on Monday got in line, he couldn't stand it anymore.

Opening his lockbox, he pulled out three hundred dollars. When he saw Gracie stomp by angrily, Eric close on her heels, Chase called, "Eric, can you watch my booth again?"

Eric stopped, his attention moving back and forth between Chase and Gracie, getting further away from him. "I'm kind of busy, man."

"I'll owe you one," Chase said.

Eric stared off after his prey, shrugged, and made his way over to the Jagged Rock booth. "Where are you off to now?"

Chase didn't answer as he rounded the corner toward the kissing booth, telling himself he wasn't interfering with the kissing booth out of jealousy. But as his eyes locked on Katie, smiling beautifully at the current man leaned down to kiss her, Chase knew it was a lie.

KATIE GAVE CARL Anderson a light peck and pulled back quickly. "There you go."

Carl looked disappointed. "Man, that's it?"

Katie saw Chase walking past the other guys in line, his expression dark, and her heartbeat sped up. "Yep, that's it, Carl. Scoot."

Carl left grumbling and Chase pushed the next guy out of the way. Loud curses and protests ensued from the men in line. He handed Katie a stack of bills. "I'd like to buy three hundred dollars' worth of kisses."

Katie's mouth dropped open as Chase came around to the inside of the kissing booth and yelled, "Sorry, boys, these lips are reserved!"

The men grumbled as Katie finally got her bearings. "Are you crazy? Everybody's going to be talking about this."

He kissed her and she grabbed his arms to hold on. When he pulled back, he was grinning. "Only 299 more to go."

She blinked at him. "You can't kiss me 299 times out

here. Mrs. Andrews is already giving me dirty looks, and people are going to say . . ."

He kissed her again. "Now it's 298. People are going to say what they want. So what? We can give them something to talk about, and I don't have to imagine you kissing a bunch of other guys."

It was pretty much what she'd told herself earlier, but the little part of her that hated being the object of any gossip was protesting in her brain. She didn't argue anymore, though, as he kissed her again and again. And when her time in the kissing booth was up, he still had 137 kisses to go.

CHASE ONLY HAD an hour and a half left at his booth and Katie sat with him the whole time, watching him work or just smiling when he stole another kiss.

When the fair ended, she helped him gather his supplies, fold down the rental tent, and carry the sample binders and equipment out to the Blazer. "No chopper today?"

He slammed the back of the car and came around to face her. Putting his hands against the Blazer on either side of her head, he said, "Nope. Can't carry all that stuff on the back of a motorcycle." He kissed her again. "I think that's 118."

"You can stop counting now."

His mouth caught the last bit of her sentence. "That would be 117. No, because I want to make sure I get my money's worth."

Wrapping her arms around his waist, she asked, "Wanna see something?"

"Sure," he said, pretending to look down her shirt.

"Let's go then," she said, ducking out from under his arm.

"Where are we going?"

Her look was flirtatious. "You'll see," she said, climbing into the passenger seat.

Opening up the door to the SUV, he hopped behind the wheel. "All right, where am I going?"

"Head out to Old Mill Road. Those clouds look pretty dark, but we won't be long. I need to be back at the community center by six. Just enough time to show you my favorite spot," she said.

"Oh yeah? I can't wait to see where sweet Katie spent her youth." He started the Blazer and said, "I'll have you back on time. Wouldn't want to miss the swimsuit competition." He moved just in time to avoid a slap on the arm and added, "Now, now, temper, temper."

She stuck her tongue out at him and grinned and Chase put the Blazer into gear. He drove away from town toward the farms until she told him to take a dirt road into the Snake River Canyon. The road was barely one lane, with no guardrail along the edge, and it made him a little nervous. He had never been comfortable with heights, even as a kid. Looking over the edge of a cliff was something he avoided, even in a car.

As he descended into the canyon, she pointed. "Follow the road back there. Eventually there will be nowhere left to go and we'll just park."

He did what she said, winding back through tall weeds and bushes until the road dead-ended in a small circle. He put the car into park and shut the engine off. Turning to her, he asked, "So now what?"

Katie leaned over and kissed him hard and fast. Before he could grab her back, she opened her door and hopped out. "Now we walk."

"Are we going to get shot for trespassing?" he asked, getting out of the Blazer and looking around for some hidden assailant.

Laughing, she headed onto a very narrow trail surrounded by tall bushes and grass. "I haven't, but you never know. I'd be more worried about snakes."

Chase stopped. He hated snakes, had always been a chicken shit around them. "Yeah, I'm not much of a hiker," he called.

She stopped suddenly and walked back to him. Reaching out, she took hold of his hand and laced her fingers through his.

So much for not holding hands.

"Stay close, city boy, and just listen for the sound of a rattle. Like a *chickchick bzzzz* sound," she said. "Oh, and watch for poison ivy."

Looking around at the jungle of vegetation, he said, "What the hell does that look like?"

She pointed to a plant about a foot from his leg and he pictured his death by poisonous snakes and oozing sores.

Chase let her lead him by the hand like a child, checking around his feet for anything slithery. Every once in a while he'd hear something scurry into the bushes, making him jump. Katie would squeeze his hand and give him a smile until he started to relax.

Suddenly, Katie stopped, leaned up to give him a kiss, and whispered, "That's 115."

After that he figured a little oozing death was worth it if it meant he could kiss her 114 more times.

Chapter Seven

KATIE HADN'T BEEN to Rainbow Falls since high school and she couldn't wait to see Chase's face when he saw it. They came into the clearing surrounded by bushes and trees and she squeezed his hand. "We made it."

The large spring waterfall came out several feet below the canyon rim and formed a clear pool that ran down into Snake River. The sun hit the water in such a way that sprays of color arched down to the middle of the pond. She looked up at Chase's face, delighted to find him smiling.

"Cool huh?" she said.

"Yeah." Dropping her hand, he surprised her by reaching down to take his shoes off. "What are you doing?" she squeaked.

Tossing each shoe by a bush and pulling his socks off, he asked, "Can't a guy take off his shoes for no reason?" As he straightened up, he started unbuttoning his jeans.

"It's hot out here. Thought maybe it would be a good time for a swim." He pushed the jeans off his hips and said, "You did want to try skinny-dipping. Figured we could cross one more thing off the list."

"But it's still light out!" she said.

Katie watched him slip his jeans over powerful thighs, and when his hands reached for the bottom of his shirt, her mouth watered. "So?"

The T-shirt came up and off, revealing tanned skin with several tattoos on his biceps and one on his chest. He slipped his thumbs into the waistband of his boxers and bent over as he dropped them to the ground, his stomach muscles bunching.

Chase stood up and raised one eyebrow at her. "Are you coming?"

She stared at him, naked as a jaybird and so amazingly put together her heart kept stopping as her gaze traveled over him. He had nice arms, just the right amount of definition to make them hard, but not too bulging, and his pecs were a thing of beauty. A light, happy trail started below a set of abs that would make a saint stare, and below that . . .

Blushing, she averted her eyes. He was already standing at attention and she hadn't even stripped yet. Besides the fact that he was the most beautiful man she'd ever seen, she'd never really been naked in front of someone in broad daylight. There had been mornings with Jimmy, but they had been under the covers and in the moment. Never just putting all her goods out for anyone to see.

And that was another thing: someone could discover

them, and she was surprised that the thought was more exciting than scary. More than anything she wanted to show this man that she could be daring. That she could let loose and be wild. That she knew how to have fun.

With steely resolve, Katie reached up to take her hat off and set it on top of the nearest bush. Turning her back to him, she slowly started undoing the straps to her halter top. She was a little self-conscious of her lack of a bra beneath, but the open back of her top hadn't allowed for one. Tossing the shirt on the bush to join the hat, she kept her back to him, kicked off her cowboy boots as gracefully as possible. Her hands unsnapped the buttons of her jean skirt and she shimmied out of it, shaking it out when it touched the ground. Laying the skirt out on the bush, she bent over to take off her socks, knowing that his eyes were probably glued to her lace-covered butt in the air and trying hard to ignore it. Standing up again, she took a deep breath and wiggled out of her underwear, her last shield of modesty. Bared to him and anyone else who might happen along, she stood back up, folded her arms over her breasts, and took a deep, bracing breath before facing him.

Chase looked her over from head to toe, his gaze filled with hunger. A strangled groan escaped him and he moved toward her across the dirt. He'd barely taken a step before he yelped and picked up his foot. "Shit, there're stickers. Hold on."

She watched him yank out the sticker and slip his shoes back on. Walking to where she stood, he picked her up in his arms, holding her high against his chest like a knight carrying his lady. She'd never been carried before and she felt an overwhelming giddiness spread through her, taking away some of her nervousness. The heat of his bare skin and muscles sent tingles of awareness through her, and she wanted to run her hands over him.

Snuggling closer, she said, "You know this is really gentlemanly and romantic. Like Rhett carrying Scarlett up the . . . oof!"

Suddenly she was flying through the air toward the pond. Chase had tossed her in. She took a breath right before she hit the cool water and spluttered to the surface a moment later, yelling, "You cretin!"

Laughing as he kicked off his shoes again, he dove in near her, and stayed down long enough to swim up behind her, saying, "You were getting all mushy. It had to be stopped."

Turning to face him, she knew he was right. They had agreed to keep things light and casual. She had almost demanded it. So why did it hurt her feelings that he hadn't wanted to hear her compliment him? She had called him chivalrous, which, in her opinion, was high praise. Did it make him uncomfortable because he wasn't used to someone seeing his sweet side? There was so much she didn't know about him, yet here she was, naked as the day she was born, and frolicking in her favorite childhood spot. Why wasn't she freaking out? And why did everything about being with this man feel so right?

Katie couldn't really be mad at him, but she could seek revenge for his callousness. She reached up and tried to push down on his head, but he didn't budge. He was too tall to dunk, and his laughter was getting on her nerves. Finally giving up on plan A, she swam away from him and proceeded to plan B: splashing him in the face. Chase stopped laughing, wiped the water from his eyes, and swam toward her with an evil grin. Shrieking, she tried to swim, but he caught her a few feet away and picked her up as if he was going to toss her again.

Wrapping her arms around his neck like a barnacle, she cried, "No, please, please, please, I'm sorry, don't!"

She squeezed her eyes shut and took a deep breath, but she didn't feel the familiar rush of air or the sting of the water. Instead his body started shaking, and she opened up one eye to see him laughing again. Relieved that the danger seemed to be over, she cried, "I hate being dunked and tossed. Steph's brothers used to love to torment me because I was a screamer."

Chase's laugh faded and she was suddenly aware of her naked breasts pushing against his hard chest. The sensation of his skin against her erect nipples made her shiver, and she watched his eyes darken like the ominous clouds forming to the south. Their mouths were so close she could feel his breath on her lips when he asked, "Are you cold?"

Katie shook her head. "No. Not even a little."

When he dropped his head to kiss her, she met him halfway. He tasted like sunshine, spring water, and Chase. She slid her hands from his neck over his wet shoulders, while his big hands rested on her butt before running over her thighs, squeezing her muscles as their mouths played.

It had been so long since she'd had a man touch her, and part of her was still surprised by what she was doing. Letting him touch her so intimately, and here, in her special place, where anyone could come upon them . . .

No one is going to come here with a storm rolling in. Don't be paranoid.

Putting a few inches between them, he moved his other hand up to skim her stomach and circled her nipple with his finger. Opening his hand to cup her flesh, he squeezed and teased her breast as he made love to her mouth. Forgetting her reservations, she moaned as he rubbed between her legs, and she felt his erection pressing against her sensitive flesh.

She didn't register the thunder, it was so faint at first, but she did start to feel a chill in the air right before the first raindrop hit her cheek.

"It's raining," she said, coming up for air.

"It's just a little drizzle," Chase said, trying to bring her mouth back to his.

As if the fates were working against them, the sky burst open and started dumping buckets of rain.

"Shit!" he said, laughing.

"Let's get out of here!" Pulling away from him, she started swimming toward shore. They climbed out of the water, and she tried to walk gingerly toward her now-soaked clothes, but halfway there she stepped on a sticker and winced. It wasn't the first time, but it still wasn't pleasant.

Chase's hand rested on her back and he yelled over the pouring rain, "Are you all right?"

"Yeah, I've stepped on these things a million times." Holding on to his arm, she bent over to pull it out, trying to see through the downpour and ignore the sounds of rumbling thunder getting closer to them. She let go of Chase's arm to walk the last few steps cautiously and grabbed her boots, struggling to slip them onto her wet feet. Gathering her clothes, she held them against her chest and turned, laughing when she caught Chase hopping from foot to foot, trying to put on his own wet shoes.

Swiping his clothes from the bush, she waited until he stood back up and thrust them at him. He gave her a wide grin and, using his free arm, reached out and yanked her into his arms, taking her mouth in a hard kiss. She would have stayed right there, kissing him in the rain like every girl's fantasy come true, except she could hear the thunder closing in. Storms in Idaho could come on quick and change rapidly, and although they were pretty safe from lightning in the canyon, she didn't want to take any chances.

When the next crack of thunder caused the earth to shake, she pushed him away and grabbed his hand, tugging him toward the trail. The sound of their feet couldn't be heard over the deafening rain and as they reached the SUV, she ran to her side and jumped into the passenger seat. She started to retie her halter top just as Chase dove into the driver's seat and threw his clothes in the back.

He gave her a weird look and asked, "What do you think you're doing?"

"Putting my clothes back on?" she said, pausing to

look at him but releasing the straps when she saw his intense stare.

Moving across the seat, he slipped his hand into her wet hair and gently pulled her toward him. "Why the hell would you do that? I'm not done with you yet."

She didn't know what was pounding harder, the rain on the roof or her heart as he covered her mouth with his. Chase yanked Katie's top off, his hands wreaking havoc over her skin, sending hot waves of ecstasy with each soft touch. She leaned her head back as his mouth found the sensitive skin of her neck and he breathed across her collarbone. "Let's take this to the backseat."

Giddy, nervous, and excited at the same time, she kicked of her boots and tried to climb gracefully over the middle console but ended up face first on the backseat with her feet in the air. She twisted around and dragged her feet back, watching as Chase followed her, his naked muscles flexing as he moved. She couldn't believe she was going to do this in the back of a car like some crazy teenager.

Chase sat next to her on the bucket seat and reached for her. As their hands moved over each other's bodies, he slid one between her legs to play with her wet folds. Moaning, she moved her head to the side as he kissed along her neck, collarbone, and finally down to take her nipple into his mouth while he fondled her.

Katie arched against his hungry mouth and felt pressure building as his clever fingers manipulated her in swift, sure strokes. It was just as intense as it had been in the laundry room, maybe more so. She cried out when he slipped a finger inside her and rubbed his thumb quickly over her clitoris, working her inside and out. Unable to hold on to a coherent thought or come up with one reason why what they were doing was wrong, her breath came in short gasps as she felt that muscle-tightening throb that told her she was close. As the orgasm hit her hard, taking her higher than she'd ever gone, she cried out, "Chase!"

When she finally came back to herself and stopped trembling, one coherent thought struck her. *Maybe it doesn't feel wrong with Chase because he's the right guy for me?*

GOD, HE WANTED to hear her cry out his name again.

It wasn't like he hadn't been with other women, and maybe some of them had even called out his name, but when Katie did it, it was like an awesome song. Watching her fall apart as she came and that one, desperate cry, was something he could listen to over and over again.

Reaching down to his wallet and pulling out a condom, he kissed her parted lips, murmuring, "You are so beautiful."

Her blue eyes opened slowly and the smile she gave him was soft and sexy. "So are you."

Smiling in return, he ripped the condom package with his teeth and slipped the latex over his erection. Once he was sheathed, he pulled her into his lap and tongued her nipple again until she made soft, mewling sounds. Rubbing against her wet flesh, he teased her with his touch, stopping only when Katie reached down and wrapped her hand around him. He let her take the lead as she adjusted his cock until he was pushing against her opening. He wanted to go slow, to make it good for her, but then she whimpered, "Please, Chase, I want you . . ."

It was all he heard before he was thrusting up and inside her tight, honeyed warmth, lifting his mouth away from her breast to shout with pleasure. He held on to her hips as he pumped into her, and she leaned forward to kiss him as she met his movements. Chase could feel how close he was and sweat broke out on his forehead as he groaned. "Firecracker, I'm not going to last."

"It's okay, I can't go again anyway," she whispered. He tried to concentrate on her expression, not how good she felt, and saw she really believed that.

Adjusting his hips and pulling out of her for a moment, he watched her start to frown. "What are you . . ."

He reentered her hard, and knew by her surprised gasp that he'd done something right. "Wanna bet?"

Her eyes widened as she got his meaning, and she wrapped her arms around his neck. "Hey, no complaints if you want to try, but I never have before."

Pulling out a little again, he countered, "That's because you weren't with the right guy."

Thrusting deep, he started alternating his rhythm between quick, shallow strokes and deep, slow ones until she was making fast, panting sounds. The inner walls of her passage tightened around him and he kept going, wanting her to finish again before he did. When her muscles spasmed around him, he let go, pumping into her as he hollered his release. To his relief, he heard her cry out again as she came and collapsed against his chest, her lips pressed against his shoulder. More than anything, he wanted to please Katie.

When his galloping heart finally slowed, Chase moved his lips over her cheek as he reached between them. Cupping her chin in his hands, he tipped her face back and kissed her softly, sliding his tongue inside to explore every sweet surface.

You just haven't been with the right guy.

His words rushed back through his head and he struggled with what they meant. When had his feelings for Katie started to change from mild curiosity and lust to this feeling of . . . completeness? When he was with her—hell, even when he thought about her—it was like the sun was shining. He felt warm, content, and . . . home.

Crazy talk, dude. You just had amazing sex. It's the sex talking.

Whatever it was, he needed a chance to think, and she needed to get dolled up for her pageant. He patted her thigh and said, "I should probably get you back to town so you can smile, wave, and kiss babies."

Frowning, she pinched him and said, "Hey, pageanting is hard work. I'd like to see you stand around in heels for hours, showcasing your talent, and talking to a crowd of people who are either mocking or ogling you."

She turned away to grab her clothes from the front seat and he asked, "So why do it if you hate it so much?"

"I didn't ever want to do them, and after tonight I never will again," she said as she looked over her shoulder. "My mom loved pageants. She used to do them when she was a kid with her mom, and she enjoyed seeing me up there, all decked out. She said they were a great confidence builder for me and it was, as long as I said the right things and always held my tongue."

"When did she die?" he asked, grabbing his T-shirt and pulling it over his head.

"Three years ago."

"Why did you do it last year?"

She blushed. "Jimmy wanted me to."

"I see." And Chase hated it. He hated that Katie had done the pageant for Jimmy. The guy hadn't deserved her.

And you do? You aren't exactly a good guy either.

"Do you see my underwear?" she said, frowning as she shook out her skirt.

Looking along the floor with her, he didn't see them. The thought of Katie standing on stage in a pageant dress after wild sex with him and missing her panties was enough to make him want to start all over. "No, I don't."

Pulling her skirt over her legs with a grumble, she started to work it up over her bare thighs while he watched hungrily. Trying to distract himself, he prodded, "So your mom wanted you to be confident and have opinions as long as they went along with hers?"

She stopped and glanced at him sharply. "My mother just wanted me to be polite and have the right morals and values."

Swiping his boxers off the front seat, he stepped into them and pulled them up. He didn't know why that comment rubbed him wrong, but it did. "I'm guessing

Mommy Dearest wouldn't have approved of me, then. I'm not exactly the boy next door."

Her expression changed from mildly annoyed to darkly furious in a flash. "First of all, do not call my mother that. She was a wonderful woman who just wanted what was best for me. She might have been strict, but she was also there for me, always. And second, I don't know why you're attacking me, but if I didn't want to be here, I wouldn't be."

Chase wondered what life would have been like if his mother had been more like Katie's. Would he have spent so much time alone and still discovered art? Or would he have ended up playing football and becoming a lawyer? Who knew? He liked his life, was proud of the things he had done, but he realized that despite her mother's wacky ideals, he actually envied Katie. Growing up with a parent who only wanted you to be happy and succeed?

Must have been nice.

"I thought it was just because I offered," he said.

"No, you idiot, I'm here with you because I like you. You are handsome, accomplished, and I'm happy when I'm with you," Katie said.

Her words hit him like a ton of bricks and he reached out for her, surprised she came so willingly when a few seconds before she'd looked like she wanted to throttle him. He stroked her wild curls and kissed her hair. "I'm sorry I was being a dick. You aren't like the other women I've been with. You're . . . well, nice."

"Well, thanks . . . I think. Why would you date mean women?" she asked.

"Just the type I usually attract," he said.

"Lucky you," she said sarcastically. "I usually attract selfish, cheating buttheads, so I guess we both have bad taste." Snuggling against his chest, she added, "I'll give you a pass this time on account of you usually dating harpies. Next time, though, you're in trouble, mister."

"Are you going to punish me?" he asked.

He felt a light nip on his neck. "Oh yeah, big time."

"Spanking?"

"Possibly."

"You are such a tease." He groaned.

Pulling away, she looked up at him, raising one perfectly arched eyebrow. "Who said I'm teasing?"

She just kept surprising him: sweet and warm to feisty and flirty in zero to sixty. Chase liked that about her.

Moving out of his embrace, she reached up front for her purse, grabbing the strap and pulling it back into her lap. She stuck her hands in to grab her phone and sighed. "Great, it's 5:43. I have to be at the community center in fifteen minutes to get ready or Mrs. Andrews is going to have my head."

Chase pretended to shudder. "That woman is terrifying."

"Tell me about it." Katie, fully dressed, bent all the way over and peered along the floor. With a groan, she sat back up. "I give up! I have no idea where they went."

"What? Your underwear? They'll turn up when I clean this thing out," he said.

"That doesn't exactly help me now," she said, starting

to crawl over the middle console. With her cute little rear in the air, he couldn't resist giving it a pat.

She flopped into the front seat and he caught her glare as he grabbed his jeans. "Sorry, couldn't help myself."

"Do you know how cave-mannish it is to slap a woman's butt? Next you'll be yelling, 'Honey, can you get me a beer?'"

"I think 'Barmaid, get me a beer' sounds better," he said, pulling his jeans up and zipping them with a grin. "Too bad I don't keep beer in the Blazer."

"You're incorrigible," she said.

Gathering up his socks and shoes, he crawled into the driver's seat and said, "No, I'm recidivous."

Katie blinked at him. "What does that mean?"

Giving her a smacking kiss, he said, "Incorrigible."

"You think you're so smart," she said, fighting back a smile.

"And I've got the college degree to prove it, Firecracker." He had managed to pull on his socks; they were pretty soaked, but he could deal. His shoes were a bit harder to finagle in the cramped space, but he finally managed and put the keys in the ignition.

As he started the engine, he looked out into the blurry landscape and could hardly see even with the wipers on. The rain was really coming down hard.

"I can't believe I lost my panties. What if I dropped them along the trail?" she said.

He grinned. "Then some lucky teenage boy will find them and use them when he gets"––she smacked him and he rubbed his shoulder—"ow, cold! I was going to say he could use them for a hat."

"Sure you were," she said dryly.

He wiggled his eyebrows and fingers at her. "Besides, I like you this way. Easy access."

She sat back with a groan and said, "Let's go before you make me late. If I get an earful from Mrs. Andrews, I'm going to make you suffer." As if anticipating his naughty comeback, she added, "And not in a good way."

Chase backed up the SUV, laughing, and the car struggled along the muddy back road. He kicked it up to four-wheel drive and joked, "I guess I see now why everyone drives big redneck trucks around here."

"Didn't you have the same type of thing where you grew up? Nevada isn't so different from Idaho," she said.

The car swerved as it fought for traction along the bumps and grooves of the road. "I was more of an indoor man. Played a lot of video games. I'd draw and write. I think the only thing I did outside was swim. Loved swimming." He leered. "Especially naked."

As they started along the uphill slope of the canyon, his hands gripped the steering wheel nervously. The one-lane road was a smoother ride than the bottom had been, but still, the cliff growing beside his window made his palms sweat.

"Are you scared of heights?" she asked.

"No. Why?" he said.

"Because you're white knuckling that wheel," she said.

Loosening his grip a little, he felt a rush of relief as they made it to the top.

He looked over at Katie, who had a little smile on her face, and slid his hand over to rest it on her knee.

"What are you smiling about?" he asked.

She turned that seductive smile on him and reached down to cover his hand with hers. "Nothing. Just you."

Trying to concentrate on the road was difficult with her hand over his. "What about me?"

She shrugged. "I'm just really happy right now. I've been so miserable trying to make it, trying to survive one day at a time, but with you, I can just relax and have fun. Be myself." She squeezed his hand and added, "You are the reason I'm smiling. So thank you."

He turned his hand over and laced his fingers through hers. He couldn't remember the last time he'd held hands with a woman, but with Katie it felt right. Her palm was warm and soft against his, and he trailed his thumb over her silky skin.

The last few miles, Chase shifted his eyes from the road to look over at the woman who was beginning to get to him. Her smile, which brightened every room she entered. Her laugh, sometimes accompanied by the cutest snort at the end, and when it escaped, her cheeks would turn pink, which he thought was adorable. How unselfishly she put other's feelings before her own, even the ones who didn't deserve it.

He pulled into the parking lot of the community center and parked by the back entrance. Katie unlocked her seat belt and started to get out, but he reached across to stop her. She smiled at him in that soft, happy way and he had to kiss her, had to show Katie she was the most amazing woman he'd ever been with and that he didn't want anyone else.

Cupping her cheek in his hand, he brought her lips to his and tenderly covered her mouth, hoping his actions would show her exactly what he wished he could say. Expressing his emotions had never come easy to Chase, but as a man of action, he hoped she understood that this thing between them wasn't just casual or simple anymore.

And if nothing else, he wanted to show her that she made him happy too.

Chapter Eight

KATIE COULDN'T BELIEVE her day. So far she'd broken every one of her so-called rules to keep this thing between them uncomplicated, and she'd loved every second of it. Kissing Chase in his booth, by the bathroom, at the waterfall . . . their incredible sex in the Blazer, and now they were making out in the parking lot of the community center. She couldn't seem to pull away, and if her phone hadn't started screeching, she could have stayed right there all night.

Reluctantly, she broke the kiss and reached into her purse for her phone. Mrs. Andrews's number was flashing across the screen and she groaned.

"I'd better get in there," she said, grimacing.

Chase's hand smoothed back her hair and he gave her a quick kiss on the nose, something that should have made her feel like a kid but instead made her feel cared for. Like Chase felt more for her than just lust.

"I'm going to go home and shower, but I'll be back. Maybe after the pageant you can come over to my place and we could watch a movie or . . . something?" he said, smiling suggestively.

She returned his smile. "I'd love that."

"All right, then, you'd better go before dragon lady comes looking for you."

Laughing as she opened the door and jumped out of the Blazer, she raced for the community center door, the rain pouring down over her, soaking her to the skin. Yanking it open quickly, she made her way toward the sounds of angry women and high-pitched laughter.

"Where have you been?" Mrs. Andrews's voice practically burst Katie's eardrum, it was so loud and shrill.

Katie looked at her phone. "It's only 6:08. I have plenty of time to get ready."

"Just look at you! That shirt, what there is of it, is practically see-through, and you're not even wearing a bra! You look like you've been out necking in a hayloft with some boy."

Actually, it was the backseat of an SUV, and he definitely wasn't a boy. Katie tried not to smile as she said, "I got caught in the rain, Mrs. Andrews, and I'm freezing, so if you don't mind letting me dry off and change, I would appreciate it."

"I saw you with *that man*. Kissing him like some floozy. And I heard about the little show he put on at the kissing booth. He is a bad element, and you are too nice of a girl to get involved with him," Mrs. Andrews said firmly.

Katie didn't feel like smiling anymore. Instead she felt like grabbing the nearest glass of water and seeing if the witch would melt. How dare she treat her like an errant child, like *her* errant child! Even on her worst day, her mother had never come close to Mrs. Andrews's obnoxious, overbearing attitude.

"Mrs. Andrews, as you are neither my mother nor my boss, I would ask you to keep your opinions to yourself." Katie said it as calmly as she could, but even she noticed the tremble in her voice. Doing her best to distance herself from the situation, something her mother always told her helped during a conflict, she started to turn her back on the older woman. Too bad New Katie took over just long enough to say offhandedly, "Oh, and by the way, it was the backseat of his car, not a hayloft."

Mrs. Andrews gasped and Katie walked away, a mixture of horror and pleasure warring within her. She'd always been taught that talking about sex and intimacy was a private matter, but the look on the nosy old bat's face had been so ... satisfying. She'd probably regret it later, after Mrs. Andrews had told anyone who'd listen, but for right now she felt good, like she was ten feet tall and bulletproof.

She walked past all of the young girls and women, barely noticing their curious glances as she reached a storage room, which doubled as her private dressing room, and opened the door.

Becca and Steph were inside and they turned to her simultaneously. Becca closed and locked the door while Steph hissed, "Where have you been? Mrs. Andrews has been walking around asking everyone if they've heard from you."

"I took Chase to see Rainbow Falls."

"That's code for sex, right?" Becca asked.

"Oh my God, you had *sex* with him?" Steph shrieked.

Katie wanted to bang her head against something. God knew she loved small-town life in most instances, but the nosy, gossipy way everyone was in everyone else's business made her crazy sometimes. Even when one of the nosy neighbors was her best friend. "Okay, yes, we did; no, I don't want to talk about it right now and, may I ask, why are you two back here anyway?"

Becca grabbed a garment bag hanging from a metal shelf of cleaning supplies and said, "I could not let you wear that gangrene-colored monstrosity of a dress again, so I brought you something else."

"And I thought I could help you with your hair and makeup, just like in high school," Steph said innocently, but Katie didn't buy it for a second. Her suspicions were confirmed when Steph continued, "And I wanted to know what happened with Chase. Everyone is talking about him dropping three hundred bucks at the kissing booth and—"

Katie interrupted. "I will tell you everything later, but for right now, can we just get me dressed so I can do this stupid thing?"

Steph frowned at her. "Are you serious about him? I thought this was just a casual thing."

That's what Katie had thought originally, but now she wasn't so sure. "I like him. Not sure about anything else, but can we discuss it later? I am so late."

Steph remained silent, but Katie could tell by the stubborn tilt of her jaw that they weren't done discussing it.

Becca, bless her heart, unzipped the garment bag with a flourish and grinned. "Let's do this thing!"

CHASE WALKED UP the aisle of the community center, feeling out of place with the people in the crowd staring at him. He recognized the back of Becca's multicolored head and took the empty seat next to her. "Have I missed anything yet?"

Becca shook her head and held out a little bag of popcorn. "Nope, still have a couple minutes before it starts. I love beauty pageants. Want some?"

"No thanks. I'm surprised. I would've thought you would despise them," he said.

"Nope, love them. The fashion. The competition. The drama. It's better than anything Hollywood could dream up." She shoved a handful of popcorn into her mouth, and the lights dimmed. She elbowed his side. "Wait until you see Katie. She looks smoking hot."

Chase looked past Becca and saw Steph glaring at him but didn't have time to ask her what her problem was before the stage lit up and Harold Martin grapevined into the spotlight. Harold did the afternoon show at LMKZ 105.9, the local country station, and his smooth voice called, "Who wants to see some foxy ladies tonight?" The crowd cheered. "Yeah, that's what I like to hear! I just want to thank everyone for coming out tonight to support the thirty-sixth annual Canyon

Queen Pageant. These women aren't just beautiful, they are smart, talented, and some of them even laugh at my jokes. How sweet is that?" A few chuckles. "Just a reminder that the fireworks have been canceled due to the rain, but as soon as we can figure out the best day to light up the sky, we will announce it. Now, I'd like you all to welcome last year's Canyon Queen, Ms. Katie Connors. Louder, everyone, she needs to feel the love in here!"

Chase watched Katie glide onto the stage like she was floating, her hair pulled back from her face and twisted into a fat bun high on the back of her head, her tiara placed in front of it. The black dress she wore wrapped up over one shoulder and hugged every curve of her body until it hit mid-thigh, where the skirt split into strips of fabric, dancing along her legs like black flames. In her hands was a clear box that held another tiara, probably for tonight's winner. She looked amazing and he wanted to jump up on stage and hide her away from the other men's eyes. He had never been the jealous type, but as he scanned the crowd and saw several men sit forward with interest, he clenched his fists.

Becca leaned over and whispered, "Isn't she gorgeous?"

He only nodded as Harold greeted Katie and asked, "So, Katie, how do you feel about giving up your crown tonight?"

"Actually, I feel really good about it, Harold. I enjoyed being Canyon Queen, but I'm ready to relinquish the honor to the next worthy candidate." She smiled out at the crowd and when her gaze landed on Chase, it brightened.

He returned her smile as Harold said, "Well, let me just say, she is going to have some mighty big shoes to fill. You are quite a beauty. I hope your guy appreciates you."

Chase could see Katie's blush from his seat. "Thank you, Harold. I'll be sure to tell your wife how lucky she is to have such a charmer."

Harold turned to the crowd and said, "You hear that, Wilma? I'm a charmer!"

A woman's voice shouted a reply that Chase couldn't hear, but laughter ensued from her side of the room. Harold gave the crowd an uh-oh look and said, "Well, I guess I better get on with it before my wife decides I'm sleeping in the doghouse tonight! Katie, may I escort you to your throne, Your Majesty?"

The crowd chuckled as Katie gave him a shallow curtsy and said, "Why thank you, sir."

Harold led her to her throne, a giant gold chair with red cushions, and deposited her smoothly, while Katie nodded her head at him regally and shooed him with a wave of her hand. Harold made a great show of continuing to bow as he backed away, and when he turned back to face the crowd, he said, "Why do I feel like I should be wearing a fool's hat?"

There was more laughter from Harold's wife's side of the room, and he called out sternly, "Woman, you better be nice to me or . . ." he paused, "well, I've got nothing. Let's welcome our first contestant to the stage, everyone!"

The crowd cheered as contestant number one walked

out onto the stage, and Chase watched Katie smile as the girl came over to greet her and kiss her cheek. The girl seemed a little unsteady on the high heels she was wearing, and Chase kept waiting for her to biff it, right on her face.

Harold, as if anticipating her unsteadiness, rushed toward her and held out his hand. "Ladies and gentleman, may I introduce you to the lovely Jenny Andrews? All of seventeen, Miss Andrews has managed to score a scholarship for the Boise State music program and hopes to one day play professionally. Now Jenny, I believe you're going to play us something mighty fancy on that fiddle of yours."

"Yes I am, Mr. Martin," Jenny said, smiling nervously.

"Well, let's get it started then," Harold said, stepping back to stand beside Katie as Jenny set up for her talent.

Chase leaned over and asked, "Is that the dragon lady's daughter?"

Becca choked on her popcorn and a couple of people behind them shushed. Steph leaned over Becca and said, "Yeah, she's the youngest."

Steph's tone sounded sharp and irritated, and he looked at her again. Her expression was fierce, and all that annoyance was directed at him. Sitting back in his seat, he grimaced. Chase wasn't sure exactly what he'd done to piss Steph off, but he knew when someone had a bone to pick with him. He'd seen it enough times to know the signs. Now he just needed to wait until Steph made her move and fix it. Because if he wanted to continue to see Katie, he couldn't have her best friend hating his guts.

Jenny started to play a classical piece on her violin that at least sounded in tune to Chase, although he was no expert. His gaze moved over to Harold and Katie, who were smiling and whispering. Once Jenny finished, the next contestant was called, and he caught Katie looking bored during her very bland rendition of a monologue from *Romeo and Juliet*. When she caught him watching her, he gave an exaggerated yawn and she covered her mouth to hide a smile.

Contestant number three, Marissa Channing, did a cheerleading routine, and four, a weird "interpretive" dance that had Becca and him trying to cover their laughter with coughing fits. Steph scolded them, but even that didn't stop the grimacing and groaning that took place when contestant number five sang "On My Own" from *Les Misérables* and hit the high notes at a pitch so off it could make ears bleed. Chase saw Katie was still smiling, although she kept touching her ears discreetly, and shook his head. When the girl finished, Katie clapped the loudest, and he loved her good heart.

Once all fifteen contestants had finished the talent portion, Harold called each one back up on stage to answer a series of questions. By the time the last girl had been interviewed, Chase was ready to bail. He kept waiting for Harold to call an end to it, but it seemed like a never-ending parade of tight curls, clown faces, and ruffle dresses.

"All right, folks, we are going to turn our final decision over to our wonderful judges, Gracie McAllister, Kirsten Winters, and Daphne O'Neal." The crowd applauded the three women, and after ten minutes of deliberation, and some really bad jokes on Harold's part, Gracie handed him an envelope.

"My queen," Harold said, bowing to Katie, "would you like to help me announce the winners?"

Katie stood up gracefully and moved forward, accepting the white envelope Harold held out to her. "Thank you, Harold, I'd be delighted." She pulled out the little card and after looking at it for a moment, spoke into the microphone with a smile. "The second runner-up is Ms. Lindsey Lawrence."

Applause and whoops sounded to Chase's right and he leaned over to ask Becca, "So what do the winners get?"

Becca shrugged. "Probably a gift card to get their nails done or something."

"Lindsey, here is your gift certificate for a free pedicure at K.C.'s Salon. I've heard the place is fabulous," Katie joked, hugging the younger girl. "Congratulations."

Harold hugged the girl, who looked like she was going to start weeping at any moment, and helped usher her over to the winner's side of the stage. "Wasn't she outstanding, folks?"

Once the applause for the distraught girl quieted, Katie called out, "First runner-up for the crown, who will take over if our queen cannot fulfill her duties, and the winner of a dinner for two at Stampede Pete's Steak House is . . ."

Chase asked, "Is that place any good?"

"I wouldn't know; I don't like red meat, but it's always packed when I drive home," Becca said.

"Maggie Palmer! Congratulations!" Katie said as a frowning girl allowed Katie to hug her. When Harold came over to walk her across the stage, the girl brushed past him and stomped her spiked heels as she disappeared behind the curtain.

Harold, collecting himself, said, "Well, folks, there's all kinds of queens out there. Queen Bees. Evil queens. *Drama queens*. Katie, why don't you announce our winner and we'll see what kind of queen she is."

Chase clapped along with everyone else, thinking that if he got the chance to take Katie out on a proper date, he would take her to that steakhouse. If she was interested, that is, and after the things she'd said to him on the way to the pageant, he had a suspicion she would be.

"And now for the winner and your next Canyon Queen ..." Katie smiled as she announced, "... Jenny Andrews!"

Jenny screamed and jumped up and down in her heels excitedly until a loud snap echoed through the large auditorium. With her arms spinning like a windmill, she toppled over into the contestant next to her. That girl grabbed the next contestant, Marissa Channing's dress, as she fell, ripping the fabric to reveal the poor girl's corset-clad upper body. Struggling to her feet, she wrapped her arms around herself and hobbled off the stage wailing as the crowd roared with laughter and sympathetic cries. Jenny scrambled to her feet and, with her face in her hands, limped from the stage on her broken heel after Marissa.

Katie, shoving the microphone at Harold, followed

the distraught girls off stage. Harold stood red-faced, trying to control his chuckles. Finally calm, he cleared his throat, and said with a straight face, "Did I mention how graceful they were?"

The guffaws from the audience started all over again, especially from Becca, who was howling beside Chase. "What did I tell you? Drama and laughs!"

"Yeah, you did," he said, standing with a smile. "I'm going to go backstage and see if I can catch Katie."

"Oh, give her a kiss for me," she said, pursing her lips and smacking them together.

"Thanks for coming out tonight, folks, and hope you enjoyed the excitement! See ya next year," Harold said as people started to get up.

Chase laughed and started toward the stage, rounding along the edge and through the people moving about. Suddenly, a hand grabbed his arm just as he was about to make it backstage, and he turned to face Steph.

"Oh hey, Steph, I was just heading back to see Katie."

Steph's look wasn't friendly. "I don't know what your deal is, but you need to leave Katie alone. She's too good for you."

Chase was surprised by Steph's outburst, and he suffered a severe case of déjà vu. How many times had he been told he wasn't good enough for something? A girl? A scholarship? It hurt, but he'd never let someone's low opinion keep him from what he wanted. "Look, Steph, Katie is a grown woman, and if she doesn't want to see me, I'm sure she'll put on her big-girl pants and tell me."

"Katie likes you. I can tell. But after the last scumbag

she cared about crushed her into a million pieces, I told myself I wasn't going to let her get hurt again. So you're going to leave her alone before she gets attached and you break her heart," Steph said.

Chase was caught between anger, respect, and excitement. He was pissed that Steph had the nerve to tell him to stop seeing Katie, but he could understand it. She was just protecting her best friend. However, if she was worried that Katie had feelings for him, that meant Katie had said something, right? He liked the thought of Katie telling her best friend she was into him; a shock in itself, but there it was. He didn't know what was going on with them yet, but he wasn't going to put up his hands and step back from Katie just because Steph didn't like him. Forget playing nice; he was all for being cool with her, but he wasn't going to take shit from someone when he didn't deserve it.

"Look, Steph, I get that you want to protect her, and I swear I will do my best not to hurt her. But you're not going to dictate my life or Katie's."

He didn't give her a chance to reply, and she didn't stop him as he walked away. He wanted to see Katie and find out if there was something to Steph's observation. Were Katie's feelings stronger than she'd let on?

And why did that please him so damn much?

"OH, I RUINED everything. They'll probably take my crown away."

Katie squeezed Jenny's shoulders reassuringly. She

had followed the younger girl backstage and had been trying to calm her down, but she just kept crying. Even when she'd put the shiny new tiara on Jenny's head, it still hadn't lifted the poor girl's spirits. "Hush, they will not. It's not your fault your heel broke. No one blames you."

Katie saw Mrs. Andrews, heading for them looking like a thundercloud, and braced herself for the storm.

"Jennifer Lynn Andrews, what have I told you about decorum and serenity? Now, because you acted like a three-year-old on Christmas, poor Marissa has locked herself in the bathroom." Mrs. Andrews's hands slammed down on her ample hips as she prodded, "Well, don't just sit there; we need to go apologize to everyone."

Katie held tight to Jenny and said, "Mrs. Andrews, she was just excited. It's not her fault that . . ."

Mrs. Andrews's eyes narrowed on Katie. "I'll thank you to release my daughter and mind your own business. The last thing she needs is to be under the influence of a rude hussy with the moral fiber of a cat in heat."

"Mother!" Jenny yelled.

"Do not scream, Jennifer, I am merely stating the facts. She told me earlier, and I've seen her all over that lowlife Chase with no regard for anyone except herself. How Quinn Connors could have raised such a loose girl, I will never know," Mrs. Andrews said.

"You will apologize to Katie right now."

Katie was partly relieved to hear Chase coming to her rescue but also humiliated that he had heard every vile word Mrs. Andrews had said. And that he was making it worse.

Katie couldn't speak as Chase descended on them like a dark, avenging angel and put his hand on her shoulder. His angry gaze was directed at Mrs. Andrews, whose nose had lifted four inches into the air. "I am not going to apologize for speaking the truth, you insufferable boar."

Chase took a step toward the older woman and Katie dropped her arms from Jenny, moving forward to grab his hand, hoping to defuse the situation. "It's not worth it, Chase. Let's just go." He ignored her, his focus still glued on Mrs. Andrews's defiant expression, and she squeezed his hand. "Please, Chase. People are staring."

He eased back a bit slowly, but his voice was cold as he said, "Katie is too nice to really give you what you deserve, but I'm not as nice or as good as she is. If I was a good man, I'd leave before I called you a bigoted, small-minded waste of space. But I'm not that good."

Katie was relieved when Chase turned his back on Mrs. Andrews's red-faced anger and led her toward the back exit. The rain hit her face, and she let the tears she'd been holding back flow. She shouldn't have let Mrs. Andrews's insults hit her so hard, but when she'd caught the various looks on the other faces around her, it had killed her to hold back her hurt. There had been looks of sympathy, people looking away to avoid eye contact, and then nods of agreement accompanied by disapproving scowls. It was terrible that so many people who had known her since she was a baby would stand by and let her be bullied.

She let Chase open the door and help her up into the Blazer. Slamming the door behind her, he ran around the front of the SUV to climb into the driver's seat. Shaking his head like a dog spraying raindrops everywhere, he asked, "Are you okay?"

Trying to be discreet, Katie wiped at her tears. "Yeah, it was my fault anyway. I was inappropriate and antagonized her earlier, when I knew better."

He cupped her cheek, turning her to face him and interrupting her excuses. "I don't care what you think you did to deserve that, but you didn't. You are the kindest, funniest, and most amazing girl I have ever met, and no matter what you might do, you would never deserve that."

His words made her stomach flip-flop. When he kissed her softly, tenderly, her eyes teared up all over again. She'd known most of those people her whole life and the only person who had defended her was a man she barely knew.

"So, do you still feel like coming over?" he asked, pulling away to brush her cheek with his hand tenderly. "Waiting out the rain?"

"Yes," she said, nodding to emphasize how very much she wanted to be with him right then. "There's nothing I want more."

With a grin, Chase started the Blazer. "Besides, I already told you I had this fantasy about the prom queen. And with that cute little tiara on your head, well, I have a feeling that my fantasies are about to become a reality."

Katie reached up to touch her tiara and said, "And who are you in this little scenario?"

Taking her hand in his, he raised it to his lips. "The luckiest guy in the world."

Eyes beginning to blur once more, she tried to tell herself he was just making her feel better. That it didn't mean anything, even as he wormed his way just a little bit more into her heart.

CHASE HAD BEEN driving the car one-handed since they left the community center five minutes earlier, his other hand covering Katie's. She couldn't help feeling content, safe, and cared for, and she was done pretending this wasn't serious. She was falling in love with Chase, and if he knew what she was thinking, he'd probably drop her on the side of the road and drive as far from her as he could get.

Or maybe he feels the same way you do. You could ask him.

Turning in the seat to study him, she cradled his hand in hers as she pondered that. They had taken the back roads out of town and hadn't really said anything. Katie was a little worried he was regretting his earlier chivalry and was quietly panicking next to her.

As he turned off onto a short gravel road leading to a large, white ranch house with a wraparound porch and a barn, Katie sucked in her breath.

It was her dream house. The type of house she could imagine raising her kids in. The kind of porch on which she could set two rocking chairs, one for her and one for her husband. They'd spend their evenings rocking together, holding hands and talking about their lives, their kids, their love . . .

"So what do you think?" Chase's voice broke into her fantasy and she blushed.

"It's a great place," she said.

He opened his door and jumped out, slamming it behind him. When she opened hers and started to step down, though, she noticed the huge puddle of muddy water under her door.

Great, on top of looking like a drowned, puffy-eyed princess, I'm going to ruin my new heels.

Chase came around the door quickly, ducking his head against the rain, and said, "Need some help?"

"I can't walk through the mud in these shoes. I can take them off, but then I have to hold the dress up and I'm afraid of falling," she said.

Wrapping one arm behind her shoulder and the other under her knees, he lifted her up against his chest and said, "You know, if you wanted me to carry you, you could have just said so instead of hinting and hee-hawing."

Rain pelted her face and she protested, "I wasn't hee-hawing. I was just talking out loud. I wasn't trying to get you to carry me, especially after the last time you tossed me in the pool . . ." Her rambling stopped when she felt him start to toss her up a few inches and catch her again. "Chase!"

He looked like a seven-year-old who had been caught pulling a girl's hair. Mischievous and innocent. When they reached the top of the stairs, Katie said, "Okay, you can put me down now."

Shaking his head, he rebalanced her so he could reach out to open the screen door. "Uh-uh, Firecracker. I'm carrying you all the way back to my bed, where I plan on doing all kinds of things to you."

"What kind of things?" she asked.

He pushed the wood door open and said, "The kind of things good girls don't do. Unless they happen to be at the mercy of a very, very bad boy."

Carrying her through the kitchen and down a narrow hallway, the look he shot her was intense. Licking her lips, she whispered, "Am I at your mercy?"

"Yes, Firecracker, you're completely at my mercy."

A FEW HOURS later, Katie lay across Chase's chest in the dim light of the bedroom, running her hands over his body. Lightning flashed and the whole room lit up.

"So why did you get this one?" she asked, pointing to the sun tattoo on his chest.

He smiled. "Why does there have to be a reason?"

She shrugged. "I don't know. I was just curious if there was."

"You want the truth? It's pretty cheesy." He grabbed her hand and laid it flat over the tattoo.

Kissing the skin over his heart, she said, "Hit me with your best cheese. I won't laugh. I promise."

Chase stroked her face and said, "When I was a kid, my mom used to sing me 'You Are My Sunshine' all the time. After my dad left us, she stopped singing. She stopped caring about anything but finding a new man to take care of us. Each guy was just a new tool, and when she got too clingy, they screwed her. One guy actually stole her car when he left. She worked her ass off at the diner up the road from our trailer, sometimes taking double shifts for days just to make rent. Or avoid me." She could hear the pain in his voice and she wanted to take it away.

He cleared his throat, obviously getting a handle on his emotions, and said, "Anyway, I was drunk and seventeen and I kept thinking about that stupid song, and how my mom used to be. I told you, cheese balls."

Her eyes were burning with tears when she kissed his palm. "I'm so sorry, Chase."

Running his thumb under her eye to catch her tear, he chuckled. "Ah, Firecracker, you're such a softy. Don't worry about it. I got over it a long time ago and dealt with my demons. I may not have had the most functional parent, but I turned out okay. And she's got her life together now, been happily married for the last eleven years to an ex-naval officer who thinks the sun rises and sets on her."

Katie lifted her head. "You don't know where your dad is? Has he tried to contact you?"

He shook his head. "Nope. Woke up one morning to my mom crying and he was gone. Not a card, letter, or call in twenty-eight years. She never could tell me why he did it, but it doesn't really matter. He left us. Makes him worth less than nothing to me."

"Were they married?" she asked.

"No. Yours? Where's your dad?"

"Yeah, they were married, not that it mattered. My dad left when I was too little to remember him. Mom never told me anything about him, but I found a box in her closet after she died. It was filled with pictures and love notes. I hired someone to find him, just to see if I could meet him, but he had been killed in an accident when I was six. He'd been drinking and taken a curve to fast," she said.

"I'm sorry," Chase said.

"It's okay, I didn't know him. But when Mom died, it was like my world had been tipped onto its axis. I know she was sick for so long, and she fought hard for extra time; I should have been prepared for it." Katie's tears spilled over, as they did every time she talked about her mom.

"I don't think you can prepare for that kind of thing." His hand rubbed over her back, and it was comforting. "So she was a stickler, huh?"

Katie laughed. "Understatement. She was a first-grade teacher and famous for her 'Rules of Morality.' She used all of these old-school sayings to keep her students, and me, on the straight and narrow. 'Do unto others as you would have them do unto you' was her favorite. I wasn't allowed to wear makeup—except for pageants—until I was sixteen, and I was so frustrated. All of the other girls wore it, so when I was a freshman I started getting to school early and putting it on before class. I'd wash it off before leaving school, but one day I forgot I had a dentist appointment and my mom came to pick me up early."

"Busted." He laughed.

"Way busted. I got the whole Oh-what-a-tangled-web-we weave-when-first-we-practice-to-deceive lecture and she grounded me for a month. It sucked," she said.

"My mom never grounded me. I didn't even have a curfew. It was like living with a roommate for most of my life," he said.

She had hated being grounded and sometimes her mother had been a bit too strict, but she always knew her mom loved her. Chase hadn't had that, though. She was surprised he was as successful as he was with his up-bringing. "So how did you get into art?"

He chuckled again. "You're awfully curious tonight."

Katie sat up and straddled his abdomen. "Considering we just became very well acquainted with some very private parts of each other's bodies, I would think sharing a few fun facts shouldn't be too much to ask."

"Hey, I was just making an observation; don't get your panties in a wad."

"I'm not wearing any panties, remember?" She felt wicked saying it, but with Chase, her filter seemed to have disappeared completely. His eyes darkened and she slid her hand over the ridges and planes of his six-pack. "So art . . ."

Chase trailed his fingers up her thighs and said, "You expect me to concentrate on anything but your lack of panties?"

"Yes." Leaning over and teasing his earlobe with little nibbles, she said, "Tell me and I'll . . ."

The things she whispered to him were way too bold for Old Katie. When she pulled away, the mix of shock and desperation on his face made her laugh as he quickly spilled his guts.

"My English teacher in sixth grade. She caught me

doodling, and instead of giving me detention, she pulled some strings to get me into a seventh-grade art class," he said.

She walked her fingers down his stomach and prodded. "And your comic books?"

He was running his hand over the bare skin of her back and she wanted to purr like a cat. "I started it my senior year and showed it to the guy who owned the comic-book store in town. He helped me find out how to submit it, and after about eight rejections, I got a letter saying they wanted to publish three issues."

Katie shook her head. "That is amazing."

"So now you. Why did you pick cosmetology after giving up law enforcement? Kind of a weird jump." He ran his finger down her nose and over her lips.

"Yeah, well, I decided I liked making my own hours and making good money more than chasing down bad guys." She opened her mouth and he slipped his finger inside. She felt wanton and sexy as she sucked on it gently. Whatever it was about being with Chase, she liked the way she felt with him, lying in bed and not being the least bit self-conscious about the way she looked or if he wouldn't like something she did. That was the amazing thing about being intimate with him; he made her feel like everything she did was a major turn-on.

Like teasing and sucking on his fingers softly. She was just testing it out, enjoying the look on his face, until he pushed her onto her back and moved over her, staring down at her like she was a sweet piece of chocolate he wanted to savor.

Rubbing her palm over his stubbly cheek, she whispered, "I love scruff."

Chase smiled. "You do? Most girls bitch about it scratching them."

She shook her head. "Not me. A little scruff to darken the cheeks. I think Hugh Jackman, when he's all scruffy, is the hottest man on the planet."

He scowled. "Hugh Jackman is a pansy."

"Um, have you seen his body? The man is a God." She laughed.

He started to roll off her. "Okay, I'm done, lost all interest."

Katie hooked her arm around his neck and leaned up to kiss him. When she had him sufficiently relaxed, she said, "You're a liar."

"How's that?" he asked.

Lying back, she lifted her hips to rub against him and said, "You're still interested."

"It's only hard 'cause I'm thinking about Salma Hayek right now."

"Oh yeah?" She laughed and sent her fingers into his ribs.

"Sorry, not ticklish," Chase said, grinning down from his position on his elbows.

"Huh." She skimmed her fingers up and over his back, kneading the muscles, and said, "Guess I'm going to have to figure out another way to torture you, then."

Katie slid her hands down his back and grabbed his butt firmly. He sucked in his breath and she released the rock-hard cheeks to run her hands up his sides. She got to his chest and pushed him over, moving against him until her nipples were hard little peaks.

"I think I want to add another thing-I've-never-done item to my list." She moved lower with her mouth, sucking and licking at his salty skin.

"Oh yeah? What's that?" Chase's voice was hoarse as she slipped farther down until she was at eye level with his erection.

"Why don't I just show you?"

Chapter Nine

As GOOD A girl as she was to the rest of the town, Katie was amazingly bad in the bedroom. Three times, not counting the car, she had had her way with him, and he'd loved every minute of it.

Turning over to look at the clock, Chase noticed the flashing numbers. The power must have gone out at some point, but it was light enough outside now that the room was dimly lit, so it must've been around seven. He didn't hear rain anymore, but it could just be taking a break. Either way it was probably a good day to stay in bed. Possibly with some very warm company.

He rolled over to look at the beautiful woman sleeping beside him and smiled. Katie was lying on her side with her back to him, and he leaned over to rub his prickly cheek against the skin of her shoulder. He'd found out the third time they'd made love that it drove her wild to have him drag his stubble all over her body. He enjoyed hearing those sweet noises and the soft way she said his name.

He'd never been with a woman like Katie and he'd definitely never wanted a woman so much before. When he'd heard her yelling at her ex yesterday, he'd come around the corner ready to pound someone. But that look she'd given him, that boy-am-I-glad-to-see-you look, had been enough for him. He'd been fine just ignoring the little shit, but last night at the pageant had been too much. He didn't like to see Katie hurt, especially by people who weren't good enough to lick her cute little toes.

Katie moaned and stretched, turning her head to smile at him with closed eyes. "That feels amazing."

Chuckling, he slid behind her so her sweet, round ass was cupped by his groin and wrapped his arm around her waist. Kissing her shoulder, Chase said, "I'd love to make you feel more amazing, but I have no idea what time it is and I don't want you to be late for work."

Katie twisted her head toward the clock and groaned. "Ugh, do I have to go? I don't want to leave."

A zing of happiness went through him. "I wouldn't mind if you played hooky to lie in bed with me all day, but I know you're too goody-goody to do something as irresponsible as call in sick."

She turned all the way onto her back and raised her eyebrow. "First of all, I own the salon. If I want to call in, I will."

"Oh sure, if you wanted to."

Her eyes narrowed and she said, "And second of all, that sounds like a dare, Mr. Trepasso."

He leaned up on his elbow. "That's because it was, Ms. Connors."

Sitting up, she held the sheet to her chest and said, "Can you hand me my purse on the chair?"

Chase rose from the bed stark naked, knowing she was checking him out as he walked over to grab her purse. When he turned around, she was licking her lips and looking hungry. He crawled across the bed, dropped her purse in her lap, and started to lean in for a kiss. "You look like you want to eat me."

"Mmm . . . maybe I do." She reached out for him, and a rumbly noise came from her stomach, making them both laugh. "I guess I'm hungry for other things too."

Giving him a quick peck, she pulled out her phone and dialed. Chase took the opportunity to pull the sheet down and latch onto her breast, tonguing the nipple into a hard point.

Her voice came out strained as she spoke. "Hey, Kitty, it's Katie. Yeah, I think I might be getting a summer cold. My throat's a little . . . oh . . . um . . . tickly. Could you . . . um . . . cancel my appointments?"

He felt her hand go into his hair and tug. Laughing softly, he slid his hand down under the sheet to play with her in other places, and she hissed, "Stop it. No, Kitty, it's just the cat. He keeps trying to get up on the counter. Thanks for doing that for me. I'll call you later. Have a good day."

Suddenly she grabbed his hair so hard it felt like it was coming out by the roots and he yelled, "Ouch, woman!"

"You suck! If Kitty knew what was going on, I would die!"

He didn't like the way she said that. Like she was doing something wrong by being with him. Rational Chase told himself that it was just Katie being modest, but the small part of him that remembered a girl ducking down in his car so she wouldn't be seen with him was hurt.

Chase pulled away from her and stood up. "I'll see what I have in my cupboard to eat."

Grabbing his hand, she stopped him, and he saw the confusion on her face as she asked, "Hey, what did I say? I just don't want her to think I'm having sex with her on the phone."

You sure it's not that you don't want them to know you're screwing the tattoo guy?

Trying to swallow his doubt and insecurities, Chase leaned over and kissed her forehead. "I know what you meant. I'm going to see what I can scrape together."

He picked up his boxers, pulled them on, and left the room without looking at her again. He couldn't explain why he was making this more complicated. He hadn't wanted complicated. Hell, *she* hadn't wanted complicated. Yet here he was, acting like Mr. Sensitive, getting his feelings sore over nothing.

Get it together, man. So you like her more than you've liked any other woman. This thing was supposed to be fun. You need to get a grip on your balls and man up.

UNSURE OF WHAT she'd done now, Katie pulled on her clothes and went to the bathroom to wash her face. Sleeping in her makeup always made her feel grungy the next day, but once she was cleaned up a little, she went out to the kitchen to find Chase with his head in the fridge, cursing.

What had she said to upset him? He seemed to be sensitive about people being ashamed of him, but she wasn't. If she was, she wouldn't have told Rock Canyon's biggest blabbermouth how she had spent yesterday afternoon. Still, Chase had been hurt so bad, and she wanted to fix it. She wanted to show him how special he was, but she also wasn't going to walk on eggshells around him.

"That bad, huh?" she said as she set her purse on the counter.

He pulled his head out of the fridge, and his grin was sheepish. "Yeah, unless you want one egg. And I'm pretty sure it's about to hatch into something."

Whatever had ruffled his feathers, he was acting like he was fine now. Katie toyed with her purse strap and avoided his eyes, feeling awkward as she said, "It's fine. Do you mind driving me to my 4Runner? I'll just eat at home."

She heard the fridge close. "I thought you played hooky to hang with me?"

I did, but you acted like you were irritated with me.

Meeting his gaze again, she said, "You just seemed like you were upset with me, and I didn't want to overstay my—"

Chase cut off her explanation with a kiss, and she only had a second to think about her morning breath before she was kissing him back. When he finally pulled away, he whispered, "I'm sorry I was an ass."

"Yeah, you know, the ultrasensitive, sexy rebel thing only goes so far with me," she said, only half kidding. Maybe as they spent more time together and got more serious, she would be able to help Chase work through his issues.

Wait, what was she saying? The minute he got the idea in his head that she wanted to take things to the next level, he was going to take off.

"I'll try to work on that," he said, running his hands down to intertwine their fingers. "Please, stay. I don't want you to go."

"Yeah, I got that now," she said, leaning into him to give him a soft kiss. "Although I don't know how we'll survive the day without food."

Even if he had been grumpy, he was definitely adorable in the morning, half naked, with his hair sticking up all over his head. He seemed younger, even with the dark stubble beckoning to be caressed. He looked like he was thinking hard about their dilemma and Katie laughed. "Okay, don't strain yourself."

His fingers tickled her ribs. "I was just thinking that we could go to Boise for the day. Do something there. Get out of town."

"It sounds wonderful, but . . . isn't it still raining?" she asked, looking toward the window.

"Nope, the sun is coming out to play and it will be a beautiful day to take a long drive on the chopper."

Katie gulped a little at the thought of riding on a motorcycle for longer than three minutes. "I need to go home first. Shower and change."

He sighed. "Okay, I'll take you to your car and then I'll pick you up with breakfast."

Now that sounded perfect.

KATIE TOOK THE fastest shower of her life and wrapped her hair up in a towel. Heading into her bedroom, she decided to spend very little time primping, since a two-hour motorcycle ride would wreak havoc on her hair anyway.

She was just grabbing her light black jacket and her Skechers when someone knocked on the door.

"Great." She looked at the clock and frowned. Chase was fifteen minutes early. Didn't he know a girl liked to take her time?

Walking out to the front door, she looked through the peephole and saw it wasn't Chase but Steph.

Pulling the door open with a confused smile, she said, "Hey, what's going on?"

Steph cocked a perfectly arched brown brow and looked her up and down. "Well, you don't look sick."

"Oh, like you've never called in to work?" Katie said.

"Sure I have, but *you* don't. Ever. Unless you're dying, and only then because you don't want to get anyone else sick." Steph walked past her into the house, and Katie closed the door. "What's up, Katie? This isn't you. You don't do weird things with your hair or dress like a . . . well, actually, the clothes are cute, but still. And the guy . . ." Steph said.

Katie was caught between surprise and anger. "What is wrong with Chase?"

Steph snorted. "Besides the fact that he's got heart-break tattooed on his forehead?"

"In case you don't remember, I had my heart broken about eight months ago and I'm finally over it." Katie laughed bitterly and said, "You should be happy for me."

"I know that you were broken up over Jimmy and I was worried," Steph said, reaching out to squeeze her shoulder. "And if a little fling with a hot guy gets you back in the swing of things, then great. I just don't want you getting attached to him and getting hurt all over again. And I don't like the influence he's had on you. You aren't acting like yourself, and I feel like I don't even know you."

That stung a little, and Katie wondered why Steph was being so dramatic. "Why are you being so down on Chase? You don't even know him. I dated Jimmy for years and you never liked him, but you were never this adamant. Is this really about Chase, or something else? I don't think I've changed that much, and if I have, it's because Chase makes me stronger. He makes me not want to be the meek little mouse and stand up tall and say what I think. What's wrong with that?"

"It's not *wrong*. You just used to care if you hurt people or made them feel bad, and now it just seems like you're only out to please yourself," Steph said.

"And what's wrong with that? I have done what other people wanted my whole life. Why can't I, just once, do what I want? Be happy and not constantly worry about what other people think!" Katie said, her voice rising.

"Because you're better than that!" Steph yelled back.

"God, I am so sick of everyone saying that. I'm too

good, I'm better than this and that and whatever. It's my life and I want to live! You of all people should get it and support me. You're my best friend, Steph, not my mother," Katie said firmly, trying to calm down.

Steph's face went red and she snapped, "Yeah, well, if she was here she'd be ashamed of the way you're acting."

Katie felt like she'd eaten six bad tacos and they were all making her sick at once. She had never been a violent person, had never even been in a fight before, but right now all she wanted was to slap Steph's horrified face. Of all the things Steph could have said to her . . .

And part of you thinks she's right. Your mom would *be ashamed of you.*

It was one thing for Mrs. Andrews to say something like that, but for Steph, it was almost unforgivable. She had said the one thing she knew would hit Katie the hardest . . . and hurt her the most.

Katie's eyes stung as she growled, "Get out of my house."

"Katie, I'm sorry . . ."

"I want you out of here now!" Katie yelled, her vision blurred with unshed tears.

Steph turned with what sounded like a sob, opening the front door with a jerk, and burst out of the house. Katie slammed the door behind her and leaned against it, trying to stop the tears from overflowing. Straightening up, she walked into the living room to sit down on the couch, swiping at her wet cheeks.

Steph was wrong about her. She was just having fun. Trying something new. And as far as Chase went, they were good together. She was happy, and Steph hadn't respected that. Hadn't respected her.

I'm sure she didn't mean it. She was just worried about you.

Katie knew that Steph was protective of her. They had been friends since preschool, and Steph had always been there to support and defend her. While Katie had smiled and taken things with all the grace her mother had instilled in her, Steph had been outspoken and sometimes impulsive, shooting off her mouth without thinking. She had been Katie's champion more times than she could count, but that didn't give her the right to push her opinions on Katie now. Especially about what her mother would say or do.

Steph had loved Katie's mother too, but that hadn't stopped her from telling Katie that she needed to stand up to her. Tell her she was an adult. Funny how Steph had forgotten all that rebellious talk today and tried to use her mother to control her.

But it had worked, like kryptonite; Katie couldn't stop thinking about what her mother would say.

"Didn't you learn your lesson the first time, Katie? Boys only want one thing and if you give them that, you might as well show them the door."

Another knock pulled her out of her own self-doubt, and she tried to sound normal as she called, "It's open."

Katie heard the rustling of bags and Chase said, "So I got you a caramel mocha and a chocolate chip muffin, since Gracie said that's your usual. And I was actually thinking we could take a drive to Hailey instead of

Boise . . ." He was standing by the couch and she tried to hide her red eyes, but he'd already seen them. "What's wrong?"

"Nothing," she answered, wishing her voice didn't sound so nasal.

Setting the food down on the end table, he sat next to her and turned her face toward him. "Why are you crying, Firecracker?"

She shook her head. "That's a stupid nickname."

He tilted up her chin, studying her. "Maybe so, but I don't think me calling you Firecracker really bothers you; you're just changing the subject."

"I'm fine. I just had a fight with Steph is all."

"Already? What happened?" he asked.

She stood up and said, "I don't really want to talk about it, okay? I want to get my hands on this mocha you promised me." She grabbed the mocha off the end table and walked away from his penetrating gray eyes and his questions. She wasn't in the mood to deal with either of them right now.

CHASE LET THE fight go, but he knew that something was really bugging her. They ate their muffins in the kitchen in relative silence, though he was afraid he knew why Steph and Katie had been fighting.

"Please, Chase, you can barely afford lunch. How are you going to pay for prom?"

Emily Wilson had said that after having sex with him in the back of his mother's van. They had hung out for a little over a month senior year before he'd found out exactly what she really thought about him.

"You're a hot guy, but I could never really date you. I mean, you live in that run-down trailer and you have no ambition. You're going to end up stuck in this town with the rest of the losers."

He came back to the present with clenched fists. Emily had spent a month with him and never knew a thing about him. She'd seen a boy her daddy would hate and a way to make him squirm. She hadn't even known he was leaving for Berkeley at the end of the summer.

But Katie wasn't like Emily. She was sweet and she was interested in him, in who he really was. When she wasn't constantly worried about what everyone in this pissant town thought, she was fun.

More than fun.

But whatever Steph had said had to have been about him, and about the way Katie had changed. If Steph had thought warning him off wouldn't work, going to the source would have been her next stop. It wasn't like he didn't know Katie was just experimenting. He knew she was going to wash the streaks out of her hair and always keep her tattoo hidden from view, and when it was all over, she'd move on with her life.

Without him.

Chase knew this was all temporary. He just got to be the lucky guy in the right place at the right time, but he didn't like thinking about Katie not being around for him to touch. That she wouldn't be there to laugh at his outrageous comments or run her hands over his scruffy face.

He liked Katie. Maybe someday it could be more than like, but he would never know.

"All you are is trailer trash, Chase, and that's all you'll ever be," Emily's voice said, taunting him from the past.

Katie wrapped her arms around his waist and nuzzled his chest. "I'm sorry that I've been such a bummer this morning. You want to back out? Find something else to do?"

He looked down into those clear blue eyes and slid his hands into her hair, kissing her softly. "Nope. Nowhere else I'd rather be."

She snuggled closer. "You say the sweetest things."

Only to you.

That thought brought with it a rush of panic. He had to stop entertaining these serious thoughts about Katie. Adventurous and ballsy he might be, but he wasn't stupid. Especially when it came to women, and to putting himself out there. Which is how he had lived thirty-three years without a single broken heart. A few dents to his ego, but nothing that couldn't be fixed with a couple of beers and a warm, feminine body. But if he let Katie become special to him, he was setting himself up for a whole world of pain.

Come on, man, you're just fooling yourself. She's already special.

Breaking the moment, he slapped her ass playfully and said, "All right, since it is already close to ten and I have to open the shop at five, what do you want to do?"

She rubbed her injured posterior with a grumble, "Wow, I cancel my appointments for the day and you can't even close your shop for a few hours? Nice."

He saw the challenging look on her face and conceded. "Fine. We'll put a note on the door as we head out of town."

KATIE REALLY DIDN'T want to ride two hours on the back of Chase's motorcycle, but she sucked it up and got on. The road to Hailey from Rock Canyon was an easy drive on a two-lane highway with lots of open space around them. Chase had brought a helmet for her, though even the extra protection didn't calm her fears. She held on tight to his waist and tucked her head against his body.

After an hour she was squealing and yelling, "This is awesome!"

Of course she stopped yelling once she got a bug in her mouth, but she still loved the feel of the wind and the warm sunshine.

And the hot, solid man in her arms.

Chase parked along the main stretch once they reached Hailey and she got little tingles when he squeezed the hands she'd wrapped around him. "You okay?"

The helmet got in the way of leaning forward to kiss him, so she just said, "Yeah, except for the one bug who found its way into my mouth. Now I have bug breath."

He laughed and turned his head to catch her lips in a kiss. When he pulled back, he teased, "You taste fine to me. Not buggy at all."

Laughing, she reached up to unclasp the helmet and swung off the chopper. Catching his grin, she asked, "Why are you smiling at me like that?"

He slipped his arm around her waist to pull her against him, "Nothing, you just look good in my helmet. Very sexy."

I'm trying so hard to keep things casual, and then you go and say something like that.

Wrapping her arms around his shoulders, she said, "I've always fantasized about a tall, handsome bad boy taking me for a ride on his bike."

He shook his head. "I've told you before, Firecracker, it's not a bike."

"Chopper, then. Are you going to kiss me or not?"

He kissed her and she leaned into him, not caring if anyone was watching.

I don't want this to end.

Katie knew it would, though; he wasn't the type of guy to stick around. He'd told her himself he didn't like to stay in one place too long. He'd lived in six towns in the last twelve years, and when it got to the point that he was ready to go, he did.

Although he did say the house in Rock Canyon was the first one he'd ever owned. That meant something, right? Even on a subconscious level?

"I think your kisses are like crack," she murmured.

Chuckling, he said, "If I'm crack, then you're sugar. Probably why I can't taste the bug. You're so sweet."

Katie melted at his words and pulled away reluctantly. "So, what do you want to do?"

Swinging off the motorcycle, Chase stretched out his arms and back, making his muscles twist and ripple. He was so wonderfully made; it was like a bunch of women picked all the best parts of a man and put them together to build him. Even the small studs in his ears added to his sex appeal.

"What do you say we just walk around? I haven't really been up here except for snowboarding back in February."

Of course he snowboarded. "Yeah, I don't do that. Snowboard, I mean. The only thing I do in the snow is sledding down very small hills."

Her stomach rolled excitedly when he draped his arm around her shoulders and said, "Well, maybe we'll have to change that."

She glanced up at him, and he looked a little surprised, like he couldn't believe he'd said that. He might be regretting the slip, but it gave her hope. If he was imagining them doing things together in six months, maybe he wasn't thinking this was just a casual thing anymore either.

Chapter Ten

CHASE PULLED UP to Katie's house at half past ten and she was yawning as she swung off his chopper. He'd had a great time with her, making her try sushi, and laughing when she'd made a twisted, disgusted face. They'd checked out the town, and she'd told him about the different stars who lived in the area, even taking him to what she said used to be Bruce Willis's house.

Afterward she'd shown him this beautiful place, where a creek ran just under the majestic Sawtooth Mountains year-round. They'd sat under a pine tree, him leaning back against it and her leaning back against him. She'd told him more about her mother, about watching her friends dye their hair or get second holes in their ears, and her mother telling her that employers didn't want to hire people who didn't look professional. She'd never wanted to do anything major, but her mother had not been a big fan of anything that altered the appearance unnaturally.

"That's what started my list at Buck's," she'd said. "I was just sitting there thinking how I'd done almost everything she had wanted and I was alone, while other women who had done everything else had husbands and families. It wasn't fair."

He'd hugged her. "It's not about how good you are or how many rules you follow. You just have to meet someone you can stand to live with for a lifetime and go for it."

"Gee, that's romantic. Not someone I can love, just stand," she'd said.

"Girls always want to talk about their feelings and beat a subject to death, whereas manly men like myself like to just say, 'Hey baby, you wanna do this thing?'" he'd said.

She'd burst into that charming laugh, ladylike snort and all. "Not all guys are like that."

"Uh, yes they are, unless they've conformed to the romantic-comedy standard of what a relationship should be."

"I'm not looking for the perfect rom-com relationship. I'd just settle for someone to love me for me."

"You mean the sweet, docile version of you who cuts hair and never steps out of line, or the quick-witted, naughty girl who isn't afraid of anything?" he'd asked.

"I want to be both. I can follow my mother's ideals without letting people take advantage. And I can tell people how I feel without being brutal. I just need to find a happy medium," she'd said.

After that, the subject had changed to her work. How much she loved cosmetology, creating something that brought people so much joy and confidence.

"That moment when I'm done blow-drying or curling and I show them their hair, it's like they're seeing themselves in a new light. They feel good and they walk a little straighter. Not that I always have happy clients, but for the ones that get that little spark afterward, that's why I love it."

He'd understood what she meant. She was an artist in her own way, just like he was.

They'd spent several hours in that place, talking, teasing, and touching. He couldn't seem to get enough of being near Katie. She was soft and warm, with just enough spice. She really didn't like to hurt people's feelings, which he had to give her mom props for. She'd raised a decent human being.

While they were in one of the trendy shops, Chase had dared her to steal something, even just a key chain. She'd made it all the way to the door and stopped. Veering left to the counter, she'd bought a cheesy pink rabbit's foot, and handed it to him for good luck. He'd taken it with a smile, knowing she wouldn't go through with it. There were some rules that Katie just couldn't bring herself to break.

While riding out of town, she had insisted they stop and try a fast-food place called The Snow Bunny. He'd stopped, but Katie's description of the amazing food had left him doubtful it could measure up. He'd taken his first bite and groaned at how good the burger was. She'd laughed as she dipped her fries in the homemade fry sauce. "I told you it was yummy."

They'd taken their time on the drive home, stopping to explore. Chase had rolled his eyes when Katie kept taking pictures of them on her phone, but it actually made it all seem more real. He'd slipped up earlier, suggesting he'd teach her to snowboard, but something about the way she'd looked at him made him think she hadn't minded. That maybe she'd been thinking about them as more than just hanging out too.

Back at her house, she flipped on the light, and Chase caught a glimpse of a black fluff ball meowing nasally. When he spotted Chase, the cat's gold eyes narrowed and he hissed before crawling down the hallway on his belly.

"Well, I guess it's safe to say your cat hates me."

"Slinks hates everyone but me," Katie said, smiling. "I found him hiking four years ago, this tiny black kitten in a skunk trap, covered in filth. I brought him home and gave him a bath, but it took him two weeks to get to the point where he would come to me willingly. He hated Jimmy with a fiery passion, and he's only just started letting Steph touch him."

Chase came in behind her and shut the door. "Speaking of, still don't want to talk about what happened with you two?"

It's none of your business. Let it go.

She put her purse down and said, "She just said something hurtful about my little changes. I don't really want to talk about it, okay?"

He came up behind her and wrapped his arms around her waist. "Want me to go?"

"No. Stay," she said, leaning back against him.

"We could try out some of that edible massage gel," he said, running his hands over her stomach.

Twisting around in his arms, she kissed his neck. "Is that you trying to get me to give you a massage?"

"I am a little stiff from the drive." He grimaced to emphasize his point.

She slid her hands around to his abdomen and started moving lower. "Mmm, I can feel that."

Considering where she had her hands, he hoped so. "So maybe we should take this into your bedroom and work on easing some of my tension."

"I think that is an excellent plan, Mr. Trepasso."

"Lead the way, Ms. Connors."

Katie moved in front of him down the hall, and when they reached the bedroom, he sat down on the edge of the bed. She walked over to her dresser and opened the top drawer.

"Look what else I got."

Turning, he saw she was dangling something from her fingers. It was a pair of fuzzy pink handcuffs.

"You want to cuff me, Officer?" Chase held out his hands jokingly.

She walked to him and stood between his legs. "Actually, I want you to strip down and lay back full length on the bed. Then I'm going to cuff you to the headboard."

"And what are you going to do once you have me naked and defenseless?" he asked.

Her fingers slid up into his hair and she said softly, "I'm going to make you beg."

"And if I don't let you?"

Her face fell. "Really? Because you said anything on my list and . . ."

Reaching up, he brought her mouth down to his. "I'm just kidding, Firecracker." Moving with fast, jerky motions, he pulled his shirt off, tossing it across the room. His pants, shoes, and socks followed moments later, and with a teasing grin he flopped onto the bed. "I'm ready. Do your worst."

KATIE WOKE UP early the next morning to run to the store for bagels and cream cheese, rushing back to get ready for work quietly, trying to let Chase sleep. She left a note on the counter with the bag of bagels next to it and headed out the door.

When she walked into the salon at nine, Kitty gave her a sly smile. "So, how are you feeling?"

Putting her purse below her station, Katie said, "I'm feeling better. Must have been allergies."

Kitty came over and leaned on the back of her chair. "Yeah? That's good, because I was headed out to Hank's last night for karaoke and I thought I saw Chase's chopper in front of your house."

Trying for nonchalance, Katie said, "Oh yeah, he brought me some soup and . . . ointment . . . for my tattoo."

"Oh my God, *you* got a tattoo?" Kitty said.

Crap. "Um, yeah. It's no big deal."

"Let me see. Where is it?" Kitty started trying to pick up her shirt, and Katie grabbed her hands.

"Whoa! Not here."

Leading the way, Katie snuck around the corner to the product closet and Kitty closed the door behind them. Katie picked up her shirt and Kitty squealed, "Oh, that is so cute, and he did such a good job! I'm going to have to go to him for my next one."

Kitty pulled down the top of her shirt to expose her shoulder and said, "See, I love fairies; isn't she pretty?"

The tattoo was gorgeous and intricate, but it was so big. "It's beautiful."

Kitty pulled her shirt back up and Holly peeked her head in. "What are you two doing in here?"

"Katie was showing me her new tattoo!" Kitty said.

"Shut up, you've got a tat? Let me see!"

Katie lifted the back of her shirt without another word.

"That is awesome, did Chase do it?"

"Yeah, he did," Katie said.

Holly gave her a curious look. "I heard you guys were a thing."

"From who?" Katie asked.

"A couple of people around town. Oh, and that new gossip column said so too," Holly said.

"I'm going to burn that paper." Katie felt her cheeks warm at her stylist's scrutiny. "I'm not sure what we are yet."

"Well, all I know is, if I was seeing a stud like that, I'd make sure he was all mine. Brand him like a baby cow," Holly said.

"You are so bad!" Kitty giggled.

"I'll be out in a minute. I just need to grab a few things," Katie said.

The other girls headed out and Katie lifted up her hair. In the small mirror on the door, she looked at the purple hickey Chase had left toward the back of her neck. She had always thought hickeys were disgusting, but the feel of Chase's mouth latched onto her skin last night, sucking and kissing . . .

Well, it made her ache all over again.

She closed her eyes, thinking about the way they'd taken turns in the cuffs, using nearly all of both the edible gel tubes, eating the liquid off each other's skin. She'd loved the feel of him straining under her when she'd cuffed him to the headboard, trailing her lips over his body until he had practically begged her to let him go. Once he was free, he had rolled her onto her stomach, cuffing her while he used his stubble on her back, making her squirm and writhe. Chase had undone the cuffs right before he brought her knees up and slid into her from behind, curling his body over hers. He'd kissed her neck while he'd slipped out of her slowly, running his erection in low and out high. Katie had pushed back against him as he'd used one hand to play with her breast and nipple. Bringing his other hand up, Chase had held both of her breasts in his hands while he kissed, licked, and sucked at the skin of her neck. Nuzzling her hair aside, he'd whispered just under her ear, "I can't get enough of you, I . . ."

The door flew open and Katie, brought back to where she was, dropped her hair into place.

Kitty gave her a strange look and asked, "Are you okay?"

"Sure, just needed some stuff," Katie said, hoping her burning cheeks didn't make her look too suspicious.

"Okay, well, your first appointment is here."

"I'll be right there," Katie said.

Yeah, I'll be there, once I get my raging hormones under control.

Taking a deep breath, she walked out of the supply closet with a few bottles of gel. She saw Gemma Carlson standing by the reception desk and smiled at her.

Unfortunately, Jimmy was also there, looking sheepish, and her smile disappeared.

What in the name of all that is holy is he doing here?

"Hey Gemma, why don't you head on over to my chair and I'll be there in a bit," Katie said.

Gemma patted her arm as she passed. "Thanks for fitting me in. If you need me to pull the hurry-up-I-got-to-pick-up-my-kid card, I'm on it."

Katie laughed. "I think I can handle him, but I appreciate it."

"Well, it's none of my business, but you just let me know," Gemma said.

"What can I do for you, Jimmy?" Katie said, moving to stand in front of him.

"Can we talk outside? There's something I want to say, but not here," he said.

Katie hesitated, not wanting to cause a scene. "I've got a client waiting."

"Please, it'll just take a second," he said.

New Katie wanted to tell him to go to hell, but Old Katie, the one who gave people the benefit of the doubt, said, "Okay, let's go out front."

He held the door open for her and followed her to the simple wooden bench in front of the shop window. Katie sat down and asked, "So what did you want to tell me?"

Jimmy sat next to her and reached out for her hands. She jerked them back and glared. "What are you doing? You said you wanted to talk!"

His brown eyes darkened and his mouth twisted into an ugly frown. "I was just trying to apologize again. For the other day and for . . . well, for before."

Okay, New Katie was about to rear her angry head. "Before what, Jimmy? Before you wasted seven years of my life? Before you dumped me after cheating on me for God knows how long? Or was it before you sent me your wedding invitation? Tell me, which *before* are you talking about?"

"Damn it, why do you have to make this so hard?" he said.

She stood up and snapped, "I'm sorry, was I supposed to make this easy for you? What you did was reprehensible and unforgivable. You showed absolutely no remorse for the way you treated me before, so I have to wonder why you're here now. The apology is just a little too late."

"Please, Katie, don't go. I just want to talk," he said.

"You talked, I listened. Now, I have a client who has to pick up her kid, so if you'll excuse me." She turned away from him to walk back inside.

"What's going on with you and that pretty boy?" Jimmy asked.

Facing him, she couldn't believe his gall. "Are you serious? You came here to ask about my personal life?"

"That guy isn't right for you. You're too good for him," he said.

Of all of the ridiculous, absurd . . . "You're an idiot."

"He has earrings like a chick, for fuck's sake," Jimmy shouted.

"Well, I think his earrings are sexy! So why don't you get the hell out of here, go back to your perky little fiancée, and keep your opinions about my love life to yourself?"

"Come on, Katie-bear . . ." he pleaded.

"Do not call me that. Like I said before, you are nothing to me now, Jimmy. Just a walking, talking reminder of some really bad decisions." She reached out to grab the door and threw it open, stomping into the salon, and avoiding the wide, curious eyes following her as she walked to her stylist chair.

Katie stopped behind Gemma, breathing hard, and said, "I'm sorry about that. Are you ready to get started?"

She barely heard Gemma's answer, she was so focused on why Jimmy was acting so bizarre. He almost seemed jealous of Chase, but that made no sense. He had cheated on *her*, dumped *her*, and was currently *engaged* to someone else. So why was he coming around trying to give her dating advice?

"Men are moronic," she grumbled.

Gemma let out a quiet chuckle. "Yeah, it's tough. Can't

live with them, can't shoot them. Unless you've got a real good place to hide the body."

Katie laughed, feeling a little bit better. "Well what do you say we swap man troubles over some bleach and a Coke?"

CHASE WOKE UP alone in Katie's room and looked at the clock. 9:36. Swinging his legs over the side of the bed, he picked his boxers off the floor, sliding them up over his hips. Padding out to the kitchen, he saw the bag of bagels and the slip of paper.

> *Morning, Hotstuff,*
> *I didn't want to wake you, you looked so peaceful.*
> *There's cream cheese in the fridge and I'll call you*
> *later.*
> *Have a good day,*
> *Katie*

Chase plugged in the toaster and grabbed the cream cheese, whistling with a grin. Last night had been incredible, but at one point he'd had an epiphany so wild, it was like being kicked in the gut.

He wanted Katie to be his only, and he was having a hard time figuring out how to put that into words.

Tonight was his late night, and he probably wouldn't see her. The idea of not being with her was a major mood killer. He finished his bagel and headed back to her bedroom to grab his clothes. He saw Katie's evil-looking cat sitting on top of his jeans, glaring at him.

"What's your problem, cat?"

The black animal hissed and scrambled past him down the hallway, his belly to the floor.

Chase shook his head, picked up his jeans to pull them on, and jerked his hand back.

They were wet.

He sniffed his hand and gagged.

"You're dead, cat!"

A hiss came from somewhere, as if the creature was saying, "Screw you, asshole."

Chase left Katie's house slamming the door and texted her, *Your cat pissed on my jeans.*

Stuffing his phone into his pocket, he swung into his seat to drive home and shower. Would it ruin the jeans to bleach them?

He'd risk the bleach, and remember to pick them up off the floor next time.

Smiling in spite of his wet, pungent leg, he tried not to dwell on the fact that he was already looking forward to seeing Katie again.

KATIE WAS STILL laughing as she left work that night. She felt bad that Slinks had peed on Chase's jeans and she had texted him to say so. The cat was possessive and a little psycho, but he was her baby and didn't like to share her. Chase had texted her back that they may have to limit their overnights at her house unless he bought another couple pairs of jeans. Katie had almost told him he was lucky all Slinks had done was pee, but she'd refrained.

Chase would probably veto all overnights at her place if he knew Jimmy had gotten a number two in his work boots once.

The Rock Canyon Independence Day Extravaganza planning committee had arranged to meet today to re-schedule the fireworks, and although she wasn't looking forward to being in the same room as Mrs. Andrews, she'd made a commitment and she was going to honor it.

She parked her car and started walking toward the building.

"Katie, may I speak to you for a minute?"

Turning around, she tried to keep her voice mild as she faced Mrs. Andrews. "Sure, I was just heading inside to go over the rescheduling of the fireworks."

"In light of what transpired between us at the pageant, I think it would be best if we not work together," Mrs. Andrews blurted.

Katie was taken aback. She'd actually been expecting an apology from her, not a resignation. "Well, I'm sorry you feel that way, Mrs. Andrews. I know we both said some things we didn't mean, and I apologize for my inap-propriateness, but you don't have to quit the committee."

"You misunderstand me, *dear*. I am here to tell you that it's *you* who is no longer welcome on this commit-tee," she said.

How dare you try to undermine me? Katie thought as she tried to control the lump in her throat. Every time she got angry or upset, she felt like she had swallowed a jawbreaker. "You can't kick me off the committee; I'm in charge."

"I've spoken to the council and informed them you

had some issues that you needed to work out before you could take on any more town projects. They were very understanding," she said.

Katie said, "Was there something wrong with the way I organized the parade and the fair?"

Mrs. Andrews glared. "There were no major problems, no."

"So this is personal. This is because you don't like who I'm dating or the way I'm behaving?" Katie wanted to scream at the older woman, but she was managing to keep her voice just above a harsh whisper.

"You are not behaving like yourself. You're usually so responsible and easy to work with, but the way you've been since . . ."

Katie interrupted. "Just because I don't automatically agree with everything you say doesn't mean that I can't do my job. It just means I'm finally tired of people treating me like someone who should be seen and not heard. So with all due respect, Mrs. Andrews, you need to leave the committee until you can apologize for your lack of professionalism."

Mrs. Andrews's mouth dropped open. "You can't . . ."

"Oh, you bet I can. You have done nothing but try to make me feel incompetent and small since this whole project started. I was trying to be nice before, but the way you spoke to me at the pageant was inappropriate and unacceptable. So you need to go home and think about the way you have been treating everyone in town who doesn't follow your rigid view of what's right. Once you're willing to apologize, you may come back."

Katie didn't wait to listen to any more spluttering the older woman had in her. She felt good. She had said what she needed to and hadn't been rude, only firm.

She walked into the community center with a weight off her shoulders and announced loudly, "Good afternoon, everyone! Mrs. Andrews will not be joining us for a few days, and if anyone else has a problem with the way I manage this committee or my personal life, they are welcome to leave now too."

Several older women and one man stood up and left, but instead of feeling bad about it, she just said, "Anyone else? All right then, let's get to planning."

Chapter Eleven

KATIE CLIMBED INTO her car after the meeting and drove past the Jagged Rock to see if Chase was busy at work. Looking in the window, she saw several guys inside with him. Not wanting to interrupt, she pulled into The Local Bean parking lot to turn around. The last thing she wanted was for someone to notice her car driving up and down the road like some weird stalker.

As she pulled back out onto the street, she saw Becca leaving her shop and almost ducked down. Becca was too sharp not to know she had been making a pass to see Chase.

But she had already seen Katie and was waving. Rolling down her window and stopping along the sidewalk, she said casually, "Hey, so is my advertising helping?"

"Well, considering that I've made more in the last four days than I have in the last month, I'd say so," Becca said.

Katie pulled over and parked her 4Runner as Becca

came to her window. "That is so great! I am glad it's working."

"You on your way over to see Chase?" she asked, leaning in.

No, I already checked and he's busy. "No, I was just on my way to Twin Falls when I remembered I forgot my Costco card," Katie said, pretty sure that was a logical enough explanation for driving up and down the street.

"Oh, I see," Becca said, giving her an assessing look. "Be careful with him."

Katie tensed, waiting for Becca to start giving her a warning about how he was going to hurt her, but she didn't. "He's not as cool as he thinks he is. He likes you. I can tell."

Katie's heart twisted and fluttered. "That wasn't what I expected. I thought you were going to tell me he's no good."

Becca smiled. "Like Steph?" Katie gave her a surprised look, and Becca added, "It's amazing the things women will tell you when they're shopping for lingerie. It's like all the boundaries are gone and they start spilling their issues."

Katie laughed. "Yeah, same goes when you're doing hair. You become a therapist."

"Oh yeah. Anyway, she told me that she acted like an ass."

Katie gripped the steering wheel. "Putting it mildly, but yeah."

Becca shrugged. "Just my two cents, but you guys have been friends since diapers, right?" Katie nodded and Becca said, "Give her a chance to grovel. Best friends should get a free pass every five years."

Katie thought about the times when Steph had said something to piss her off and she'd just let it go. Just smiled and moved on. Steph had been given plenty of free passes, but she had also been there for her through every major letdown. She might have overstepped in a major way, but they had been friends for a long time. Was she ready to just give up on that?

No, she wasn't, not yet. "All right, if she shows up groveling, I'll hear her out."

"Then my job is done. You going to the fireworks next weekend?"

"Yep. Figured since I helped plan them, I might as well enjoy them."

Becca grinned. "I'd like to tag along with you, if that's okay."

Katie laughed. "Deal."

KATIE WAS LYING on her bed watching a DVR recording of *The Vampire Diaries* she'd already seen twice, when her phone beeped. She picked it up and there was a text from Chase: *Hey Firecracker, what are you wearing?*

Laughing, she looked down at her sweatpants and tank top and texted: *Nothing. ;-)*

Slinks jumped up on the bed, and his loud, rumbling purr came with him. He crawled up to her side and flopped down, rolling over to expose his fat belly for rubs.

She couldn't resist him and cooed, "You are such a

bad boy, but you're Mommy's bad boy, aren't you? Yes you are."

Her phone beeped again, and she said, "Look, it's your favorite person."

The big cat just kept rubbing against her as she checked the message. *Such a tease. Why do you have to mess with me?*

Fingers flying over the keys, she wrote back: *In bed with another guy too. He's super sexy and likes when I stroke his belly.*

Beep. *You better be talking about that damn cat.*

She laughed. *Maybe. Would it bother you if I wasn't?*

Slinks crawled up on her chest and she tried to read the next text around his head. *Yeah it would.*

She was smiling so hard it hurt. *I'm wearing sweatpants and tank top and yeah, Slinks is lying on my chest. How're the tats going?*

Giving Slinks a hug, she cooed in her best baby voice, "So cuddly tonight. Were you jealous of the hot guy last night? Is that why you peed on his pants?"

A knock sounded at the door and Slinks bolted off the bed, nicking her with his back claws.

"Ow, crap," she said, rubbing her chest as she got up and walked down the hallway scowling. "I swear, you are the most high-strung cat I have ever had."

She peeked out the peephole and saw Steph. Taking a breath, she pulled the door open. "Hey."

Steph gave her a tentative smile. "Hey."

Katie wasn't feeling particularly gracious. "So what do you want?"

"Wow, that was direct," Steph joked, and when Katie didn't even crack a smile, she continued. "I'm so sorry for what I said. I didn't mean it, I was just so frustrated because you were just starting to get better after Jimmy left and I was just worried that you were going to end up in a funk again if Chase hurt you." She paused and added, "Plus I was a little jealous."

"Jealous? Of me?" Katie said, flabbergasted.

"Of course you. You have always been this sweet, tiny thing who everyone always raved about. My own mother used to ask why I couldn't be more like you. And it was okay, 'cause you were my better half, and we had the same plan of getting married and having a family. But this whole thing with Chase made me realize that you were free to do anything you wanted while I was stuck here. And I was a little jealous of that freedom," Steph said.

"Steph . . ." Katie's coolness melted a bit at her best friend's confession.

"Don't get me wrong, I love Jared and there is no better guy in the world for me. No one else would put up with my drama or my mess, but every once in a while I wonder how my life might have been different," Steph said. "And I just felt like you might decide that the plan wasn't what you wanted anymore and move on, leave me behind."

"Steph, I have been jealous of you for years. You are living the dream, my friend. You met your soul mate. That hardly ever happens anymore." Katie understood where Steph was coming from, but she needed to realize that Katie could handle herself. And her love life. "And part of the reason I am finally coming out of that funk is because of Chase. He makes me happy. I don't know what's going to happen with us in the future, but right now I am the happiest I have ever been. Even happier than I was with Jimmy."

Steph snorted. "Of course, anyone's a step up from Jimmy." She shook her head. "I do want you to be happy, and I am really, really sorry."

"You won't bad-mouth Chase anymore?" Katie crossed her arms over her chest.

Steph held up her hand. "Scout's honor."

Katie stepped back and said, "Too bad you were never a Girl Scout."

"Mom said it was too time-consuming." Steph came into the house.

"Wanna watch *The Vampire Diaries*?" Katie asked, shutting the door.

"Sure, which episode?" Steph asked.

"Does it matter? I have two words for you. Klaus and Damon." Katie said, smiling.

"I'll make some popcorn."

"I'll grab the sodas."

CHASE LEFT THE parlor and locked the front door. Pulling his phone out of his pocket, he checked for a message from Katie. Nothing.

Making his way down to where his chopper was parked, he climbed on and realized the last thing he wanted was to go home. After spending the last couple of nights with her, being alone in his big old house just didn't sound fun. Maybe he'd head over to Buck's and play a little pool.

Weak, Trepasso. You're just hoping she calls.

He started up the chopper and rode down to the outskirts of town. Parking in front of Buck's, he climbed off and strode to the front door. He walked in and sat down at the bar, nodding at Eric, who handed him his usual draft. "What are you doing here? Thought you'd be out with Katie."

Chase shook his head and took a drink of his beer. "Nope, just stopping by on my way home."

Eric grinned. "Well, word is you guys were getting pretty hot and heavy. Guess she ditched work to be with you?"

Chase made a disgusted face. "This town is too damn small."

Eric laughed. "Yes it is. We have no secrets here."

Chase's phone rang and he saw Katie's picture flash on the screen. He took another drink of his beer and picked up the call. "Hey, Firecracker."

"Hey, you done?"

He tossed some bills on the counter and gave Eric a little wave as he left. "Yeah, I just stopped by Buck's for a beer."

"Oh, well, I'll leave you alone . . ."

"No, I'm done." *Please say you want me to come over. . .*

"Oh, are you sure, 'cause . . ."

He straddled his chopper and said, "Katie baby, were you calling to see if I was coming over?"

Silence stretched over the line and he almost didn't catch her "Yes."

Grinning, he gave an air punch like a geeky kid. "I'll be there in ten minutes. But warn your cat that if I see him, he's going to end up as a pair of slippers."

Her gasp turned into a laugh, and she said, "No, he's not."

"You just tell him, and I'll see you in a bit."

"Be careful."

He chuckled. "It's a three-minute ride. I'll be fine."

"They say most accidents . . ."

"Damn it, Firecracker, you want to give me a lecture now? The longer you keep me on this phone, the longer it's going to take for me to get there, and I want to kiss you bad."

She was quiet for a minute and said, "Hurry."

Chase drove through the side streets until he reached her house and parked in the driveway. She opened the door just as he stepped up on the porch, grabbed him by the shirt, and yanked him inside.

He laughed as she wound her arms around his neck and kissed him. Cradling the back of her head with one hand, he used the flat of his other hand to lean against the wall behind her.

Kicking the door closed, he mumbled through kisses, "I would have come straight here if I had known you were waiting."

"I had company," she said, lifting her shirt up and over

her head. "Steph left a while ago, and I knew you'd be done around eleven." Eagerly, she reached for the bottom of his shirt and pulled it up, and he helped her take it off, tossing it away. Reaching out for her topless form, he pulled her against his chest, groaning at the feel of her pressed so close.

Kissing her neck, he helped her pull her yoga pants down and asked against the skin of her collarbone, "You guys make up?"

"Mmm hmm," she said as she slipped her underwear down and reached for his jeans.

Kicking his boots off, he moved his hands to brace his weight against the wall as she yanked open his belt. "Good. I'm glad." They managed to slide his jeans down together, and he stepped out of them quickly. His boxers joined his discarded jeans and he lifted her against the wall, pinning her there with his body. Heart pounding with anticipation, he took her hard nipple into his mouth to play with it.

"Me too," she said as she wrapped her legs around his waist and held on to his shoulders, moaning as he tongued her.

Releasing her breast, he slid one hand down her body and rubbed against her wet folds. "God, I want you so bad."

"Me too. Please, Chase, please."

Angling his cock up and into her warmth, he groaned as the satin sheath stretched around him and he pushed further inside. "Am I hurting you?"

"God no."

He took her at her word and worked inside her, thrusting and withdrawing, his mouth taking hers. He caught every cry, every moan against his tongue and lips and was so turned on he couldn't have left her if the house had been on fire.

Katie cried out and tensed around him as she came, and it pushed him over the edge, her clenching muscles bringing him hard. He collapsed against the wall, pressing her further into it, and kept gulping for air. "That was . . . that was . . ."

Her chest was pushing against his as she took quick, deep breaths. "Oh my God."

"Yeah, 'oh my God' just about covers it." He chuckled breathlessly.

Lips against his shoulder, she whispered, "I've never . . . it's never been like . . . this before."

Pushing himself off her, he let her slide down and kissed her nose. "No. For me either."

Her blue eyes were dreamy, but he saw serious thoughts lurking behind the haze. "What does that mean?"

He panicked; he couldn't help it. It was one thing to think about feelings and being exclusive, but actually having the conversation . . . Terrifying.

So he did what any other guy would do when faced with a beautiful, naked woman wanting to discuss the fate of their relationship. He dumped her over his shoulder and said, "It means that we should do it again. Immediately."

Walking down the hallway with his laughing prize, he dropped her on the bed and proceeded to distract her from any kind of "talks." There would be plenty of time for that later.

THE NEXT MORNING, Katie came out of the bathroom with towels around her hair and body but stopped when she saw the rage on Chase's face as he held up his jeans.

"He did it again. He pissed on my jeans again"

Katie bit her lip. It wasn't funny. At all. "Why did you leave them on the ground?"

"Really? You're blaming the victim?" he said with disbelief.

She laughed and took his jeans, leaning over to give him a kiss. "I'll wash them for you."

That got a smile out of him. "Oh, I've always wanted my laundry wench."

Reaching out, she yanked on his earlobe. "I am just trying to keep the peace. I love Slinks and I'd hate to see him turned into a hat."

"I said I'd turn him into slippers. There isn't a head in the world big enough to wear that cat. What do you feed him, small dogs?"

She almost swatted him with his jeans, but she wouldn't like being hit with cat pee pants, so she settled on excusing Slinks's obesity instead. "He was traumatized as a kitten and he seeks comfort through food. He's just a little beefy."

Chase chuckled. "He's not fat, just big boned?"

"Exactly." Taking his pants down the hall, she transferred laundry, ignoring his mocking laughter. A basket of clean clothes in her arms, she came back into the room, set them on the bed, and pulled some under things out.

"So, where are you off to this morning?" he asked.

"It's Sunday. I go to church, and then I'm going over to Steph and Jared's for a barbecue," she said.

Chase nodded. "Got it. I'll just grab my jeans when they're done and go."

"You could come with me," she said, moving closer to him as she took the towel off her head.

Chase snorted and said, "Sorry, Firecracker, but it would probably bring about the next apocalypse if I attended church."

Reaching out to rub his shoulders, she said, "I'm sure whatever sins you've committed couldn't be that bad."

Wrapping his arms around her waist, he brought her down onto his lap. "Damn, you're cold." He ran his hands over her arms. "I'm a heathen. We never went to church when I was a kid, and I just haven't found any use for it."

"Do you believe in God?" Katie didn't really know anyone who didn't go to church. There were several churches of different faiths around town, and everyone she'd grown up with attended one of them.

He shrugged. "I don't know. I remember having this friend in grade school who was really religious, and he tried to save me, but nothing ever stuck."

She kissed his cheek, disappointed, but she wasn't going to force him. Maybe some distance would be a good thing. Maybe it would temper some of her crazy thoughts that there was something more to this. "Well, I won't mention it again, then. It will be good to spend some time apart today. It's not like we haven't seen each other every day for the last week."

"Are you getting sick of me already?" he asked.

"No, but I've already played hooky from work to be with you. I'm not going to miss church too." She gave him a little smirk over her shoulder, "That would be something I would never, ever do."

Grinning, he said, "Oh yeah? So I should add 'miss church to stay in bed with Chase' to the list?"

"Nope. Never gonna happen." She dropped the second towel, pulling up lacy red boy shorts and then slipping the matching bra into place.

Chase's gray eyes turned the color of storm clouds as he asked, "Won't lightning strike if you walk into church wearing fire-engine-red underwear?"

Katie laughed as she went to her closet and pulled out a simple black dress with red tulips along the hem. "I don't think God or anyone cares what color my underwear is."

"I do," he mumbled.

She slipped on her red heels and walked past him to the bathroom, saying, "Well, I guess it's a good thing you aren't coming, then."

Reaching his arm out, he pulled her back onto his lap, facing away from him. "So, if I go with you today, what do I get?"

Leaning back against him, she offered, "The satisfaction of no longer being called a heathen?"

"Hmmm … not something I'm concerned about." His lips nibbled at the back of her neck and she shivered.

"How about you get to be with me all day?"

Chase slipped his hands under her dress and said softly, "Hmm, getting warmer."

She grabbed his hands, laughing. "No. I do not have time for your shenanigans."

He trailed his finger over her thigh and used his other hand to move her damp hair off the back of her neck. Leaving a trail of hot kisses over her skin, he whispered, "But you like my shenanigans."

"Not on Sunday. I'm not going to show up to church all rumpled."

Sighing he released her. "All right. No rumpling."

Getting up, Katie went into the bathroom to fix her hair and makeup. Slipping a bit of lip gloss on her lips, she came out fifteen minutes later to find him gone.

"Chase?"

"Making coffee," he called from the kitchen.

The more she thought about it, the more she was sure that space was the last thing she wanted. Chase really was as addictive as a drug, and his side effects included euphoria, giddiness, and other yummy feelings.

She caught him in the hallway and wrapped her arms around his waist. "All right, so are you coming with me or not?" By the pained look on his face, she took that as a no. "Okay, so no church, but do you want to go to the barbecue with me? I could come by your place and pick you up around two."

Looking resigned he said, "There's no getting out of this, is there?"

She kissed his chest. "Come on, it will be fun. You'll

love my friends, and if you're a really good boy, I'll give you a cookie."

He grumbled as he gave her a kiss. "Better be a big cookie."

"The biggest," she assured him as she kissed him back.

When she left for church ten minutes later she was slightly rumpled, but it had been worth it.

CHASE PULLED ON a pair of cargo shorts and a blue T-shirt. Checking the clock, he put some gel in his hair and pulled on his tennis shoes.

Katie knocked on the door at ten to two wearing a black halter top with little red cherries on it, red shorts, and black jeweled wedges. Her hair was down around her shoulders and her lips were painted a lush red. Big black sunglasses covered her eyes, and she smiled widely.

"Hey, are you ready to go?"

He couldn't stop staring at her mouth. The lush, red lips took his thoughts in some very dark directions, and the last thing he wanted to do was spend hours at her friend's house, staring at that mouth and fighting a hard on. "How long do we have to stay at this thing?"

Cocking her head to the side, she said, "I don't know, why? You got something else to do?"

Coming out of the house, Chase closed the door and pulled her against him. The shirt was backless and he ran his hands over her warm skin slowly, watching that smile melt into a little *o*. "Yeah, you. What possessed you to wear something like that when we're going to hang with your friends for hours?"

She licked those lips, making his Johnson jerk. "Wow, talk about dramatic. It's summer, it's hot, and I'm among friends. Plus I love my new clothes and I want to wear them all."

He slid his hand over the little tie in the middle of her back. "Yeah, but all I'm going to be thinking about all afternoon is kissing you and untying the strings of your shirt and . . ."

Covering his mouth with her hand, she said, "Stop it. Is that all you ever think of?"

"When you show up with red shorts, a backless top, and kiss-me-bad lips, yeah, that's all I think about. It's like waving a red flag in front of a bull," he said, and, removing her hand from his mouth, he kissed those beckoning lips, pulling her up against his chest. She didn't fight him, didn't try to tell him they needed to go, just slipped her hands up behind his neck to run her fingers along his skin.

When Chase finally moved away, her lips were still bright red and he rubbed his hand over his mouth. "How are they still that red?"

"Color stay. Doesn't rub off."

Alarm shot through him. "So if I get it on me, I'm going to have ruby red lips for days?"

"Relax, you don't have any on you. It was already set when you kissed me."

What a relief. The thought of walking around with bright red lipstick on his mouth all night . . . well, at least people would know it was from making out with Katie and not just because he liked the color.

He did like the color, but on her mouth only.

Squeezing his hand, she said, "Let's go. I've got potato salad and brownies in the car."

Following her down the steps, he didn't release her hand until he got into her SUV and asked, "So, Steph and Jared know I'm coming?"

"Yep. They're excited to get to know you."

Having already met and heard her best friend's opinion of him, he highly doubted it. But if it made Katie smile, it was worth a little discomfort.

Chapter Twelve

ALTHOUGH KATIE WAS nervous about being around a bunch of her friends with Chase, she tried not to show it. Jared shook Chase's hand right off the bat and took him to grab some beers, while Steph and Katie watched them amble away. Both men were tall and short-haired, but Katie thought that Chase was the handsomer of the two, and that wasn't just her being biased. Jared was good-looking, but Chase was a little bit taller, a little broader, just a little . . . more.

"So how did you get him here today?"

Katie looked at Steph innocently and said, "I just asked him."

Steph snorted. "There is no way I would want to go to some guy's friend's house when I barely knew anyone unless I was getting a really big favor."

Katie laughed and said, "How do you know? You've only ever been with Jared."

Steph shrugged. "But I can imagine the awkwardness."

Katie looked over at Chase, who was laughing with Jared and a group of guys. "He seems to be doing okay."

Chase caught her gaze, and his eyes were smoking with heat and desire. She had to mentally tell herself not to fan her cheeks.

"Whoo-ee, that man wants you. If Jared looked at me like that, I'd be hightailing it out of here and getting him naked."

Katie choked. "What happened to your lack of support?"

"Hey, take my support while I'm giving it and don't ask questions. Despite my concerns, the guy seems to be totally into you, and he is sexy as hell. Why, if I weren't married, I'd be making some very inappropriate comments about his . . ."

Katie smacked her arm. "But you *are* married, and I'll thank you to keep your wandering eyes to yourself."

"I'm married, not dead, and he's a gorgeous specimen of manliness."

Katie smiled as she took a sip of her wine. "Yes he is."

CHASE HAD BEEN inside talking football with Jared and Justin when he noticed Katie wasn't with Steph anymore. He excused himself from the guys and went looking for her, hoping she was as ready to go as he was. He liked her friends, especially Jared and Justin, but crowds always made him weary.

He found her standing against the railing of Steph and Jared's back porch. Slipping behind her, he wrapped his arms around her waist, resting his hands over her flat stomach. Kissing the side of her neck, he asked, "You ready to go?"

"Mmm. What time is it?" Katie tilted her head to the side and he took the invitation to kiss his way down to her shoulder.

"It's almost seven." He ran his hands farther down into the pockets of her shorts and whispered, "If we hurry, we could go back to my place and watch a movie."

"What kind of movie?" she asked, sounding very suspicious.

He nibbled on her ear and said, "Some girly shit."

She laughed. "Right. More like a Stephen King film or *Die Hard Infinity*."

Chase moved his fingers in her pockets and she caught her breath. His voice was harsh as he said, "It doesn't matter what it is, because I don't plan on watching it."

"What will you be watching?" Her voice was hushed.

Turning her around in his arms, he whispered, "You. I'll be watching every expression on your face while you—"

"There you two are! What are you doing lurking about?" Steph said from behind him.

Chase dropped his arms from her waist and said, "I was just telling Katie that I need to get home. Got a thing."

Steph's eyebrow arched and she smiled. "A thing, huh? What kind of thing?"

"A big thing," Chase said, waggling his eyebrows.

Steph's eyes widened and she burst out laughing. "You are a bad boy, Chase Trepasso."

Katie was covering her mouth as Chase looked at her, her eyes twinkling. She patted his arm and said, "I'm going to say 'bye to everybody else."

Giving Steph a hug, Katie went inside, leaving them alone on the porch.

Steph's friendly face changed to a hard-eyed stare. She looked like she wanted to put his balls in a vice and squeeze. Possibly crush.

Crossing her arms over her chest, she said, "Okay, I already apologized to Katie for my behavior, and now I'm doing the same for you, but I need to know your intentions."

Chase didn't actually hear an apology, but he let it go. Crossing his own arms, he said, "Intentions?"

"Yes. What are you doing with Katie? Are you just playing with her, because I swear to God, if you hurt her, I will hunt you down and castrate you. And then I will take your penis and drop it in the pit at the alligator farm."

Chase wanted to hold his boys and tell them she was kidding. "Okay, before we get into castrating and torture, I have no intention of hurting Katie. I like Katie. We're just hanging out and seeing where it goes."

"I just wanted to warn you," she said, examining her nails like she hadn't just been threatening him. "Don't want you to be surprised when you're drugged and left in a pool of your own blood."

Chase stared at the pretty brunette's pink mouth,

unable to comprehend the ugliness spilling out of it. "Has anyone ever told you that you are one scary chick?"

She tossed her hair and said, "Only people who piss me off."

"Understood. I will not piss you off."

He followed her inside at a safe distance. When Katie came over, she asked, "Are you okay? You look a little green?"

"Yeah I'm good, just . . . can you walk on the side closest to Steph?" He moved her to his left.

"Yeah, but why?" Her brow furrowed.

He shook his head and said, "Oh, just a precaution."

KATIE COULDN'T STOP giggling. "She really told you she was going to feed your penis to alligators?"

She laughed harder when he said, "I don't know why you're laughing about this. It was terrifying. I didn't think I was going to make it off the porch alive."

Rolling onto her back, she held her bare stomach as she tried to control her mirth. They'd gone back to his house and made love playfully, nipping and touching until they had sunk into each other. Afterward, they'd just been talking, and Chase had told her about Steph.

"Steph's always been dramatic. She likes to talk big."

"Yes, because I'd really hate for your best friend to put a hit out on my junk," he said.

That sent her into more giggles. "I'm sorry, but you said *junk* . . ."

He chuckled. "Are you drunk?"

"No, I just get the giggles sometimes and I can't stop." Katie covered her face and tried to calm down, but it came out more like a snorting laugh, which only made it worse.

Chase went up on his elbow and looked down at her with a grin, "Now that is a sexy noise. You sound like a hyena/pig hybrid."

Gasping between giggles, she hit his shoulder. "That is mean!"

"No, it's definitely hot. In fact, I think all girls should laugh like that." She tried to throw another light punch, but he caught her fist and kissed it. "Be nice. I have been through so much, between being threatened and hanging out with your friends."

She scoffed. "Oh come on, they weren't bad. You seemed like you were getting along with Jared pretty well."

Leaning down, he kissed her shoulder and said, "Jared's cool. They all are."

"But . . ."

He kissed up her neck and tickled her skin with his scruff. "But nothing. I had a good time."

She cupped his cheek, and he looked up at her so warmly, her heart skipped a beat. "Me too."

Smiling, he crawled up and pulled her over until she cuddled against him. "You're pretty awesome, Firecracker."

I might be falling in love with you.

Probably not the right response to so casual a statement, so she just nuzzled against his side and whispered, "I think you're pretty great too, Chase."

His grip on her tightened, and they lay there quietly until she heard his breathing even out. Lazily, she drew little hearts on his stomach with the tip of her finger until she finally drifted off to sleep too.

KATIE HAD GONE to work as usual on Monday and Tuesday but had been surprised when most of her clients had canceled. Usually she was booked pretty solid, but apparently word had traveled around that Katie had kicked Mrs. Andrews off the fireworks committee. At least, that was what her son, Mitchell Andrews, had said when he'd called to cancel his appointment, though he was in dire need of a haircut. Once Mitch's hair got to his ears, he started to look like Shaggy from *Scooby-Doo*.

"I'm sorry, Katie, but you really hurt Mama's feelings, and I can't have her mad at me. Maybe if you apologized . . ." Mitch said.

Katie had hung up on him. She wasn't going to give in to Mrs. Andrews or any of her cronies. If she wanted to act like a schoolyard bully and drag all her friends into their business, that was fine. She could take whatever the old rag dished out.

But by Wednesday, Katie was done. The new gossip column had done a piece on her "feud" with Mrs. Andrews, and how it had all started over some rather harsh words about Chase. Katie didn't know where the writer got her information, but it was dead on. If she ever found out who Miss Know It All was, she was going to give her a piece of her mind about respecting other people's privacy.

Madder than a kicked hornets' nest and with nothing to do, she left the shop by noon. Deciding to walk down the sidewalk to clear her head, she passed by Gregg Phillips and Ryan Ashton's photography studio, glanced inside for a second, walked two steps, and stopped. Backing up, she stared inside at Chase, perched on a desk, holding out some kind of magazine to Ryan.

Up until just before Valentine's Day, Ryan had dressed like a librarian and was rumored to be just as dull. She had only moved to Rock Canyon two years ago, but after she had made friends with Gracie McAllister, she'd shed her dowdy clothes to reveal a lush figure and vibrant coloring that had caused quite a stir. But on Valentine's Day, she and Gregg had gotten engaged, and they were supposed to be getting married in a few weeks.

So why was she taking the magazine from Chase with a wide smile and wrapping her arms around Chase like foil around chicken?

Stop acting crazy. Chase told you; he had a vague interest in her, nothing more.

Besides, Katie didn't have the right to be jealous. It wasn't like he was her boyfriend or anything.

Forcing herself to move away from the window, she kept walking. She could wait by his chopper, but then he might think she was being stalkerish and . . .

"Hey, I thought that was you."

Katie whirled around in surprise as Chase came out of the studio and picked her up around the waist, holding her up to kiss her mouth. When he pulled back, she was a bit dazed and he was grinning. "What are you doing over here? Don't you have clients?"

Katie didn't want to tell Chase what was going on with Mrs. Andrews, mainly because she didn't want to hurt his feelings. He was sensitive about the way people perceived him, even though he said he didn't care. Too many people had made him feel bad about being who he was, and she didn't want him to think that what was happening with Mrs. Andrews was because of him.

"Oh, I was just wound a little tight, needed to stretch my legs. Clear my head." She tried to sound casual as she asked, "What were you doing?"

"Just dropping off a wedding present. Ryan's a bit of a comic nut, and I found this limited-edition cover she wanted and had it signed for her." Chase ran his hands over her waist as he set her down and asked, "So, do you want to get some lunch?"

"Sure, love to." With his arm wrapped around her waist, she let him lead her toward the parlor. Before she could stop herself, she asked, "So what did you get Gregg?"

"What?" he said.

"Well, you got the comic for Ryan. What did you get Greg?" she said.

Laughing, he said, "A gift card to Target."

"Oh. How come you didn't just get them that?" she asked.

Stopping in front of the chopper, he gave her a funny look. "Is there something bothering you, Firecracker?"

Besides the fact that you gave a girl you were only slightly into a personal gift?

"No, of course not," she said, taking her helmet.

Holding out his hand to stop her, he searched her face, a twinkle settling into his eye. "Damn me, you're jealous."

"I am not," she said, trying to push his hand away.

Chase took the helmet and grabbed her arms to pull her against him. She struggled a little and said, "Let go, I thought we were having lunch."

"We are, just let me say something to you first," he said, laughing.

Glaring up at him, Katie stopped. "What?

Kissing her cheek, her forehead, and her nose, he finally teased her lips with his until she relaxed. When she met his gaze, his eyes were no longer laughing, and he said, "I am not into Ryan or any other woman in this town. The only woman I want to be with is you, Ms. Connors."

Swallowing the lump that his words had caused, she said, "Well then, Mr. Trepasso, would you please take me home?"

"What about lunch?" he asked.

Stretching onto her tiptoes, she kissed his mouth teasingly and said, "I was thinking we could start with dessert and order a pizza afterward."

"A woman after my own heart."

Maybe I am.

Chapter Thirteen

By Saturday, it wasn't just an idea anymore. Katie was head-over-heels, over-the-moon, heart-and-key in love with Chase. She hadn't told him, of course, although they had seen each other just about every single day, and the feelings just kept getting stronger. Not to say he was the easiest man to read. The minute the conversation got too serious or consisted of any kind of actually "feelings," he'd distract her with a snarky comment, teasing, or kissing. Except for the times when he would say something sweet and romantic, which just made her crazier.

Which she didn't really mind, except she couldn't get a read on whether they were just hanging out or getting serious. He had said he wanted only her, so were they exclusive? It wasn't like she expected him to tell her he loved her. She knew it was too soon and that she was crazy for even thinking it, but at least she wanted to know if they were heading somewhere. Chase seemed content to just let things play out and not talk about it. Which for Katie was hard. She liked to be in control. She liked to organize. And she liked to know where she stood.

Katie parked the 4Runner at the Wilsons' dairy, where they had the fireworks every year. The place was twenty acres of manure and dirt: the best place to set off the fireworks without starting a fire. People were already spreading out across the field with blankets and picnic baskets of food. Everybody knew that if you sat too close, you'd get ash in your hair, but people tried to get as close as they could. Chase had said he would try to close down shop for them but didn't make any promises. Maybe they needed a bit of time apart anyway. Time to think about how they felt.

At least he did. She knew what she wanted.

Jared and Steph were waving at her from their blanket and she waved back, weaving through the families and couples to get to them. "Hey guys, enough room on that blanket for me?"

Steph scooted closer to Jared and said, "Of course. Want a beer?"

Katie took a cold Keystone. "Thanks. What's the holdup?"

"They're having some kind of issue with the fuses," Jared said, leaning over to grab another beer.

Katie shivered. "I don't like the word *issues* in the same sentence as *fireworks*."

Jared grinned and said, "It wasn't."

"Okay, I don't like *issues* attached to *fireworks*."

Steph cupped her hands over her mouth and yelled, "Come on, dinglings, let's get this show on the road!"

Katie heard some returned curses and grinned at Steph. "Didn't anyone ever tell you not to upset men lighting explosives?"

"I doubt Sam and the rest of them will kill me over a little heckling. I'm sure I've done worse to them. I think I actually spit my beer out on Sam once when he tried to kiss me."

"What?" Jared growled, looking furious. Considering they had been together since high school and married right after, Katie could understand his reaction.

Steph waved him off, though. "It was back in high school, and to be fair, Cory Hammish did dare him. And remember, there was no kissing, only beer spitting. My lips belong to you only." She leaned over and gave him a kiss that gave off steam.

Katie turned away and took another sip of her beer. It had been hard hanging with Steph and Jared the past year, when she'd been hurting so bad, but now it was better. She still didn't want to see them examine each other's tonsils, though. "Dude, gross."

"Hey, hey, have no fear, Becca is here," Becca said, flopping down next to Katie.

Katie scooted over to give Becca more room and said, "Hey, I thought you were going to ride over with me? I tried to call you."

Becca lowered her voice. "I got a last-minute customer right as I started to close up, and you will never believe who it was."

Steph leaned over Katie and hissed, "Who?"

"Hey, nosy neighbor, personal space," Katie said.

"Hush up, I want to be in on the gossip. So who was it?" Steph asked.

Becca looked around dramatically before whispering, "Mrs. Andrews."

Katie scoffed. "Yeah right."

"Ew, that's gross. She's in her fifties." Steph made a face.

"People in their fifties still have sex," Becca said.

"I can't believe it," Katie said, still skeptical. "What did she buy?"

"Now I can't tell you that," Becca said, waggling her eyebrows. "Let's just say that I hope Mr. Andrews's ticker is in good working order."

CHASE LOOKED AROUND for Katie, spotting the back of her blond and purple head. She was sitting with Jared, Steph, and Becca, toward the front spread of people and blankets. He grabbed the sack of white cheddar popcorn from his passenger seat, knowing Katie was going to try to hog the bag since it was her favorite, but he didn't care. He liked to watch her get that sparkly smile on her face when she was happy. Especially when it was because of something he did.

Trouble. That's what he was in, but he couldn't help the way he felt. Katie was the girl he'd always fantasized about. Kind, funny, loving. Someone who wouldn't give up on the people she loved.

The first firework shot off too low, and everyone screamed, hollered, and a few even scrambled to their feet to run. He was a little afraid to sit with them now, as close as they were to the action. Maybe he would ask Katie to move back a bit. They could watch from a safe distance and be all alone . . .

Yeah, he liked that plan. He made his way through the people and came up toward their blanket.

Becca ask, "Where's your boyfriend?"

Katie said, "He was going to try to make it, but I guess he couldn't get out of the shop."

Boyfriend? Part of him wanted to beat his chest like a caveman and crow. He felt honored, proud, happy, and . . .

Then there was the part of him that wanted to back away slowly, make no sudden movements, and make a run for it.

How could he explain it? He wanted to be with Katie, deep down he knew that. But the scared guy he'd always been heard the word *boyfriend* and freaked.

"You came!" Katie said excitedly when she turned around and spotted him. Jumping up, she wrapped her arms around his waist and smiled up at him. "I'm so glad you're here, they are still trying to . . . hey, are you okay?"

"Yeah, I brought you popcorn." Another firework shot off, this one barely higher than the last.

She dropped her arms from his waist and watched him with concerned eyes as she reached out for the bag. "Thanks, but are you sure you're okay? You seem weird."

He needed to get away from her, compose himself.

"You know, I'm gonna grab another blanket from the car. This one looks a little crowded."

Turning to walk away, Chase told himself to stop being ridiculous. Katie probably thought it was easier not to correct Becca's assumption. He was panicking for nothing. Reaching into the back of the Blazer for another blanket, a soft hand fell on his arm.

Katie stood next to him, looking worried. "Hey, there's something up with you. Talk to me."

"Nothing. Just thought I'd grab another blanket and maybe we'd sit a little farther back," he said as several fireworks shot up in the air and exploded overhead.

Katie smiled and reached her arms up around his shoulders. "Aw, is a big, strong guy like you really afraid of a few little fireworks?"

Relief flooded his body as she teased him. They could stay like this, at least for a while. He could have Katie to himself without having to put a label on it. They could play and banter, and maybe down the road the thought of being called "boyfriend" wouldn't scare the holy fuck out of him.

"Me? No, why would I be scared of potentially flammable, fast-moving rockets coming toward my head?" he said, before adding, "No, I was just thinking how my idea of having you come back here with me, away from the danger zone and prying eyes, and making out all through the show was a lousy plan, just a stupid . . ."

As another round of explosives went off over their heads, she kissed him, probably to shut him up, but he didn't care. Kissing was better than his idiotic rambling or thinking about how close he was to taking the plunge with Katie. He held her against him and gave her everything he had, trying to choke down his panic.

"Well, I don't know what you're doing, man, but whatever it is, it's a miracle."

Chase pulled back from Katie, ready to lay into whoever the little turd was who interrupted them. It was Katie's ex, Jimmy, standing with a couple of cowboys, and his face was twisted in an ugly sneer.

Facing the guy, Chase said, "What's that, man?"

The scream of fireworks sounded again, but they didn't faze Jimmy.

"Katie's usually a little priss in public," Jimmy said, approaching them. "Wouldn't give me even a little kiss. But somehow with you she's more than willing to get her freak on. What's your secret? 'Cause I might just want another crack at her, if you don't mind sharing."

Chase, wanting to tear him apart, stepped toward him menacingly, his hands open like claws. "You need to apologize to her."

Jimmy and his buddies laughed. "Why? It's not her fault. When you hang with trash, you start to act like trash."

Chase moved closer to the smaller man and Katie grabbed his arm, but her attention was focused on her ex. "Jimmy, I told you when you came by the shop to stay away from me and mind your own business." She tugged on his arm and said, "Come on, Chase, he's not worth it."

Chase let her pull him back and he would have walked away, but the idiot had to get the last word.

Katie held up the bat. "If you don't think so, you're an idiot! I've got seven years' worth of reasons and a few more recent ones. Twenty . . . nineteen . . ."

Jimmy scrambled to his truck and yelled, "You're a crazy bitch, Katie! I lied; you were trash before the prick fucked you!"

Even though the cowardly little weasel had already climbed up inside his truck, Chase started forward, but Eric held him back and said, "Easy killer, she's got this."

Chase watched as Katie approached the truck with angry strides and took out one of Jimmy's headlights. Jimmy's friends scrambled forward to stop her, but Jared and Justin blocked them like a wall. Chase smiled when Justin laid the bigger cowboy out flat, while the other ran to the passenger side of the truck, throwing the door open to climb up next to Jimmy.

Katie raised the bat and brought it down hard on the hood, and Jimmy cried out like he was in physical pain. The cowboy on the ground jumped up and ran to join his buddy inside as Jimmy revved the truck backward, tires squealing out onto the road. Katie was breathing hard, her shimmery hair around her shoulders in the pink light of sunset as rockets of color exploded over her.

Chase had never seen anyone so beautiful.

She handed the bat to Jared and ran to Chase. He noticed Mrs. Andrews standing in the crowd, a look of disapproval on her face. Other people were watching Katie like they'd never seen her before and muttering in between the boom of the fireworks.

Becca and Steph were standing at the edge of the

crowd, but Katie ran past them to reach him and touched his face and body, everywhere she could. "Oh my God, Chase, your poor mouth. Do your ribs hurt? Are you in a lot of pain?"

He grimaced. "I'm okay, they just got the drop on me is all."

"What the hell is this I hear about a domestic dispute?" a voice hollered over all the noise.

Chase watched the Rock Canyon chief of police, a short, stocky man, saunter toward them, bowlegged and scowling. "What the hell happened here? Katie, are you all right?"

"Katie took a bat to Jimmy's truck!" someone shouted.

"But Jimmy and his friends were attacking Chase first!"

"And Jimmy called Katie some filthy names!"

It was chaos. A hundred people were talking at once and all of them were giving different accounts.

Mrs. Andrews pointed at Chase. "That man started a brawl, Chief, and Katie got in the middle of it. I really don't know what's come over her, but he's the one you want."

"This is why she's losing all her customers, hanging out with riffraff like him," another blue-haired battle-ax sniffed.

Chase looked at Katie, saw the red in her cheeks, and knew the woman was telling the truth. "How many of your appointments canceled this week?"

Her eyes shifted away. "I don't know. Half dozen or so. It's not a big deal, they'll come around."

Katie was standing in front of him, looking at him with concern, her hands all over him, searching for injuries, while her livelihood was going down the toilet because of him. She had run her ex-boyfriend off with a bat. Partly, he knew, because she had wanted to, but also to get Jimmy away from Chase. To protect him. He couldn't remember the last time someone had protected him. He'd always just relied on himself. She was selfless and brave, and it made him feel about ten inches tall. If their roles were reversed, would he have done the same for her? And why wouldn't she tell him about it? He was torn between feelings of gratitude that she thought he was worth taking on the whole town and guilt, because he wasn't sure if he was worth the effort.

"Now all of you shut the hell up and let me talk to Chase and Katie," the chief said, and once the crowd quieted, he asked, "All right, young man, what do you have to say?"

Another explosion lit up the sky with several colors, and Chase said, "Chief, here's what happened. Jimmy showed up with a few of his friends and said some things I didn't like to Katie. I got mad, threw a punch, and they jumped me. Justin, Jared, and Eric broke it up."

"And after all this, Katie took a baseball bat to Jimmy's truck? That how it happened, Katie?" the chief asked.

"Yes sir," she said, without stopping her examination of Chase.

"Well, if that's true, I should haul you in on destruction of private property, Katie."

Katie took a deep breath and said, "I understand, sir."

"Wait a minute! Jimmy took off. Shouldn't you at least wait to see if he presses charges?" Steph stepped in angrily.

"Plus, Chief, Jimmy did have it coming, the way he treated Katie. It was pretty shameful," Jared said, standing next to his wife.

The chief stroked his chin and said, "It can wait, I suppose, but if Jimmy wants to press charges, there's nothing I can do. Try to stay out of trouble until this blows over, okay? You enjoy the rest of the fireworks."

Chase watched the chief amble off and sucked in a breath as his ribs caught fire. Katie touched his arm gently and said, "You need to go to the hospital. What if you have internal bleeding or a broken rib? I can drive you . . ."

He interrupted Katie by grabbing her hand and squeezing it. "I'll be fine. I just need to rest for a few days. I'll be good as new by Tuesday."

"Okay, I'll follow you home and take care of you," Katie said.

Chase was aware of everyone watching their exchange, especially Steph and Becca, who stood right behind Katie. Both women had looks of warning on their faces, like they could read his second thoughts and were letting him know they weren't an option. He wasn't breaking up with Katie, though; he just needed a few days. Crazy exes, a whole town in his business twenty-four/seven . . . it was enough to make any sane man take a step back.

Especially when being with him seemed to be hurting her. He could deal with the rest, but if her business took a dive because people didn't like him, he didn't know if it was worth it.

Correction: He didn't know if *he* was worth it.

He kissed her forehead. "Really, Firecracker, I'm okay. I'll call you in a couple days." Chase pulled away from her and hobbled to his driver's side door. Wincing as he opened it and climbed up into the cab, he kept his focus on putting his key in the ignition and starting it up. The crowd around him moved as he backed up and turned around. He gave Katie a smile and wave as he passed and pulled out onto the road, his ribs screaming with the movement.

What is the matter with you? You are acting like a scared little boy.

He wasn't scared. He was petrified. Petrified that if he stayed with her, he'd start to rely on her, need to have her with him. Need her sweetness to brighten his day, his home, his life. And then have her figure out what the whole town had been telling her all along: She could do better.

And know deep down he thought she could too.

KATIE WAS SO confused and hurt, she didn't know what to do.

She felt an arm go around her shoulders and Steph saying cheerfully, "Well, that was exciting! Want to head over to Buck's for some drinks? We can relive every awesome moment of what it felt like to bust in Jimmy's baby."

Katie shook her head. "I think I just want to go home. Get some sleep."

"But . . ."

Katie saw Becca reach out and pinch Steph. "Have a good night, Katie. We'll text you later to check on you."

"Thanks, guys." Katie mouthed *thank you* to Becca when Steph was distracted. She just wanted to be alone to think.

Katie, men are like horses. You can lead them to water, but you can't make them drink. Her mother had told her that when she was fifteen and the boy she'd had a crush on didn't even notice her. Katie had cried and cried, much to her mother's disapproval.

Ladies don't caterwaul. We suffer in dignified silence.

She had already decided her mother was right. She wasn't going to cry or obsess or wait by the phone. She was going to head over to Hall's Market, grab a carton of Chocolate Moose Tracks ice cream and pop in *Sixteen Candles.* You could never go wrong with a John Hughes movie.

Or with a hot guy waiting for you with a red sports car and cake.

Although these days Katie preferred a man on a motorcycle with white cheddar popcorn, but you can't always get what you want.

GINGERLY WALKING UP the steps to his house, Chase couldn't wait to curl up in his nice, soft bed. After popping at least three Advil first. He opened the door and groaned when he moved too fast shutting it. Passing by his answering machine, he noticed the message box was flashing a bright red three.

Pressing the play button, his mother's husband, Buzz, said over the crackle of the line, "Hey Chase, it's Buzz. Look, your mother would kill me if she knew I was calling, but she's in a bad way. She's in liver failure. She'd be on the donor list, but they said family is best. She's stubborn, though, and won't call you."

Chase couldn't breathe. *Liver failure.* He'd talked to her a week ago. She hadn't said anything about being sick. Everything was fine, she had said. Liver failure was not fine. Suddenly furious with her for leaving him out in the cold yet again, Chase dialed the number Buzz had left, and he picked up on the second ring. "Chase, is that you?"

"What the hell, Buzz?"

"I know, buddy, I tried to get her to tell you, but she didn't want to be a burden. I wanted to respect her decision, but she's gotten worse, and they don't think they're going to get a donor in time."

"Where are you?" Chase's hand was shaking so bad as he grabbed a pen and paper, he wasn't sure he could write clearly. The adrenaline pumping through him made him feel on edge and he wished that Katie's stupid ex was there right now so he could use him as a punching bag. Something to make the nightmare of this day disappear.

Buzz told him the name and the address of the hospital in Reno, and Chase hung up in a panic. His mother was dying.

He walked down the hallway to the bathroom and

pulled down the Advil, tossing a couple back. Next he hit the bedroom, packed a small bag of essentials, and went into the kitchen to find paper. The first piece he grabbed, he wrote CLOSED INDEFINITELY DUE TO FAMILY EMERGENCY. SORRY FOR THE INCONVENIENCE. He would stop by the shop and tape it on the door on his way out of town.

On the next piece of paper, he wrote:

Hey Firecracker,
I need to take off for a little while, and I want you to know it has nothing to do with you. It's family stuff, but I'll call you when I get back.
Chase

Folding the note, he shoved it into his pocket. Grabbing his bag and the sign for the shop, he locked up the house and tried to run down the porch to the Blazer, but his painful ribs and hands were aching so bad, he slowed down to a limping hop. It was nearly ten, but if he drove all night he might make it in seven hours. He threw his pack in the backseat as he climbed in, grabbing his middle as a sharp stabbing pain shot from his abdomen out. Attempting to ignore the niggling voice in his head telling him to knock on Katie's door and explain what was happening, he told himself he didn't have time to get into it with Katie right now. His mom couldn't wait.

He pulled in front of Katie's house and left the engine running as he got out. Opening her little floral mailbox, he dropped his note inside and shut the lid quietly. The neighbor's yappy dog started barking, and Chase headed back to the Blazer before anyone came out to check what the noise was. As soon as his mom was stable, he'd come back and work things out with Katie. They had time, but his mom didn't. And despite how complicated their relationship was, he needed to be there for her.

Chapter Fourteen

SEVEN DAYS AND *nothing.*

Katie left the shop, her hair no longer sporting the purple streaks she had loved. She'd had them dyed back four days after Chase disappeared, but she was still rocking Becca's clothes and had even gone back for a hot, short halter dress, shoes, and a new bra/panty set. She walked around with a smile and acted like nothing had changed.

And then she went home and cried herself to sleep.

She was an emotional mess. She missed him, hated him, and loved him all at once. It was like one big, confused mixing bowl in her heart, and she wished she could just scoop out all the good things about him and just hate him, but she couldn't. She'd seen his CLOSED INDEFINITELY sign and wondered if the note he'd left was just a way to make him feel better for rushing out on her.

At first she'd told herself not to worry, he would be back. Then the third day had passed and she'd found herself constantly checking her phone for a missed call from him. Day five, all her optimism had pretty much dissolved into sadness, and she finally had to be honest with herself. If he was going to call her, if she had meant anything to him, he would have called by now.

Maybe he was getting ready to move on and wasn't sure how to break the news. It fit what he'd told her. He never stayed in one place for too long.

But this time, she had hoped he would stay.

She stopped at Rico's for pizza and Hall's Market for ice cream and a bag of Dove chocolate. By the time she made it home, she had eaten a quarter of the bag and a slice of pizza and was feeling pretty crappy.

A moment on the lips, forever on the hips, honey.

"Shut up, Mom," Katie muttered out loud, so sick of hearing her mother rambling around in her head. She opened the car door and climbed out.

Hands covered her eyes and Steph said, "Guess who?"

"My best friend pretending she's twelve?" Katie said.

"Ouch. You're in a mood." Steph dropped her hands, and Katie turned to find Becca with her.

"I always know trouble's brewing when you two are together," Katie said.

"We're kidnapping you! You need to get the heck out of that house and away from all junk food." Becca went around the other side and, before Katie could react, grabbed her pizza and other sweet goodies.

"Hey, thief!" Becca waved the food around playfully.

Katie smiled slightly. "I appreciate the gesture, guys, but I really just want to stay in and watch a movie."

"No. You are not watching any more movies so depressing they make you feel better. I know your MO, Katie. You've probably already watched *Beaches*, *Untamed Heart*, and your entire Lifetime Movie collection. It ends tonight!" Steph said.

Katie couldn't really argue with what Steph said. She did watch depressing movies just so she could say, "Look, your life's not so bad," but Steph was wrong about one thing. "I haven't watched *Beaches* yet. That's what I'm doing tonight."

"No and hell no! You are going inside, slipping into something hot, and we are taking you out!" Becca said firmly.

"Guys, really, I'm fine . . ."

"Move, woman!" Steph said, pointing to Katie's door.

Katie sighed, too tired to fight. Maybe a night off the couch wouldn't be such a bad idea. Alcohol and girl talk might be just what she needed to stop thinking about Chase for at least five minutes.

CHASE HELD HIS phone in his hands, staring at the picture of Katie hugging a wooden bear. He'd taken it when they were exploring the shops of Hailey. She'd run up to the bear and said, "Take a picture of me!" Throwing her arms around the tall, wooden carving, he had done what she commanded, and it had started a whole round of funny bear pictures, mostly on her phone, but he had snapped this one.

Texting was too impersonal, but he was afraid to call. Afraid that she wouldn't pick up or, worse, she would. And she'd tell him she was done with him.

"Chase?" Buzz said from behind him.

Chase got up from the hospital bench he'd been occupying outside, trying to clear his head. "Are the results back yet?"

Buzz nodded. "Yeah they're back, and the doctors are asking for you."

Chase slipped his phone back into his pocket and followed Buzz back into the hospital.

"WHAT THE HECK are we doing here?" Katie asked as they pulled up in front of a dark building with a bright pink sign that said PURE LOVE ENHANCEMENTS. The girls had decided to drag her to Boise for more choices in food, clubs, and, oh yeah, sex shops.

"We're getting party supplies!" Steph giggled. "You said this was one of the things on your list."

Katie cursed her big mouth. After a couple shots of the vanilla vodka Becca had bought, she'd shown them the list. Becca had decided they were going to check off everything they could on her list, and Steph had jumped on the crazy train too.

But what kind of party favors they needed to buy in a sex shop, she had no idea. "What kind of party are we having?"

"An un-bachelorette party!" Steph said, before throwing her door open and climbing out.

Katie and Becca followed her, Katie hissing, "What the heck is a un-bachelorette party?"

Becca piped up. "We dress you up like a bride-to-be, tell everyone you are getting married, and voilà, free shots all night!"

"That's dishonest," Katie said.

"Katie, stop channeling your mother and get your butt over here!" Steph said, holding the door open.

Katie walked in after Becca, and the woman behind the desk didn't look at them. Katie felt her face heat up with embarrassment at the movie posters on the walls and the large section of costumes. Steph walked over to a display of bins and pulled out a pink, sparkly shot glass on a chain. In big black letters it read I'M TYING THE KNOT, BUY ME A SHOT!

"I don't know about this . . ." Katie said.

Becca took her hand and started pulling her toward a black curtain at the edge of the room. "Trust us. This is going to be hilarious."

KATIE'S STOMACH HURT, she'd laughed so hard. Between the things she'd seen and the girls' antics to make her laugh . . .

Well, she felt better than what any sad, sappy movie could have accomplished.

They each carried hot pink bags to the car and climbed inside.

"Okay, bride-to-be, you need your veil." Steph pulled out a big white veil covered in neon condoms and adjusted it over Katie's blond curls. "There. Oh, and your shot glass."

"And your sash." Becca handed her the pink, light-up sash that read BACHELORETTE across the front.

Katie looked down at herself. "Don't you think this is a bit much?"

"Nope! Oh, we need our sashes too!" Becca and Steph pulled out two BRIDESMAID sashes, and Becca pursed her lips seductively. "What do you think?"

Katie laughed. "I think you are both nuttier than a fruitcake."

"And now, let's get this party started!" Steph yelled, throwing her bag on the backseat and starting up the car. "Wait until Jared gets a load of what I bought. He's going to be one happy man."

Katie clutched her pink bag to her chest, wondering why she'd bothered buying a sexy purple nightie when there wasn't anyone around to enjoy it.

Stop thinking about him. You are out and you are going to have fun. Forget about Chase!

THE GIRLS HAD been right. Within minutes of entering the club, a group of guys had started buying their drinks. The guys were all huge, a couple nearly six and a half feet tall, and Katie asked the shortest of the bunch, Dave, "Did you all join a club for tall guys or something?"

The guy laughed. "In a way. We play football for the Boise Grizzlies." Katie didn't follow professional football, but it sure explained the mammoth sized muscles on some of the guys.

"So what's your fiancé like?" he asked.

Her fiancé? Oh right, the veil. "He's about six foot two, with brown hair and gray eyes. He owns a tattoo parlor and writes comic books for a living."

"He's got to be a good guy to get his hands on a girl like you. He's lucky," Dave said.

Katie grabbed another shot off the table. *I wish someone had remembered to tell him that.*

Steph threw her arm around her shoulders. "Having a good time?"

Katie made sure Dave had walked far enough away before she said, "Yeah, but I'm getting kind of tired."

Steph pulled out her phone. "It's only 11:13. Are you sure you want to go?"

Katie nodded, and Steph gave her a big hug. Another pair of arms went around her, and she turned her head to meet Becca's smile.

"Hey! Group hug!" a deep voice said, and tree-trunk arms wrapped around the three of them, lifting them off the ground.

The girls laughed, and when the big guy put them down, Steph, Becca, and Katie thanked the group for letting them hang out.

Dave said, "Tell that fiancé of yours he better be good to you!"

Katie felt a lump form in her throat and thanked him. As they left the club, Becca asked, "So are you glad you came out? Did it take your mind off stuff?"

"Yeah," she said. "It was fun."

For a little while.

CHASE SAT AT his mother's side, watching the pale, thin body that used to be so full of life wince with every breath. She had railed at Buzz for calling him, yelled at him for coming, but when the results had come back that he wasn't a match for a transplant, she had cried. The doctor had warned them it was unlikely that another donor would come through in time, and Chase had wanted to smash his fist through something.

His mother was dying and he had almost missed saying good-bye.

Buzz had gone to get them coffee, and he watched his mother's light blue eyes open, bleary and pain-filled. "Chase?"

He reached out to grasp her hands. "Yeah, I'm here."

She sounded raspy as she said, "I am so sorry, baby. I couldn't ask you to come. Not after I failed you so badly."

He had heard her apologize several times, usually when her painkillers kicked in. "It's okay; you did your best."

She shook her head. "He left because of me."

He'd heard this too, several times over the last week, and said, "Mom, it's okay."

"It was just once. I didn't know. I swear I didn't."

They'd had seven days to hash out the past, and Chase really didn't know if he was better off knowing or not. His mother had confessed that she had cheated on his dad and when she wound up pregnant, she didn't think it was possible that he belonged to the other man. It had been a one-night stand, after they'd had a fight, and when she found out, she had tried to forget about it, pretend it never happened. So she had kept her secret, even as Chase has gotten older and his blue eyes had turned gray, not blue or brown like one of his parents. His father had asked her where those dark gray eyes came from, and she had said her mother, knowing full well it was a lie. Only one person she knew had eyes like that and she didn't even know his last name. For five years they lived happily as a family, but the doubt had finally been too much for his father and he'd asked for a paternity test. When the results had come back, confirming his worst fear, that Chase wasn't his, he had confronted Chase's mother. She'd confessed to her transgression, but despite her heartfelt pleas for forgiveness, his father had left, and never come back.

When he'd been five, Chase was in an accident with his dad, and they had both been taken to the hospital, where his mother had met them. His father, as a way to put his mind at ease, asked the doctor for a paternity test and the doctor had told him solemnly, that based on Chase's, his mothers and fathers blood types, there was no way he was his son. The child he had raised, built Lego cities with and kicked a soccer ball around with, wasn't even his.

His father had confronted Chase's mother that night and she'd confessed to her transgression. Despite her heartfelt pleas, his father had left, and never come back.

His mother had been overcome with guilt and grief.

She hadn't felt like she deserved Chase's love, and his presence reminded her of her mistakes. So she had shut him out and tried to make things right in her own screwed-up way, looking for a man who would love Chase like a father, even if he wasn't his.

But she had even failed at that. She had been so self-absorbed, she couldn't tell him she was sick, couldn't bear to ask him for anything.

It had taken him a day to absorb what she'd told him, and another for him to come to a decision. He'd already forgiven her. It was his father's choice to walk out on them. It was a reflection of him, not her. And as to her distancing herself from him, he had forgiven her a long time ago.

But she was so doped up on painkillers she kept saying the same things to him. The same apology over and over, and the pain and anguish she felt hurt him more than the rest of it.

"Shhh. Stop. I forgive you, Mom. Just stop." She started crying brokenly, and he held her hand tighter. "It wasn't Dad's leaving that hurt. It was that I thought you stopped loving me."

She shook her head and squeezed his hand. "You are the best thing I have ever done. I never stopped loving you."

Chase brought her hand up, kissed it, and held it against his face. He closed his eyes. His mother's voice, broken and strained with pain, started singing, "'You are my sunshine, my only sunshine . . .'"

In a hospital room, filled with the late afternoon light and the sound of his dying mother's voice, Chase wept for the first time in sixteen years.

Chapter Fifteen

THE SERVICE WAS held two days later, with just a few of his mother's friends, Buzz, and Chase attending. She had bought a plot for herself and Buzz, which he was a little surprised by, since she had always struggled with money. They buried her in the lush green grass with two white roses lying on top of her coffin.

He really didn't want to go to the funeral reception, but Buzz insisted. As he sat among a small crowd of people in their later years, he heard stories about his mother. Stories of humor and antics. Stories about how stubborn she was, or that she was the best friend in the world.

And then a short, stooped lady with blue-gray hair sat next to him, a sad smile on her wrinkled face. "Do you remember me?"

He didn't, not really, and said so. She just smiled a little wider and said, "I'm Mrs. Dowry. I lived next to you for years and would watch you after school while your mother was working."

He remembered her then, an older woman who always smelled like fresh-baked cookies and cinnamon. "Yeah, I'm so sorry, Mrs. Dowry, how are you?"

Patting his arm, she said, "Oh, I'm okay. Moved to Phoenix to live with my daughter twenty years ago to help her with her babies, and now I'm the one who needs help getting around since I had my hip replaced. These old bones just don't move like they used to."

"I'm so sorry, can I get you something?"

She shook her head and handed him an envelope from her purse. "This is for you, but I figure she probably told you everything already?"

"About my dad?" She nodded. "Yes, she told me."

"Hmph. Always told her she had more looks than brains, the way she behaved, but the girl had her demons. One thing I never doubted, though, was how much she loved you," Mrs. Dowry said.

His laugh was tinged with bitterness. "Yeah, well, I wish I could say that, but I had my doubts."

Smiling sadly, she said, "I know you did. I could see it and it broke my heart, but you gotta know she wasn't being cruel, just dumber than a box of bricks. But she took care of you, got you into that art class, paid for—"

He broke in. "No, my sixth-grade teacher pulled strings to get me into art."

She shook her head. "No, baby, your teacher called your mother to tell her that she should get you into private lessons because the seventh-grade art teacher had said no. Your mama went down to that school with your sketchbook, and she battled it out with him until he agreed to let you in."

Chase was speechless. "I didn't think she knew I could draw."

"'Course she did," she said with a snort. "She used to brag about you. Used to tell everyone down at the diner how great you were. Even framed and hung your first signed comic up on the wall."

"And her boss let her?"

Mrs. Dowry's mouth dropped open. "Boy, don't you know anything? Your mama bought that diner nine years ago. Buzz and she own it. They fixed it up and redid the whole look. She really didn't tell you?"

He shook his head. He remembered his mother borrowing money from him years ago, but she had said it was for her car. She'd paid it back fairly quick, and he hadn't questioned it. "I never knew."

She reached out and patted his hand. "You should go have a look-see. I have a feeling you're gonna be really surprised."

THE NEXT DAY, Chase took a drive out of town to check out his mother's diner. He pulled up to the little yellow building and the huge neon sign above and couldn't take his eyes off it.

Sunshine's Diner.

He got out and walked inside, staring at the cream walls. There was a wall with rainbow letters that read

COLORING CONTEST, and below that clusters of crayon-colored suns and rainbows hung cheerily. On the rest of the walls, framed pictures and artwork hung perfectly. There was the framed copy of *Destructo Boy*, with his bold signature across the bottom. There were several more framed pictures of him at Comic Con, and a cheesy one of him holding up *Destructo Boy* with a crazy grin on his face, showcasing his greatest achievement. He moved down the wall and found one of his mother and him on his graduation day, smiling for the camera like they were happy and close. Like they knew each other.

But he had no idea who this woman was. His mother had ignored him, barely cared for him. The woman who had owned this diner had taken pride in her son.

Next to the graduation picture was one of Buzz and her on their wedding day, looking happy and in love in front of a little chapel. His mom had definitely been lucky when she'd found Buzz. He was a good man.

And the last picture on the wall was one of his mom and him when he was a kid, coloring with crayons at the kitchen table. His hair was lighter, in a bowl cut, and he was missing his front teeth. His mother knelt next to him in a waitress uniform, her brown hair poufy, but her eyes were on him and her face was soft, her smile warm.

It was the same look he'd seen on Katie's face when she looked at him.

"Can I get you something ... hey, you're Lorie's boy." Chase turned to the round waitress with too much makeup and a happy smile. "Well, don't that beat all. Oh—" she lost her smile —"I was so sorry about your mama. She was a real good woman and a great boss. Buzz wanted to close down for the funeral, but we all said, 'Now, Lorie would come back to haunt us if we didn't stay open to customers.' So we drew straws to see about who would go and stay."

Chase was stunned by all of it. He reached out to the woman and gave her a hug. "Thank you."

She patted his back and offered, "Let me make you a Sunshine breakfast omelet, and afterward you can try a slice of your mama's blackberry cobbler."

He sat at the counter. Under the glass top, his mother had scattered pictures he'd sketched as a kid. Dragons, suns, and even pictures of people they knew lay beneath the protective glass. He ran his hand over the counter lovingly and said, "I'd like that."

KATIE WAS WASHING Kirsten Winter's hair when she heard Chase's name.

"I am all for him leaving town. The man is a lowlife, getting into fights and then hurting poor Katie, although I am glad to see her back to normal. I was worried about her for a while there."

Mrs. Andrews and her friend were sitting in Holly and the other stylist, Danielle's chairs, just talking to each other like the women around them didn't exist. Like Katie wasn't a few feet away, listening to every word.

Mrs. Andrews had come by a few days earlier to apologize for the things she had said, but Katie had taken it with a grain of salt. Most of the women who had started boycotting K.C.'s had only held out a few days before they were rescheduling, and Katie, being the bigger person, had magnanimously made them appointments ... for a week or so out. By the time they dragged themselves in, their hair was looking a little raggedy. Mrs. Andrews had probably just come back because she wanted the senior discount. Or was it because Chase was gone and she thought Katie was going back to being meek and mild?

Not a chance, of course, but she'd figure that out if she kept pushing her.

"Oh, I know, and what she did to Jimmy's truck? So out of character. No matter what a man does, it is important to always act like a lady."

"And it's all that Chase's fault. Bad influence, he is."

Katie started to shake with rage, especially because her stylists kept shooting worried glances her way but said nothing. Even Kitty acted like she was busy jotting down something, although her eyes were shifting back toward Katie worriedly. The rest of the women in the waiting area and manicurist chairs ignored the two gossiping women.

Katie finished with Kirsten's hair and led her back to her chair. She turned on the blow-dryer, but her attention was on the two older ladies, with their holier-than-thou attitudes and opinions. It infuriated her, the way everyone in town, young or old, treated Chase. The only people who hadn't been bad-mouthing him lately—or her, for that matter—were Becca and Steph. Even Eric had called him an idiot when she'd been in Buck's on Saturday, playing pool with Jared, Steph, and Justin. She appreciated the outrage—she was furious herself—but she could do without their opinions.

When Katie thought she heard the familiar roar of a motorcycle, she moved to the window quickly, but her heart sank moments later when she saw the blue blur of a street bike race by.

Stop looking for him. He's not coming back for you.

Eleven days without a word, wondering if he was okay, had taken its toll on her. She acted like she was fine, but she still dreamed about him, still reached for him in the morning and caught herself driving by his parlor. But she was done, completely done with him. When he got back, she was going to ignore him, or better yet act friendly, like it was no big deal. Like she'd never fallen in love with him and he'd never broken her in every way.

And maybe she would eventually believe it and stop eating every piece of chocolate in sight before she ended it up in her fat jeans.

She turned off the dryer and started curling Kirsten's highlighted strands.

"You must miss him."

Kirsten's comment made Katie meet her eyes. They were filled with sympathy, and she cleared her throat past the lump that had formed. She hated when people pitied her. It made her want to cry more. "Yeah, I do."

Kirsten nodded. "I'm sorry. About the way people talk about him. And you. I love that cherry top you wore the other day. Sweet Tarts has such cute stuff."

"Yeah, it does, and Becca's lingerie is awesome sauce." Katie laughed.

"Oh, I know." Kirsten lowered her voice and asked, "Have you ever been back in the curtained section?"

Katie shook her head. "Not yet. Have you?"

"Yeah. It's got some great stuff." Kirsten's cheeks flushed.

Leaning down, Katie whispered, "Did you know if you spend a hundred in there, she gives you a fifty-dollar sample bag from the black-curtained room?"

Kirsten squealed. "Really? Oh, I'm going to go over there next. I bought this cream that . . ."

"What are you two whispering and screeching about?"

The question came from behind Katie and she turned to face Mrs. Andrews. "We are talking about dildos, Mrs. Andrews."

Titters and giggles erupted from the other women in the salon, and Mrs. Andrews companion's eyes widened with her gasp. She had come in with Mrs. Andrews and Jenny, who was getting a pedicure with some of her friends.

Mrs. Andrews's eyes narrowed and she said firmly, "Young lady, you do not talk about those things in public."

Katie pointed her curling iron at her and said, "With all due respect, you asked, I answered. And as you are not the shop owner, I suggest that if you don't want to hear about it, you cover your ears or leave. You seem to have no problem discussing inappropriate things when it suits *your* needs. Kirsten and I were whispering, trying to protect your delicate sensibilities, while you were blatantly discussing my private life as loudly and with as much ignorance as you like."

Mrs. Andrews's friend looked uncomfortable, which made Katie think more charitably of her.

Mrs. Andrews just lifted her nose indignantly and countered, "If you don't want people to talk about you, then you shouldn't behave so coarsely. Throwing yourself at that man in public and dressing like a common slut; it's a travesty for someone like you. You were always such a good girl, and how your poor mother . . ."

Katie stepped toward the older woman. "If you dare bring my mother into this, I will brand you with this curling iron. You do not have the right to tell me what my mother would say. Good or bad, my mother loved me, and she would have wanted me to be happy."

Mrs. Andrews watched the curling iron warily and said, "But that man left you without a word, proving exactly what a miscreant he is. How happy can you be?"

Katie set the curling iron down. "Forget what Chase did to me, you didn't like him before." She turned her attention to all of the women, "All I've heard over the last few weeks is how I'm too good for him. That he wasn't worth my spit, but he is a good man. He's an artist, went to college on a scholarship, and is funny and charming. He has overcome a lot to become a successful man. Chase is a great guy, and when you say I can do better, it just makes me feel like an idiot. You judge him just like you do anyone who hasn't lived here their whole life or doesn't fit with your sense of normal."

Just that moment, Becca walked through the door and Katie pointed. "And Becca. She's been here almost two months and it wasn't until she dragged me into her store that I really got to know her. She makes the cutest clothes, in all sizes, and she tells it like it is. No bullshit. She is awesome, and none of you have bothered to get to know her or look at her clothes. Oh, except for the ones who loved the clothes I bought. Then it's okay, because Katie likes them. Katie, who is all sweet and doormat-y and will just let you say whatever you want. Just because my mother raised me to be polite and respectful, you act like I shouldn't ever make mistakes."

Becca interjected, "Ummm, I don't know what I walked into, but . . ."

Katie waved her hand and continued. "We put people in these little boxes of preconceived notions and we don't like it when they don't fit. We need to stop acting like our shit doesn't stink, because we've all fucked up at one point, even you, Mrs. Andrews."

The place exploded with applause, and Jenny Andrews shouted, "Mama, I don't know why you hate Chase so much. Daddy told me about that tattoo you got in Panama City when you were in college."

Mrs. Andrews's face turned red as she shouted, "Jenny Lynn!"

Jenny shrugged from the pedicure chair and responded, "What? You try to make the rest of the town feel bad because we aren't as perfect as you, but wanna know what else Daddy told me?"

Mrs. Andrews gritted out between clenched teeth, "Don't . . . you . . . dare."

"Mama smoked weed at a Hank Junior concert!"

The women of the salon let out gasps of surprise but

quieted down when Mrs. Andrews's companion raised her hand. "I followed around a very hot band and had a torrid affair with their drummer. Before my marriage, of course." She mouthed the name of the band, and the majority of the women, minus Jenny and her friends, were impressed.

"I like girls," Becca called out, grinning.

"Me too!" Kitty said, and Becca looked at her with interest.

One by one, each woman made a confession, and Katie was laughing and cheering along with everyone else. When everyone had spoken, Katie said to Mrs. Andrews, "Come on, Mrs. Andrews, your daughter confessed for you. Is there anything else you might like to share?"

Mrs. Andrews looked at Katie, as if trying to see inside her brain for what ace she had up her sleeve. When Katie's face remained placid, she looked around at the others and mumbled something too quiet for anyone to hear.

"What?" her daughter yelled.

Mrs. Andrews glared and shouted, "I've been inside Sweet Tart's Boutique's black-curtained room."

The room fell silent before whistles and cheers met her announcement, and she smiled slightly. Mrs. Andrews's brown eyes caught Katie's and she nodded.

It was the best apology she was going to get from the stubborn rag.

Becca yelled over the noise, "Anyone who comes in today for a purchase will get a 'naughty confessions discount' of fifteen percent off! Hell, let's make it twenty!"

When the cheers rose up again, Becca waved her hands for everyone to quiet down and asked, "So Katie, what's your confession?"

I'm the biggest idiot in the world when it comes to men.

Katie looked around at the expectant faces and said, "I recently got a tattoo."

The whole place burst with excitement and Katie smiled. Sometimes living in a small town wasn't so bad. At least you had a community that cared about you, even if some people had a backward way of showing it.

Chapter Sixteen

FOUR DAYS AFTER his mother's funeral, Chase and Buzz
left the lawyer's office, and Chase felt like he could sleep
for days, he was so exhausted. The emotional drain of
getting to know his mother for the first time, really, and
discovering all her secrets had taken its toll.

Buzz squeezed his shoulder and said, "I know your
mother wasn't always right when it came to you, but she
was proud of you."

"I just wished she'd told me instead of everybody
else," Chase said as he walked to Buzz's car. He opened
the door and sat in the front seat of the cherry-red con-
vertible, leaning his head back with a sigh.

Buzz shook his head as he climbed into the driver's
seat. "Women do crazy things when they love someone,
just like men do stupid things. I guess you'll learn that
when you find a woman to love."

Chase's thoughts drifted to Katie and he said, "I already did, but I messed it up."

Buzz gave him a look. "What'd you do?"

Chase smiled sheepishly. "I thought she was too good for me. That I didn't deserve her. And I took off without giving her a good explanation."

Buzz chuckled. "Guess you're more like your mother than you thought."

Chase looked at Buzz, taking a second to get his meaning. His mother had treated him shabbily because she thought she didn't deserve him. And she'd been wrong.

"Think she'll forgive me?" Chase asked.

"Can't tell you that, son, but if you don't try, you're gonna miss out. 'Cause when you meet that one person that you're meant for, it's one hell of a ride."

Chase hesitated before asking, "Was that my mother for you?"

Buzz smiled. "I married my best friend when we were eighteen and I had twenty-five great years with her before she died. When I met your mother, I was lonely and scared, and she made me feel alive again. Mary was my best friend, I loved her, but Lorie was . . . Lorie was my match. She was my passion. Yeah, your mother was meant for me and me for her. And if that's what this girl is for you, then you gotta make it right."

Buzz was really a great guy and his mother had been lucky to have him. When the lawyer had announced their dual ownership of the diner, Chase had felt guilty accepting it. It was Buzz's livelihood and he didn't feel right taking that away.

After a long pause, weighing his options, Chase blurted out, "If you want me to sign over my half of the diner to you, I will."

Buzz shook his head as he pulled out of the parking lot. "Your mama wanted you to have it, and when I'm gone the whole thing will go to you. Mary and I never were blessed with children."

Chase looked over at the older man and said sincerely, "Thanks for making her happy, Buzz."

Buzz grinned. "It was my pleasure, son. I was a lucky man for a little while."

Those words haunted him as he packed his bags to head back to Rock Canyon the next morning. He didn't want to be lucky for just a little while. He didn't want just a few weeks with Katie.

He wanted a lifetime.

At five in the morning, he got up and showered, leaving his scruff in case it helped him win Katie back. He walked out the door with a hug from Buzz and a warning not to be a stranger. He hugged him back, accepting a back slap. Then he pulled away and walked down the driveway to his Blazer. After loading up his bag, Chase climbed into the driver's seat and settled in for the long drive. If he hurried, he could be back in Idaho before Katie got home from work.

"KATIE, YOU HAVE a phone call!!" Kitty called from the front of the salon.

"I'll get it in the back," Katie said, trying to be heard over the blow-dryers and laughter. She headed to the office in back and picked up the phone. "This is Katie."

"Katie, don't hang up," Jimmy's voice pleaded on the line.

Katie wanted to bang her head against something. "Seriously, what could you possibly have to say to me besides 'I'm suing you'?"

"I'm sorry. About the things I said and for coming at Chase like that. I just went a little crazy seeing you together and I realized that I was jealous," he said.

Oh hell no . . . "Honestly, this is just getting weird. You dumped me eight months ago. You are getting married. This has to stop."

"I'm not getting married. She called off the wedding," he said.

Of course, no wonder he's all apologetic. Nothing like having a safety net. "That's too bad, Jimmy, but it has nothing to do with me anymore."

"Katie, wait . . ."

She hung up. No, she'd been waiting too long for a lot of things. Waiting to start a life. Waiting to get married and have kids. Waiting to meet the right guy.

She was done waiting. She wasn't going to mess around with jerks and commitment-phobes anymore. The next guy she dated was going to be solid and dependable. Someone who wouldn't take off when things got heavy.

Katie's mind was made up. Until she walked back up front and saw a familiar Blazer roar by the shop window.

Chase was back.

Part of her was happy he was back, glad he was okay, but the other part, the new, no-filter Katie who busted headlights and back talked her elders, wanted nothing more to do with him.

But the other part, the girl who was still in love with him, wanted to go to him and hold him. And beg him to never leave again.

KATIE FINISHED GETTING ready that night, her stomach feeling tight and churny. A group of them were heading to Buck's to celebrate Justin's birthday, and Katie had put on her slinky new halter dress for the occasion. Not because she thought she would see Chase. She could care less if he showed up on her doorstep with flowers; she was done with him.

So over him you've been looking out the window all afternoon, hoping he'll show up?

She grabbed her keys and purse, ignoring the taunting voice. She opened up the front door to find Chase at the end of her driveway, hands in his pockets.

"Hi," he said.

Turning away to close and lock the door, she tried to think of something clever to say, but all she came up with when she faced him again was "Hi."

His mouth tilted up into a small smile, making her heart skip a beat of its own volition. Drat the man and his ability to make her melt.

"Guess I caught you at a bad time," he said.

Fiddling with her keys, she said, "I'm heading out to Buck's. It's Justin's birthday and we're meeting up for drinks."

Chase lost his smile. "So are you two dating now?"

She realized he'd taken that to mean just the two of them, but she didn't correct him. "After two weeks without a word, do you really think you have the right to ask?"

"I deserve that. I did leave you a note, explaining," he said.

Melty smile or not, that was the wrong answer. "Oh yes, the note that said you had a family emergency and we'd talk when you got back. Not an 'I'll call you to-night' or even an 'I'll text you when I get there.' And then nothing for two weeks. Were you abducted by aliens and couldn't get cell service? How is it okay that one minute you're talking about wanting more and the next you are taking off with no word?"

"My mother was sick and when I got her husband's message, I just panicked," he said softly.

She took a step toward him, hearing the pain in his voice. "Chase, is she okay?"

Chase shook his head. "She died. I couldn't do any-thing to help her and she just . . ."

Katie came all the way down the step and wrapped her arms around him. He buried his face in her hair and his shoulders shook with sobs. Her own eyes teared up sympathetically as she said, "I'm so sorry, Chase."

She rubbed his back as he clung to her, and she felt a bit of her resolve to not forgive him chip away.

After long minutes of her just talking softly, he pulled away and said, "I'm sorry for breaking down on you. I don't deserve your sympathy or your kindness after the way I treated you."

Being this close to him, gazing into his eyes, she'd almost forgotten. "I thought you were gone for good."

"No, I just handled things badly." He reached up and tucked her hair behind her ear. "Would you give me a chance to make it up to you, Firecracker?"

No. No way! Absolutely not! "I don't know, Chase."

"What do I need to do to prove to you that I'm in this? I'll do anything you want," he said.

She pulled back from him and said. "I'll think about it." Walking around him to her car, feeling his gaze following her, she got an idea. Reaching her door and unlocking it, she looked up at him over the hood and said, "Chase?"

"Yeah?"

Smiling, she said, "Maybe you should make a list."

He looked confused. "What kind of list?" he asked.

"Surprise me," she said, opening the door and climbing inside.

CHASE DROVE HOME from Katie's house, resisting the urge to go to Buck's to make sure Justin kept his hands to himself, but the last thing Katie wanted was him making a jealous scene.

He pulled into his driveway and turned off the car,

flopping his head back as he tried to think. Maybe he'd make Katie a list of his good and bad qualities. She had asked about those when they first met.

Sitting up again, he opened the Blazer door and hopped out. He walked toward the house, trying to think of some other ideas. As he climbed the porch, he thought about a list of reasons he fell in love with her. That was romantic.

Come on, man, get creative. You can do better.

Two hours later, the idea came to him. And it was perfect.

KATIE GOT OUT of her car on Monday morning and walked toward the salon door. Opening it with a smile, she called, "Kitty, for the record, I usually don't like to take clients this . . . early." She stared at the flower arrangements set up around her station, various colors and shapes exploding from vases and pots. They could have opened a florist shop, there were so many bouquets. "Kitty!"

Kitty peeked her head out from the supply closet. "Yeah, boss?"

"Where did all of these flowers come from?"

Kitty shrugged. "I'm sure there's a card somewhere. Delivery guy brought them by twenty minutes ago."

Flabbergasted, Katie walked over to the first vase of beautiful yellow roses mixed with sprigs of small flowers and greens, and started the search. It wasn't until she made it to the brightly painted vase of gerbera daisies that she found a small card. She opened it impatiently and read:

One. I have never given a woman flowers. Ever.

Tears filled her eyes as she looked around at the flowery apology. As far as lists went, it was a very good start.

Chapter Seventeen

FOR THE NEXT week, Katie was surprised with another item checked off Chase's list every day. On Tuesday morning she found a CD on her windshield that read "Katie's Mix." She'd put it into the CD player of her car and smiled as The Band Perry's "Better Dig Two" came on first. It was the song they'd first danced to at Buck's, and she was beyond giddy that he'd remembered.

The rest of the CD had been a mix of country and pop, all songs she had mentioned. Except for two of them: "T.N.T" by AC/DC was one of Chase's favorites, and The Backstreet Boys's "If You Want to Be a Good Girl (Get Yourself a Bad Boy)," which had her laughing hysterically. Josh Turner's "Firecracker" was the last song and was a favorite of hers, not just because she loved his voice but because it featured Chase's nickname for her. She used to think it was silly, but now . . .

She had missed hearing him say it.

The note attached to the CD read: "*Two. I've never made a mix CD for a girl. A classic romantic gesture, right?*" Funny, she'd watched *Pretty in Pink* a thousand times and never fantasized about someone making her a mix tape.

On Wednesday he'd shown up at the salon with take-out from Jensen's Diner and asked her to have lunch with him. Bacon burgers in hand, they had headed over to the park, and Chase had pulled out a blanket and a cooler. After the blanket had been spread and their burgers consumed, Chase handed her a small card and grabbed the ice chest. She read the card, which had a simple pink rose on the front, and smiled. *Three. I have never fed a woman chocolate-covered strawberries.*

Chocolate-covered strawberries were her favorite dessert. She'd almost grabbed the ice chest from him as he slowly lifted the lid and pulled out a plate of perfectly dipped, red strawberries. He'd held one out for her and when she tried to take it, he'd shaken his head.

"Ah, ah, ah, it doesn't count if I don't feed them to you," he'd said teasingly.

"What if I don't like to be fed?" she said.

He started to put the strawberries away and she'd almost cried. "Fine! Okay, you can feed them to me."

"Close your eyes." His tone was soft and sinfully sexy. Katie did what he'd asked and felt something hard and cool against her lips. "Open your mouth."

She did, and the strawberry slid into her mouth. She bit into the sweet, juicy fruit and moaned. She protested when he pulled it back, but seconds later his warm mouth replaced the strawberry, his tongue sweeping inside. The kiss had taken her breath and made her heart thump, but before she could decide whether she wanted the kiss to continue or not, he was gone.

Opening her eyes to find his dark gray ones searching her face, as if looking for something, had been frustrating. She'd waited for him to try again, wanted him to just do it, not ask her if it was okay. Because if he asked, then she would have to think about it, and what he had done. Katie leaned forward, giving him permission, but he had just held the half-eaten strawberry out to her and grabbed one for himself. He'd started talking about how good they were, and said that when he'd seen the chocolate at Hall's Market, he knew she would love them.

She had finished off a half a plate of strawberries before she realized he'd done it on purpose. He'd teased her into a confused, wanting state, and unless she made a move, he would just sit back and blabber about whatever. Well, she wasn't going to be manipulated, and he was just going to have to try a little harder.

Her resolve not to be so easily seduced was almost forgotten on Thursday when he'd stood outside her house with the Rock Canyon High School Glee Club and band and sang "Hard To Say I'm Sorry" by Chicago. If she hadn't been standing in her monkey-see-monkey-do pajamas and the neighbors hadn't started screaming, it would have been the most romantic moment of her life. As it was, her neighbor, Mr. Jefferies, had fired a warning shot in the air that sent the kids running.

Chase had merely ambled up to the porch with a smile. "Nice pajamas."

"Katie Connors, what's the meaning of all that racket in the middle of the night? I ought to call the chief!" Mr. Jefferies yelled.

"I apologize, it won't happen again," she said.

The older man gave Chase a disapproving look and pointed his finger. "As for you, all that caterwauling ain't gonna make up for the fact that you broke this poor girl's heart."

"Mr. Jefferies!" Katie cried, horror and humiliation making her face flush in the dark.

Chase had taken it all in stride and said, "I know, sir, but I have to start somewhere."

"Hmmm . . . well, you just keep the shenanigans to a minimum from now on, you got me, young man?" he said.

"Yes sir," Chase said, and the crotchety old guy went grumbling back into his house, carrying his shotgun by the strap.

"I am so sorry about that," Katie had said, glad he couldn't tell how deep her blush was in the dimness of the porch light.

"Don't worry about it," Chase said, handing her a little pink card. "This is for you."

Opening the card, she read, " 'Four. I have never serenaded a woman by moonlight.' " She looked up in the sky and said, "Not much of a moon out tonight."

"I think it's the thought that counts." He'd stepped up on the porch, inches away from her, and her heart skipped and jumped.

"It does," she said, unable to look away from his lips.

"So, did you like it?" he asked, leaning his mouth down near hers.

She licked her lips and whispered, "Hmmm, I don't know. Making fun of my pajamas and pissing off my neighbors. Plus, you probably just traumatized a bunch of high-school kids."

"But you liked it?" She could feel the warmth of his breath against her lips.

"Yes. I loved it," she said.

Chase had dropped his head the last fraction of an inch and kissed her, placing his hands on her waist. She reached up to run her hands over the back of his neck and pressed her body into his. Her nipples hardened as they rubbed against the fabric of her shirt and his hard chest.

He pulled back slowly and she'd protested. "Where are you going?"

Kissing her again softly, he said, "Home."

"What? Why?"

He'd reached up and taken her hands down from his neck. "Because it's late and you need to get up for work in the morning."

Kissing her cheek and turning to walk back to his chopper, he'd started whistling. Katie had scowled and said, "Seriously, I am inviting you inside and you aren't going to come?"

"Nope. Good night." He swung his leg over the chopper and started it up. He'd given her one last wave before pulling into the street and flipping around.

She'd stomped into the house and gone to bed grumbling.

Now it was Friday morning, and as she walked out to her car, Katie found a little pink card that read: *Five. I have never told a woman no when she asked me to come inside.*

Was that supposed to make her feel special? Chase gave in to everybody else, but with her, it was so much easier to resist?

Katie got into her car with a mission. She was done with this game. He had apologized, he had romanced, and he had teased, but when it came down to it, he was toying with her.

Something had to be done.

DRIVING OUT AND making a left onto Main Street, Katie headed to The Local Bean. She parked in the lot beside the big brick building and got out of the car, walking toward the coffee house with a determined gait. Opening the door, she walked inside to find Gracie McAllister talking to Ryan Ashton over a pile of magazines.

Katie almost turned around and walked back out the door. The last thing she needed when she was feeling so agitated was to run into Chase's previous crush.

But she was caught by Gracie, who looked up and said, "Katie! Carmel mocha?"

Drat, too late. She walked to the counter and said, "Sure, that sounds amazing." Her eyes shifted to Ryan, and she asked, "How are you, Ryan? Getting excited for the wedding?"

Holding up the stack of magazines, which appeared to be all wedding related, Ryan laughed. "Can you tell? I never knew how many things were on a bride's to-do list."

"I can imagine," Katie said a little bitterly.

Ryan must have caught her tone because the look she gave Katie was pensive. "Yeah, hard to imagine that six months ago I was sure I was going to end up an old maid, living alone with lots of yarn and cats. If it hadn't been for Gracie, I probably would've."

"Please, your inner sex goddess would have come out eventually," Gracie said.

Katie smiled. "Yeah well, at the rate I'm going, you can add a bit of hoarding to my future."

Ryan's expression was confused. "But I thought Chase was back, and from what everyone has said, is wooing you like crazy?"

"He is; at least I think he is. But he can't take a hint that I'm ready to forgive him and move on. Instead he just keeps teasing and pulling back, and I just want him to man up!"

Katie's face turned red when she noticed a couple of patrons were looking at her oddly. Great, now she was having a meltdown in public.

Gracie set her caramel mocha down and said, "You know, jealousy is always the best way to push a man over that edge."

Katie took a small sip and made a soft moan. "Mmm, so good."

"That is genius, Gracie! How fast can you throw together a bachelorette party?" Ryan asked.

"Do you know who you're talking to? I'll call Gemma. All hands on deck. When are we doing this?" Gracie asked.

"Tonight!" Ryan said.

Katie had no idea what was going on, so she said, "Well, you guys have fun with that. I'm off to work."

Ryan laughed. "Hey, where are you going? We are scheming for your benefit, you know."

"Me? You hardly know me? Why?" Katie asked.

Ryan's blue eyes were slightly dreamy. "Because I think everyone deserves a happily ever after. Especially a guy like Chase. He's not as tough as he looks."

"And I like to meddle and party," Gracie added.

"But how is a bachelorette party going to help me?" Katie asked, confused.

"It's simple! Men love competition. If he feels like he's losing you to someone else, it might be just the shove he needs to seal the deal," Gracie said with a wicked grin.

Katie looked from one woman to the other and grinned. "Why not? But don't worry about decorations. I have everything you need at my house." As they sat down at a table to plan, Katie explained why she could supply a huge, puffy veil with neon condoms all over it.

Surprisingly, the other women didn't think it was strange. Gracie called an un-bachelorette party a brilliant idea and, if she never found the right guy, was going to have one of those for her thirtieth birthday. Katie laughed and found that the longer she talked to Ryan, the more her initial jealousy faded. Ryan was sweet, funny, and completely in love with her fiancé. Plus, Ryan told

Katie that when he'd dropped off the wedding gift, Chase wouldn't stop talking about her, and that she shouldn't have to push him too far to get him to declare himself.

Katie left the coffee shop praying she was right.

SATURDAY NIGHT AT work was crazy for Chase and he found himself unable to leave the parlor until eleven. As he was closing up, he looked at his phone and saw a missed call from Katie.

Chase called her and the phone rang a couple times before she picked up.

"Hello!"

"Hey, where are you?" he asked, listening to the shouts and music in the background.

"I'm at a bachelorette party at Buck's! Where are you?" she said, and he heard a collection of female voices cheering.

Chase nearly ran to the chopper, thinking about how crazy bachelorette parties could get. "I'm heading there now."

"Okay, see you soon," Katie said cheerfully.

Chase heard a guy's voice say something that made Katie giggle. Jealousy shot through him like a lightning bolt. He didn't want anyone else making Katie do that cute little snort laugh. Hanging up the call, he got on his motorcycle and headed to the bar.

Seven minutes later he walked into Buck's and almost exploded.

Katie was up on the bar, wearing a short jean skirt,

cowboy boots, and a brown tank top that had a lace-up front. She was dancing to Miranda Lambert's "Mama's Broken Heart," and a group of guys stood beneath her, enjoying the show.

Chase marched over to Eric and shouted, "Couldn't you have stopped her?"

Eric passed beers off to a couple of guys next to Chase and said, "No, she told me to fuck off."

Chase blinked. "Katie told you to fuck off? Katie doesn't say *fuck*, ever. And why did that stop you from hauling her down and sending her home?"

Shrugging, Eric said, "You're here now. You can do the hauling."

"Who did she come with?" Chase asked.

"The bachelorette party," Eric said.

"What bachelorette party?"

Eric pointed to the back of the room where Ryan Ashton stood, wearing a huge white veil with neon condoms on it. She caught sight of him and waved. One by one, the group of ladies turned to look at him, giving him mixed looks of disapproval and resentment. Chase caught Steph's eye and pointed toward Katie. She threw up her hands as if to say "Oh well."

What the hell was wrong with everyone?

Deciding it was up to him to get her down from there, Chase walked purposefully to the edge of the crowd surrounding Katie and pushed his way to the front. He looked up at his firecracker as she did a little turn and dip, almost knocking out a couple of "whooping Toms."

He reached up and said, "Come on, Katie, let me take

you home." His suggestion was met with boos and hisses from the men around them.

Chase ignored them, his eyes glued on *his* girl, who had stopped dancing and was smiling at him.

"Chase! I'm just checking flirting and drinking too much off my list. Who knew dancing on the bar would be so easy? I was sure I would have fallen off by now."

Chase held his hands up again. "Well, now you have, so why don't you come down?"

KATIE REACHED DOWN and put her hands on his shoulders as he swung her to the floor, feeling giddy as he frowned at her. She'd watched him from the minute he walked in, and by the look on his face he was furious. Gracie had said she needed to make him jealous, and she was pretty sure she'd succeeded.

"Whooo. That was fun," she said, leaning against him purposefully, pushing her breasts against his chest.

His eyes flickered down to where their chests met and she almost grinned at the strained look on his face. It was nice to see Mr. Cool's iron-clad control slipping.

"We need to talk," he practically growled at her.

"Mmm, can it wait until tomorrow? I'm suddenly really tired," she said, pretending to yawn.

"Why don't I drive you? We can talk on the way," he said.

"I think we've done a lot of talking this week. I feel kind of talked out," Katie said, trying to move out of his arms.

Releasing her, he threw his hands up and shouted, "I don't understand what you want from me! All week I've tried to make it up to you, tried to earn your trust again, and you come out here, trying to complete your list. Can't you see I am trying to show you how I feel? I thought we were finally getting back to where we were, but if you aren't going to take me seriously, then why did you even ask me to make that list? Are you trying to make me crazy?"

He turned away from her and started for the door.

This wasn't how it was supposed to go. He was supposed to be so overcome with jealousy, he would tell her he loved her and haul her off to his place for incredible makeup sex.

Before he hit the door, she yelled, "I loved everything you did, but enough is enough!" He stopped and she continued, "I've waited thirty years to find you, and I don't want to waste another minute! You're my soul mate, the one guy who was meant for me, and I'm done playing games." Finally he faced her again and, sucking in one last breath, she asked, "So do you have anything else on that list, or can we get out of here and really start making up?"

Chase's feet ate up the distance between them, and he reached out to cup her cheeks in his hands. "Just one more thing," he said, leaning down to kiss her softly. She would have deepened the kiss, but he pulled back too soon. "I love you, Katie. I have never said that to another woman, but I couldn't help myself. You are irresistible, beautiful, and keep me on my toes. You make me want to be a better man, and I need you. You are my first, last, and only love, and I never want to be without you again."

Katie laughed and threw her arms around him, kissing him with all the love in her heart.

When he broke the kiss, Chase said, "Well, don't you have something you want to say to me?"

With a wicked smile, she said, "Hey baby, do you wanna do this thing?"

Swinging her up into his arms with a loud laugh, he said, "Yes. Let's do this thing."

Epilogue

One year, seven months, and eighteen days later

CHASE SAT IN the big oak rocking chair, humming out loud to the tiny pink bundle he held in his arms. He rocked his nine-week old daughter, Lorie Quinn Trepasso, slowly as he sang, "You Are My Sunshine."

Lorie's sweet blue eyes opened briefly and she made a soft noise. Chase couldn't get enough of his baby girl and snuck into her room to ogle her as much as he could. She was perfect.

"You know, everyone says that's how babies get spoiled."

Chase turned to smile sheepishly at his wife, who stood in the doorway with her lips pursed and her arms crossed. "That's an old wives' tale. Besides, I heard her fussing, and I thought I'd let you sleep."

Katie uncrossed her arms with a smile and padded

over to give him a soft, lingering kiss. "I have such a thoughtful husband."

Chase stood up with Lorie in his arms and said, "Yes you do."

She laughed and kissed their daughter's forehead. Katie had been the one to suggest they name her for both their mothers, and he had been thrilled with the idea. He laid Lorie down in her crib and her eyes stayed closed as they snuck out. Chase wrapped his arms around Katie's waist as they tread quietly back to their room.

Katie had sold her little house and moved in with him four months after their reconciliation and two months later they had been married in her church. Chase still grumbled about going to services every Sunday, but he did it for Katie. Because he loved her.

He ran his lips down her neck and teased, "Wanna play around a bit?" He laughed when she yawned and answered his own question, "Guess that's a no."

She turned around and said, "I'm sorry, I'm just so tired. Today I almost forgot to pay for milk at the store, I was so out of it."

"Well, then, you would have been able to cross off another item from your list," he teased.

She leaned her head back to look at him with pursed lips. "The list has been over for a long time, sweetie."

"Of course, but only because you stole something already," Chase said.

"What was that?"

He moved away from her. Dramatically, he held his hands against his chest. "My heart."

"Ugh, gag me. Cornballs." Opening her mouth wide, she stuck her finger inside to emphasize.

He dropped his hands and said, "Geez, you used to think I was romantic."

"That was before I went through twenty-two hours of labor and started getting only five hours of sleep a night," Katie said.

"Okay. Okay, let's just cuddle."

Giggling, Katie pointed to their bed, and Chase saw Slinks curled up on his side. Reaching out to move the devil cat, Chase chuckled as Slink's lifted his head and gave a very whiny meow.

"No way, dude. I told you, you start hocking hairballs and you can't sleep in here." He scooped him up, and the cat cuddled against him, purring loudly. About the time Katie was seven months pregnant and cranky as hell, Slinks had started warming up to Chase, rubbing against him and purring. Maybe it had to do with him scooping the litter box, but Chase had welcomed the cat's affection. Anything to stop the constant ruination of his clothes.

He put Slinks outside the door and the cat glared at him before swishing down the hall with his tail in the air.

Closing the door again, he padded toward the bed and Katie said, "He loves you now."

Shrugging as he climbed in and pulled her close, he said, "Or he just knows who's boss around here."

They snuggled under the covers and she whispered, "Have I told you what a good father you are, Mr. Trepasso?"

His heart squeezed and he held her tighter. "A few times, Mrs. Trepasso."

"It's really sexy." He felt her hand start to drift.

Grinning in the dark, he said, "I thought you were too tired?"

Her hand started doing extraordinary things and she responded, "What can I say? Being here with you does things to me."

Sliding his hands into her hair, he said, "Me too, Firecracker. Me too."

See how the romances of Rock Canyon began!
Continue reading for an excerpt from Codi Gary's

THE TROUBLE WITH SEXY,

available now in Kiss Me:
An Avon Books Valentine's Day Anthology.

An Excerpt from

"THE TROUBLE WITH SEXY"

Available in Kiss Me: An Avon Books Valentine's Day Anthology

She's got a hot new makeover ... and a boss to seduce! For prim and proper Ryan Ashton, sexy has always been an elusive quality. But with a little help from a new friend, she just might snag the one man who can set her seductive side loose ...

GREGG CAME AROUND the corner and nearly swallowed his tongue. Ryan was wearing the same type of wool slacks she wore to work most days, her flame-red hair pulled back into a no-nonsense bun and her face free of any makeup. Her nose had a little bump on the bridge, and she had a heart-shaped face with full lips. His eyes traveled down to where her buttoned-to-the-neck top should have been and instead, in its place, a slinky white camisole showed a lot more than it covered. It was usually hard to discern what her figure looked like under her drab clothes, but in the tight top tucked into the slacks he could see that her breasts were firm, more than a handful, and it made his palms itch to reach out and cup them. Her waist was slim and indented, and if he had to hazard a guess, they probably flared quite nicely under the sexless pants.

His imagination was taking a dangerous turn and his mouth dried out as he pictured her in nothing but that sexy little see-through top. When he opened his mouth to speak, it came out a little ragged. "What happened to your shirt?"

"Oh good, you brought my sweater." Oblivious to his pained expression, she grabbed the cardigan and slipped it over her arms and shoulders. She buttoned the sweater, covering the upper portion of bare skin he'd been admiring, and said, "While Cammie and Joel picked out the pictures they wanted, I offered to hold Dylan, and the little booger puked on me. I tried to just wipe it off, but apparently baby puke is toxic. I couldn't get the smell to go away and it was making my stomach turn."

He tried to forget about what he'd seen under the dowdy black sweater, and choked out, "So is it just the puke you object to? Or is it the actual kid you find distasteful?"

She shook her head and walked around him. "No, I love kids. I would love some of my own someday, lots of them, but the only puke I want to clean off me is theirs. Or my husband's, depending on how much I love him."

He wasn't sure he'd ever love anyone enough to let them puke on him. He tried imagining Ryan sitting in a rocking chair surrounded by a dozen little cherub faces, and the scene made him smile. She'd make a wonderful mother, being so patient with the kids who came into the studio.

"So how many is a lot?"

She smiled as she sat down at her computer. "I don't know, maybe four? I always wanted a big family. My mom had complications when she had me so she could never have any more kids, and it was always kind of lonely by myself. We didn't live in a neighborhood, so I didn't really get to have friends until school, and I had a few really great ones but I was always a little . . . awkward."

Gregg knew that Ryan had a hard time talking to people outside of her job, and it always puzzled him. She had been a little nervous during her interview with him when she responded to his help-wanted ad, but she warmed up quickly. Of course, they had been talking about photography, which Ryan was very passionate about, but after that he hadn't had any trouble having a conversation with her. In fact, she was actually really funny and could give as good as she got.

This wasn't the first time Ryan had brought up her awkwardness, and for some reason, the thought that she couldn't see herself the way he did bothered him. To him she was funny, sweet, and easy to talk to. Their constant banter was one of the things he looked forward to most days.

He leaned over her shoulder and whispered, "Well I don't know if it counts for anything, but I think that you have definitely grown out of your awkward stage."

She looked up at him. "You really don't think I'm awkward?"

He stared down at her, drowning in her eyes. "Not at all."

She swallowed a little. "Gregg, we're friends right?"

He cocked his head and gave her a small smile. "Of course."

She twisted her hands in her lap. "And you'll be honest with me?"

He sat on her desk and nodded. "Sure."

She cleared her throat and whispered, "Do you think I'm sexy?"

He froze above her and his mind started searching for something to say.

She turned away from him quickly. "I'm sorry, please forget I said anything."

He hadn't liked the flash of hurt in her eyes, and blurted, "No! I mean, you just surprised me. I think you have a lot of really great qualities. You're smart. You're funny. You are really artistic. You're attractive. You have a great work ethic. You're a good person." He paused and took in her blank expression. "Yes, you're sexy."

He could tell by the look on her face that she didn't believe him, so he continued, "The trouble with sexy is people have different tastes. Some guys like girls in flashy, skimpy clothes with big hair and cowboy boots. Other guys think shy girls who are less obvious are more desirable. Some guys check out a woman's body and others look at her face. It's all about personal preference."

"What kind of girls do you like?"

Was she kidding? He didn't really have a type, unless you counted busty redheads with blue eyes who liked to wear a lot of wool, but he wasn't about to say that. Besides accepting his kiss at New Year's, Ryan had been nothing but professional, and a good friend. He wasn't going to jeopardize that by opening his big fat mouth. "I like girls who are confident. They need to be funny and like the same things I do—"

She interrupted him. "Yeah, but that's not what makes you approach her, right? Are you a leg man or a breast man?"

"What?" He couldn't help the bark of laughter that escaped.

"It's a simple question. Does a girl who walks into a bar wearing a miniskirt get you going or a low-cut top?"

This conversation was leading into some very dangerous areas, but he answered her anyway. "Low-cut top."

She blushed at his quick reply, and at that moment he'd have given more than a penny to get a real good look at those thoughts.

About the Author

CODI GARY has been an obsessive bookworm for twenty years and dreamed of writing romances since her first Sweet Valley High book. She writes best with a white mocha in one hand and the sound of female country singers in her ears. She lives in Idaho with her family.

You can find her online at www.codigarysbooks.com or on Facebook at www.facebook.com/CodiGarysBooks.

Visit www.AuthorTracker.com for exclusive information on your favorite HarperCollins authors.

Give in to your impulses . . .
Read on for a sneak peek at four brand-new
e-book original tales of romance
from Avon Books.
Available now wherever e-books are sold.

LESS THAN A GENTLEMAN
By Kerrelyn Sparks

WHEN I FIND YOU
A TRUST NO ONE NOVEL
By Dixie Lee Brown

PLAYING THE FIELD
A DIAMONDS AND DUGOUTS NOVEL
By Jennifer Seasons

HOW TO MARRY A HIGHLANDER
By Katharine Ashe

An Excerpt from

LESS THAN A GENTLEMAN

by Kerrelyn Sparks

New York Times bestselling author
Kerrelyn Sparks returns to romance during
the Revolutionary War with the sequel to her
debut historical novel, *The Forbidden Lady*.

Matthias gazed up the lattice to his balcony. As youngsters, he and his cousin had used the lattice to sneak out at night and go fishing. Of course the doors had not been bolted back then, but climbing down the lattice had seemed more exciting.

Matthias wasn't sure the lattice would hold his weight now, but with Dottie's restorative coursing through him, he felt eager to give it a jolly good try. Halfway up, a thin board cracked beneath his shoe. He shifted his weight and found another foothold. The last thing he wanted was to slip and tear Dottie's stitches from his shoulder.

He swung his legs over the balcony railing and landed with a soft thud. *How odd*. His door was open. *Of course*, he reminded himself. Dottie had gone there to fetch his clothes. She must have opened the door to air out the room.

He slipped inside. Moonlight filtered into the room, glimmering off the white mosquito netting. He strolled over to the secretaire, then kicked off his shoes and dropped his breeches. When he draped the breeches on the back of the chair, he noticed something was already there, something thick. He ran his fingers over the folds of cotton. The scent of roses drifted up to his nose. His mother's perfume. Why would she have left one of her gowns in his room?

Odd. He pulled off his stockings. He'd talk to his mother in the morning. For now, he simply wanted to sink into a mattress and forget about the war.

He unwrapped his neck cloth, then removed his shirt and undergarments. How could he forget the war when he had so much to do? Ferryboats to burn. Supplies to capture. He untied the bow from his hair and dropped the thin leather thong on the desk. And those two missing females. *Where the hell could they be?*

He strode to the bed and slipped under the netting. With a sigh of contentment, he stretched out between the clean cotton sheets.

The bed shifted.

He blinked, staring at the ghostly netting overhead. He hadn't budged an inch. There was only one explanation.

Slowly, he turned his head and peered into the darkness beside him. The counterpane appeared lumpy, as if— He listened carefully. Yes, soft breathing.

He sat up. A soft moan emanated from the form beside him. Female. His heart started to pound, his body reacting instinctively. Good God, it had been too long since he ...

What the hell? He drew his racing libido to a screeching

halt. This had to be another one of his mother's plots to force him to marry! Even Dottie was in on it. She had insisted he bathe and go to the Great House. Then they had locked up the house, so he would be forced to climb the lattice to his bedchamber. Straight into their trap.

He scrambled out of bed, batting at the mosquito netting that still covered him.

The female gasped and sat up. "Who's there?"

"Bloody hell," he muttered. His mother's scheme had worked perfectly. He was alone and naked with whomever she had chosen for his bride.

Another gasp, and a rustling of sheets. The woman climbed out of bed. Damn! She would run straight to her witnesses to inform them that he'd bedded her.

"No!" He leapt across the bed and grabbed her. "You're not getting away." He hauled her squirming body back onto the bed. Her sudden intake of air warned him of her intent to scream.

He cupped a hand over her mouth. "Don't."

She clamped down with her teeth.

"Ow!" He ripped his hand from her mouth.

She slapped at his shoulders.

He winced as she pounded on his injury. "Enough." He seized her by the wrists and pinned her arms down. "No screaming. And no biting. Do you understand?"

Her breaths sounded quick and frightened.

He settled on top of her, applying just enough pressure to keep her from escaping. "I know what you're after. You think to trap me in wedlock so easily?"

"What?"

He could hardly see her pale face in the dark. His damp hair fell forward, further obstructing his view as he leaned closer. The scent of her soap surrounded him. Magnolia blossoms. His favorite, and Dottie knew it. This was a full-fledged conspiracy. "I assume you brought witnesses with you?"

"Witnesses?"

"Of course. Why would you want me in your bed if there were no one to see it?"

"My God, you're perverse."

"You're hoping I am, aren't you?" He stroked the inside of her wrist. "You're hoping I'll be tempted by your soft skin."

She shook her head and wiggled beneath him.

He gulped. She was definitely not wearing a corset beneath her shift. "You think I cannot resist a beautiful, womanly form?" Damn, but she *was* hard to resist.

"Get off of me," she hissed.

"I beg your pardon? That's hardly the language of a seductress. Didn't they coach you better than that?"

"Damn you, release me."

He chuckled. "You're supposed to coo in my ear, not curse me. Come now, let me hear your pretty little speech. Tell me how much you want me. Tell me how you're burning to make love to me."

"I'd rather burn in hell, you demented buffoon."

He paused, wondering for the first time whether he had misinterpreted the situation. "You're . . . not here to seduce me?"

"Of course not. Why would I have any interest in a demented buffoon?"

He gritted his teeth. "Then who are you and why are you in this bed?"

"I was in bed to sleep, which would be obvious if you weren't such a demented—"

"Enough! Who are you?"

She paused.

"Is the question too difficult?"

She huffed. "I . . . I'm Agatha Ludlow."

An Excerpt from

WHEN I FIND YOU

A TRUST NO ONE NOVEL

by Dixie Lee Brown

Dixie Lee Brown continues her
heart-racing *Trust No One* series with
a sexy veteran determined to protect
an innocent woman on the run.

"Okay—now that I've got your attention, let me tell you about my day." Walker resumed his pacing. "I've been up since four-thirty this morning. I've saved your neck three times so far today, and for my trouble I've been cracked on the skull, threatened by a bear, and nearly drowned. We're through doing it your way." He stopped and pinned her with a warning glance. "I realize you're confused and you've got no idea who I am, but there's only one thing you need to know. I'm taking you out of here with me, and I don't care if I have to throw you over my shoulder and carry you out. Are we clear?"

She watched him without saying a word, looking anything but resigned to her fate.

Walker stared back, daring her to defy him.

She never even flinched.

"If you were me, what would you do?" Her strong, clear voice challenged him, while her eyes flashed with fire.

"If I were you, I'd find someone I could trust and stick with him until this is over."

"And that's you, I suppose? How do I know I can trust you?"

He made a show of looking around. "You don't have a lot of options at the moment, but, in case you haven't noticed, I'm the one trying to keep you alive." He reached for her elbow and pulled her to her feet. The cool breeze through his wet clothes chilled him, and he worried about her. Even with her arms wrapped around herself, just beneath her breasts, she still shook. No sense putting this off. She wasn't magically going to start trusting him in the next few minutes, and they had to get moving.

He held up his jacket in front of her and took a deep breath. "Get out of those wet clothes and put this coat on."

Her eyes widened in alarm and she stared at him, resting her hands on her hips in a stance that would have made him smile if she hadn't been so serious. He held her gaze, expecting her to tell him to go to hell. He couldn't afford to give on this issue, so he kept talking. "We'll head back to higher ground, start a fire, and get our clothes dried out. I have to warm you up, and this is the only way I know to do it. We don't have time to argue about this."

"You can't seriously expect me to . . . you're wet and cold, too. Wear your own damn coat." She wrapped her arms around her waist again, as though she could stop her trembling.

The fear in her expression tugged at his conscience and sent him searching for the words to reassure her that he wasn't going to jump her as soon as she undressed. The suspicious glare she fixed him with succeeded in hardening his resolve, and he lowered the coat, raised an eyebrow, and swept his gaze over her. "Either you can get out of those clothes yourself, or I can help you."

"You wouldn't dare!"

"You'll find there's not too much I wouldn't do."

Darcy glowered at him a few more seconds, clearly wishing she had a tree branch in her hand. Then she sighed and dropped her gaze, blinking several times in quick succession, obviously determined that he wouldn't see her break down. So, the woman wasn't as tough as she wanted him to believe. Her vulnerability unleashed a wave of protectiveness that washed over him and left him feeling like an ass.

He frowned. "I'm not the enemy." He held the coat higher so it blocked his view of everything but her head and shoulders. "Hurry, we have to get moving." Trembling visibly, her lips still maintained a bluish tint. She wasn't out of danger yet.

An Excerpt from

PLAYING THE FIELD

A DIAMONDS AND DUGOUTS NOVEL

by Jennifer Seasons

The sexy baseball players of Jennifer Seasons'
Diamonds and Dugouts series are back
with the story of a single mom, a hot
rookie, and a second chance at love.

JP reached out an arm to snag her, but she slipped just out of reach—for the moment. Did she really think she could get away from him?

There was a reason he played shortstop in the major leagues. He was damn fast. And now that he'd decided to make Sonny his woman, she was about to find out just how quick he could be. All night he'd tossed and turned for her, his curiosity rampant. When he'd finally rolled out of bed, he'd had one clear goal: to see Sonny. Nothing had existed outside that.

Her leaving her cell phone at the restaurant last night had been the perfect excuse. All he'd had to do was run an internet search for her business to get her address. And now here he was, unexpectedly up close and personal with her. So close he could smell the scent of her shampoo, and it was doing funny things to him. Things like making him want to bury his nose in her hair and inhale.

No way was he going to miss this golden opportunity.

With a devil's grin, he moved and had her back against the aging barn wall before she'd finished gasping. "Look me in the eyes right now and tell me I don't affect you, that you're not interested." He traced a lazy path down the side of her neck with his fingertips and felt her shiver. "Because I don't believe that line for an instant, sunshine."

Close enough to feel the heat she was throwing from her deliciously curved body, JP laughed softly when she tried to sidestep and squeeze free. Her shyness was so damn cute. He raised an arm and blocked her in, his palm flush against the rough, splintering wood. Leaning in close, he grinned when she blushed and her gaze flickered to his lips. Her mouth opened on a soft rush of breath, and, for a suspended moment, something sparked and held between them.

But then Sonny shook back her rose-gold curls and tipped her chin with defiance. "Believe what you want, JP. I don't have to prove anything to you." Her denim blue eyes flashed with emotion. "This might come as a surprise, but I'm not interested in playing with a celebrity like you. I have a business to run and a son to raise. I don't need the headache."

There was an underlying nervousness to her tone that didn't quite jive with the tough-as-nails attitude she was trying to project. Either she was scared or he affected her more than she wanted to admit. She didn't look scared.

JP dropped his gaze to her mouth, wanting to kiss those juicy lips, and felt her body brush against his. He could feel her pulse, fast and frantic, under his fingertips.

It made his pulse kick up a notch in anticipation. "There's a surefire way to end this little disagreement right now, because I say you're lying. I say you *are* interested in a celebrity like me." He cupped her chin with his hand and watched her thick lashes flutter as she broke eye contact. But she didn't pull away. "In fact, I say you're interested in *me*."

JP knew he had her.

Her voice came, soft and a little shaky. "How do I prove I'm not?" The way she was staring at his mouth contradicted her words. So did the way her body was leaning into his.

Lowering his head until he was a whisper away, he issued the challenge, "Kiss me."

Her gaze flew to his, her eyes wide with shock. "You want me to do *what?*"

What he knew they both wanted.

"Kiss me. Prove to me you're not interested, and I'll leave here. You can go back to your business and your son and never see my celebrity ass again."

An Excerpt from

HOW TO MARRY A HIGHLANDER

by Katharine Ashe

In this delightful novella from
award-winning author Katharine Ashe, a
young matchmaker may win the laird of her
dreams if she can manage to find husbands for
seven Scottish ladies—in just one month!

It would have been remarkable if Teresa had not been quivering in her prettiest slippers. Six pairs of eyes stared at her as though she wore horns atop her hat. She was astounded that she had not yet turned and run. Desperation and determination were all well and good when one was sitting in Mrs. Biddycock's parlor, traveling in one's best friend's commodious carriage, and living in one's best friend's comfortable town house. But standing in a strange flat in an alien part of town, anticipating meeting the man one had been dreaming about for eighteen months while being studied intensely by his female relatives, did give one pause.

Her cheeks felt like flame, which was dispiriting; when she blushed, her hair looked glaringly orange in contrast. And this was not the romantic setting in which she had long imagined they would again encounter each other—another ballroom glittering with candlelight, or a rose-trellised garden path in the moonlight, or even a field of waving heather aglow with sunshine. Instead she now stood in a dingy little flat three stories above what looked suspiciously like a gin house.

But desperate times called for desperate measures. She gripped the rim of her bonnet before her and tried to still her nerves.

The sister who had gone to fetch him reappeared in the doorway and smiled. "Here he is, then, miss."

A heavy tread sounded on the squeaking floorboards. Teresa's breath fled.

Then he was standing not two yards away, filling the doorway, and . . .

she . . .

was . . .

speechless.

Even if words had occurred to her, she could not have uttered a sound. Both her tongue and wits had gone on holiday to the colonies.

No wonder she had dreamed.

From his square jaw to the massive breadth of his shoulders to his dark hair tied in a queue, he was everything she had ever imagined a man should be. Aside from the neat whiskers skirting his mouth that looked positively barbaric and thrillingly virile, he was exactly as she remembered him. Indeed, seeing him now, she realized she had not forgotten a single detail of him from that night in the ballroom. She recognized him with the very fibers of her body, as though she already knew how it felt for him to take her hand. Just as on that night eighteen months before, an invisible wind pressed at her